The Yiddish Gangster's Daughter

Joan Lipinsky Cochran

P E R R I C O T
PUBLISHING

Published by Perricot Publishing
Book cover design by: PINTADO
All rights reserved
First printing
Copyright © 2018 Joan Lipinsky Cochran
ISBN: 978-0-9998280-0-7

Printed in the United States of America

About the Author

Joan Lipinsky Cochran was born in Miami, Florida
and lives in Boca Raton, Florida. She is an adjunct
professor, journalist and food columnist whose
short stories have won numerous awards.

Other Books by Joan Lipinsky Cochran

Still Missing Beulah: Stories of Blacks
and Jews in Mid-Century Miami

To access a Reader's Guide, contact Joan
through her website
www.joanlipinskycochran.com

To my family,
Michael, Eric and Ryan

1

I'm the type of woman people trust. Or so friends tell me. It's probably because I have such an open face. Brown eyes set a few centimeters too far apart. Broad cheekbones that taper to a square jaw. Curly brown hair that flops over my forehead.

It's what people politely call an *interesting* face.

Strangers in coffee shops ask me to watch their computers when they go to the bathroom. Mothers in grocery stores catch my eye and smile conspiratorially when their kids throw tantrums.

When I was a child, everyone's assumptions about my trustworthiness embarrassed me. Teachers appointed me class monitor, figuring I'd never lie about my friends' misbehavior. Neighbors asked me to babysit, confident I'd have their children in bed by eight.

By sixteen, though, I caught on to what I could pull off with an open face. I became the wise guy friends sent inside liquor stores, knowing no clerk would challenge me. When my resident advisor found marijuana in my dorm room my freshman year, I had no trouble convincing her a boy I'd just met abandoned it on my desk.

But my trustworthy appearance is not the problem.

My trusting nature is.

It's taken me fifty years to find that out.

It's a typical Sunday in August and my husband and I have driven to Miami to pick up my father for brunch. As we pull up to his building at the Schmuel Bernstein Jewish Home for the Aged, we spot the old man. In point of fact, it's impossible to miss him. He looks like a giant leprechaun in Kelly green Bermudas and an equally green polo shirt. My dad's a big man at six feet three inches and his shorts ride well above his knees. Daniel and I exchange amused glances. Then my husband rolls down his window.

"Tootsie. Over here," he yells, waving my father to the car. Everyone, including his grandchildren, calls the old man Tootsie. It's the nickname he acquired when an older cousin—another Sydney—insisted *he* was the original.

This particular Sydney a.k.a. Tootsie stands in the portico of a five-story apartment building, arms crossed and foot tapping in a less-than-subtle demonstration of impatience. He lives in one of eight identical brick buildings on the campus of what the Schmuel Bernstein's promotional brochure describes as an independent living facility—and Tootsie calls the old folks' home. It was built fifty years ago in the former hub of Jewish Miami, now a tough neighborhood comprised of car dealerships, Haitian restaurants, and a kosher delicatessen run by Nicaraguans. Every now and then, the locals spice things up with a drive-by shooting.

Though in a gritty section of town, the Schmuel Bernstein's ten-acre campus remains a Shangri-La for Miami's elderly Jews. This is due, in no small part, to the generosity of successful Israelites who want a spot to be waiting for them when infirmity strikes. On the kosher side of the ten-foot metal fence that surrounds its grounds are chrome and glass state-of-the-art medical facilities, a nursing home, independent living buildings, and paved trails wide enough to accommodate dual wheel chairs.

Virtually every building, garden path, and meeting room on campus is adorned with a brass plaque that identifies its wealthy benefactor. I tell Daniel on the drive over it won't be long before little brass testaments to donors show up inside bathroom stalls. One day, you'll be able to do your business while honoring the memory of Saul Berkowitz or Miriam Wolensky.

My father bought his apartment in the Fannie Sadowitz Residence a year ago and loves to kvetch about the old people. But he likes it here. There's a dining room, so he doesn't have to cook, and a couple of his cronies have moved in. Their poker games are rumored to be vicious.

Spotting Daniel, Tootsie ambles over and climbs in back before leaning over to kiss my cheek. "Head to Zimmerman's Deli." Then, remembering his manners, "If that's okay with everyone."

Daniel and I mutter our agreement, then I shift into first. Today marks three months since we began driving to Miami, an hour south of our home in Boca Raton, to take Tootsie out for Sunday brunch or dinner. It's a ritual we launched after my father and I made up. We argued after my mother's funeral two years ago when I said I'd never forgive him for cheating on her. But after my children left for college, I realized how much I missed being around family and reconnected with the old man. So far it's worked out.

"What's the matter? Too cheap to use the air-conditioning?" Tootsie says, reaching over the seat and adjusting the fan. The day is turning into a scorcher. It's only ten and heat radiates off the causeway, forming shimmering pools of light above the tarmac. We park in the lot behind Zimmerman's Deli and enter through the back door, passing empty orange and blue crates that line the narrow hallway. The early crowd's gone and it'll be a while before the tennis players trickle in so we're seated right away.

Zimmerman's is one of Miami Beach's oldest delis and looks it. Its dozen or so red and gray Formica tabletops are scratched and dented, and the grout between the floor's white tiles is moldy brown. Even the waitresses, with their cheap cotton aprons and tired eyes, seem worn-out. But it doesn't matter. Miami Beach's Jews are loyal. Zimmerman's draws a steady Sunday morning crowd. It's the place to be seen. I grew up thirty minutes south of here, in Coral Gables, and am glad I don't need to worry about familiar faces. I've done nothing with my hair and wear the gym shorts I threw on to walk this morning.

"Lox and bagels," I tell the waitress, echoing my father's order. Daniel, who asked for an egg white omelet, raises an eyebrow and I respond with an abashed grin. I forgot we'd had a discussion the night before about eating healthier. But the lox here is amazing.

When the waitress leaves, Tootsie pokes Daniel in the ribs. "See that broad?" He speaks in a stage whisper as he motions toward a tall, attractive blonde in her early forties. She's snuggled up to an elderly gnome with gnarled hands about three tables away. She could be the guy's daughter, except that no one goes to breakfast with their father in a leopard skin tank top that shows off her two best assets. She's positioned them under the old man's face. "Son of a gun married her a month after his wife died. Everyone knew he kept her for ten years before the old lady croaked."

Daniel shrugs. He knows how I feel about cheating. My father's serial affairs have made me a bit touchy on the subject. "She's a good-looking woman," he concedes.

"Good looking, my foot. She's a beauty. The guy, Morton Shapiro, did well for himself. Made a fortune in the underwear business and could afford the best broads in town. Can't blame him for having a little on the side."

It's the closest my father's come to the subject of cheating since we reunited and I'm uncomfortable with the conversation. "Dad, you want to drop it?" I try to distract him with news of our youngest son, Gabe, who left for college three months earlier. He has Asperger's syndrome and we've been worried about his ability to survive on his own. He's high functioning but has trouble meeting people and negotiating complex situations—like signing up for classes.

"Gabe called yesterday. He likes his dorm and professors."

But Tootsie's not biting. "Men cheat. That's all there is to it. It's not the worst thing in the world."

"Not to you, maybe. I doubt Mom would agree."

He glares at me. I pretend not to notice.

"She stayed with me, didn't she?" He curls his lip and glances at Morton Shapiro. "Your mother understood that it's unnatural for a man to be with just one woman."

There's no point in arguing with him. It would be like convincing an addict to stay off heroin.

Our breakfast arrives and we're silent as we eat. I figure we're safely off the topic of Morton and his friend. But Tootsie continues to sneak glances at the woman. She makes a production of smearing cream cheese across one half of a bagel, then layering it with bright red lox and sliced tomato before handing it to the gnome.

To tell the truth, I'm watching her too, fascinated by her diamond rings, the largest of which has to be ten carats. She's remarkably adept at manipulating the knife and bagel despite inch-long red nails. Morton's no more than five feet, two inches and his bald head barely reaches the woman's shoulder.

"Come on, Daniel, be honest." Tootsie says. "You wouldn't give your left nut for one night with a dame like that?"

Daniel frowns and laughs. "No, I wouldn't." He squeezes my knee under the table. "You're like a dog in heat, Tootsie. I never saw anything like it."

"Not every wife would mind, you know. I bet half my friends didn't bother to hide their affairs from their wives. It's what men did back then. At least I was discreet. I don't know why you get so upset when I discuss it, Becks.

Blood rushes into my cheeks. I can't help wondering if my dad's becoming senile. What kind of man talks about his affairs in front of his daughter? I decide to leave the table before I lose it.

"Let me know when this discussion is over," I say and rise. "I'll be up front reading the menu or whatever."

I pass the gnome and his wife on my way to the glass picture window that faces out to the street in front of Zimmerman's. The view is partially blocked by yellowing newspaper reviews, most of which are at least ten years old. The food's gone consistently downhill and no self-respecting food critic would set foot inside Zimmerman's these days.

Five minutes later, I'm squinting to read a faded review when Daniel puts his hand on my shoulder. "Ready to go?"

"You bet."

He takes my hand and leads me to our table, where Tootsie rises and follows us through the rear door to my car. On the ride home, I tell my father about Gabe's call Saturday. He sounded happy and excited for the first time since leaving for college. He's just a few miles away from us at the moment, at the University of Miami, but we're steering clear until he adjusts to school.

Tootsie sounds interested and asks a few questions about Gabe's call. When we reach the Schmuel Bernstein, he reaches over the seat to squeeze my shoulder. "Sorry for giving you a hard time, Doll. I'm an old man and it's hard to break old habits."

I feel guilty for being judgmental at breakfast. It's one of my nastier habits. "It's okay," I say. "I still love you."

On the drive home, Daniel and I chat about the bars and restaurants we frequented before we had kids and moved to Boca Raton. Zimmerman's was *not* one of them.

"You remember the Fontainebleau?" Daniel asks as we pass the I-195 exit that leads to the classic Miami Beach hotel. He grins lasciviously.

"What about . . ." Then I remember and, despite thirty years of marriage and two sons, feel the heat rush into my face. It was the first—and last—time the boys caught us in the act.

Daniel raises his eyebrows Groucho Marx-style. "What do you say to a repeat performance when we get home?"

I smile and stomp the gas in response.

Yes. Your typical family Sunday—full of food and memories. Little did I know it would be our last.

2

True to his word, Daniel takes my arm after we get home and tries to lead me upstairs. But there's voice mail on my cell. I must have missed it in the noisy restaurant.

"Let it go," Daniel says. "What could be so important?"

I shrug. "What if it's one of the boys? I hate to miss their calls."

I place the cell on the counter between us and press the speaker button while he opens the refrigerator and pulls out a pitcher of iced tea.

"Becks?"

The voice sounds vaguely familiar.

"It's Eva. Daniel's office manager."

I'm surprised to hear from her and glance at Daniel. He raises his eyebrows. He'd told me a week earlier he caught her stealing from petty cash and fired her. She's got to be calling to get her job back.

What comes next is the last thing I expect.

"I hate making this call but there's no point in beating around the bush. You know Dawn?"

It's a rhetorical question. She knows I hired Daniel's assistant a year earlier.

"Well, your husband and Dawn are having an affair."

A crash sounds behind me and I look up. Ice tea's all over the floor. Daniel pulls a stream of paper towel off the roll next to the sink and kneels to wipe up the liquid and shards of glass.

"Can you believe that? How could she say such a thing?" I ask.

I know she's lying. But her accusation still stings.

When my husband stands, his expression stuns me. I expect anger. Or shock. But his face is white and he's breathing heavily. "That's crazy," he says, tossing a wad of towels in the trash before shoving his hands in his pockets. "I didn't realize she was so angry at me."

"What do you think is going on?"

"She was upset when I let her go. Couldn't believe I caught her stealing. Maybe she figured lying to you was the easiest way to get back at me. And she was jealous of Dawn."

"Dawn? What did Eva have against Dawn?"

"I'm not sure. Dawn came crying to me one day, claiming that Eva was jealous and making her life miserable."

"Since when do employees confide in *you*? I thought you stayed away from office politics."

I do most of Daniel's hiring and firing and employees tend to contact me with personnel issues.

"I don't know. I guess she felt more comfortable, that is . . . maybe she wanted . . ." He waves a hand in the air, at a loss.

It makes sense—sort of. And I want to believe him. But something feels wrong. He never mentioned Dawn's outburst. And his stance, hands shoved in his pockets and back straight, seems stiff and unnatural. Worst of all, he hasn't reached for my hand or taken me in his arms to reassure me Eva's lying. For the first time in our marriage, I'm afraid to approach him. My heart races, as disbelief battles horror.

When he glances around the room without meeting my gaze, I become light headed and grab the counter.

"Something isn't right here," I whisper. "Are you telling the truth?" I've never accused him of lying and feel sick at the words. "Because—"

"How can you accuse me?" he says before I finish. "I'm hurt you'd consider Eva's word over mine. Particularly after she stole from me."

He doesn't sound hurt. He sounds angry and irritated—and steps back as though frightened of what I'll do or say. When he pulls his hands out of his pockets and crosses his arms, it hits me:

"Eva never stole from you, did she?" I say, speaking slowly as I work things out in my mind. It's like pulling taffy from an old-fashioned machine. "You fired her so she wouldn't learn about your affair with Dawn. You *knew* she'd tell me."

"Hold on there. I wouldn't lie about Eva stealing. She took five hundred dollars, for God's sake."

I stare at him. Does he think I'm stupid? That I don't see his indignation as a pathetic attempt to distract me? My stomach churns. "I can't believe this. You had sex with Dawn."

"No. I didn't—I wouldn't—" He looks me in the eye and his voice breaks. When he drops his head in his hands, I almost pity him. "I'm sorry." He speaks between sobs. "I never meant this to happen. I love you."

Sure I pushed him to confess. But now that he has, I don't want to believe him.

"You never meant to hurt me!" I say when I regain my voice. My knees are so weak I barely make it to the table to sit. "Didn't you think about what it would do to *us*? To Josh and Gabriel? Did you think I wouldn't find out?"

He looks up and his eyes are red and puffy. "I don't know. It was just after my mother died. And nothing seemed to make sense. I got caught up in the moment and—"

"Shut up. I don't want to hear it." He flinches. We've always treated each other with respect and I'm as shocked by my words as he is. I've never used coarse language around him. But everything's different now. The rules have changed.

It's funny how we worry about awful things happening, but aren't prepared when they do. I'd spoken with my friend Leisa about the anger and depression she experienced when her husband left. But she didn't say anything about the humiliation that overwhelms me. Other people know about this affair! If Eva knows, so does Mary, who handles his schedule. I imagine the pharmaceutical reps who come to his office to push drugs joking about it in Daniel's parking lot.

Successful doctor screws his nurse and his wife is the last to know it. It's a cliché. But it's happening to *me*.

I stare at Daniel, speechless. When he comes to the table and pulls out the chair across from me, I cringe.

He either misses or ignores my reaction. "I know we can get past this," he says, reaching for my hand. I jerk it away. "We need to sit down and—."

"Talk?"

"Of course. We love each other. We can work this out."

"Right. Just like that. Talk about it and the problem disappears."

"Come on, sweetheart. I'm not saying it'll be easy."

"You're damn right it won't. I want you out of here."

"You can't mean that. It's been over for weeks. You're the one I love."

"You wouldn't have slept with Dawn if you loved me," I say, my anger building. "I want you out of here tonight." Tears stream down my face.

I rise and open the door that leads from the kitchen to the garage. "I'm going for a walk. If you ever gave a damn about me, you'll be gone when I return." I slam the door behind me and leave the garage open for his departure.

As I roam the deserted streets of our neighborhood, my sobs fade. I wonder if I've done the right thing. If I should have stayed and talked it out. But my grief and anger are too raw. All I'll do if I go back is lash out at him. Memories of my parents' fights flash across my mind. My mother screaming at my father, then running to their room to cry. She invariably took Dad back. I hated her for it and refuse to turn into the doormat she became.

When I return home a half hour later, Daniel's car is gone. I race upstairs. Trousers and shirts are missing from his side of the closet. I stare at the gap in the shelf that held his suitcase. It mirrors the hollowness in my chest.

I'm not much of a drinker. But I can't think of anything else that will ease the pain. I go to the kitchen and pour myself a glass of wine. Then another. And one more. In an hour, I'm so woozy I have to hold on to the walls as I stumble down the hall to the family room. I'm planning to watch television, hoping it'll distract me, but the photo album from our family vacation in Yellowstone draws my attention. I pull it off the cocktail table onto my lap and flip through photos.

The first picture is of Daniel and me on horseback. We're smiling and waving. Daniel looks silly in a floppy, wide-brimmed hat. In the next, Daniel and the boys smile over their shoulders as they walk toward a bison at the edge of the road. In the third photo, taken by a waiter at the Old Faithful Lodge, Daniel drapes an arm over my shoulders as the boys lean into the picture. We look like such a happy, normal family.

What went wrong? When did he decide it was okay to break the rules of our life together? Everything was going so well. Josh and Gabriel were away at college. My father and I had resolved our differences. And Daniel and I were planning a week's vacation in Montreal. The photos make my loss feel worse. At six o'clock, I return the album to the cocktail table, then go upstairs and change into pajamas. Our king-sized bed looms large and empty. I pull the covers up to my neck and realize it's the first time in almost thirty years that I've slept alone.

I hate it.

3

A week later, as I drive south on I-95 to pick up my father for dinner, I consider lying about Daniel's and my separation. But it's pointless. This will be the first time in months I've come without my husband and Tootsie will know something's wrong. Better to get it over with.

"So where's the doc?" my father says as he opens the car door. "Get called away for an emergency?"

"Daniel and I aren't talking."

My father slides into the seat next to me and cocks his head. "What happened? The two of you never fight."

The old man's not far off base. We rarely argued. I always assumed it was because we got along so well. But maybe we communicated so poorly we never had a reason to fight?

"I threw Daniel out. He was cheating."

My father, who's been fiddling with his seat belt, jerks his head up. "What?"

"Daniel's screwing his nurse."

"You've got to be kidding." My father shakes his head, then laughs. "I'm sorry, Doll. I can't see Daniel . . . How'd you find out?"

"A phone call from his office manager. And he admitted it."

"Jeeze. Is it still going on?"

"He says no."

"And this is the first time he's cheated?"

"As far as *I* know."

"If it's just this once . . ." He's silent a moment. "Maybe you should let it go. It's not such a big deal."

I pull away from his building and drive through the Schmuel Bernstein's gate a bit faster than usual. My face grows hot and blood throbs through a vein in my neck. It creates an irritating tic near my Adam's apple. So much for sympathy from my father.

"He cheated on me. What am I supposed to do? Say okay. Let's get on with it?"

"You're married, what, thirty years and this is the first time he's cheated? There's nothing wrong with forgiving and forgetting."

"That might've worked for you and Mom." I glare across the seat at him. "But not me."

"Honey—"

"I don't want to talk about it."

"I know but—"

"I said forget it. Let's go to Wolfie's. And talk about something else."

Driving back from dinner, the thermometer on a bank marquee along Biscayne Boulevard flashes ninety degrees but my father insists we hang out on the front porch of his apartment building. The evening air is thick and steamy. But Tootsie's always cold so I'm out here with the alter cockers, the old folks, and my hair is plastered to my scalp with sweat. I glance at the porch's dozen or so elderly occupants, who sit in two symmetrically-spaced rows of wheelchairs and lawn furniture facing onto the black-topped parking lot. When we first sat down, my father pointed out a man who owned the Italian bistro near our house. It's hard to envision the old guy with purple-bruised arms and loose-skinned neck as the dark-haired, handsome restaurateur who greeted us at Angelo's. Most of the residents chat quietly or read magazines. No one else seems bothered by the heat. In fact, a few wear cardigans and lap robes.

We're fully engaged in digesting our pastramis on rye when an elderly woman comes trundling toward us with her walker. Her cheeks are cavernous hollows in a long narrow face, and her wispy gray brows furrow into a vee of angry determination. It's an agony to watch her struggle to lift the aluminum walker, swing it forward, and take another arduous step across the patio. I rise to help her, then, taken aback by her rage, drop in my seat. Her eyes are fixed on my father.

I'm about to ask my dad if he knows the approaching woman when she comes to a halt and plants her walker squarely in front of him. Her finely-lined face contorts into a series of gremlin-like grimaces as though she's probing the loops and tangles of her brain for a hidden memory. Finally, her features go still and her eyes focus intently on my father. He returns her stare and tilts his chin, studying her.

Then, with no warning, the woman's lips pull away from her teeth and the perplexed look she'd directed at my father turns into a coal black glare of rage. She points a skeletal finger at his face. "*Ach, ach.* Murderer. Murderer. *Du bist a rotseyekh.*" I recognize the Yiddish term for killer. Her voice is low and raspy. But there's no mistaking her horror at encountering my father.

A chill creeps up my spine at the venom in her voice. My father's no angel, but no one's ever accused him of *murder.* I assume she's blaming him for the death of someone at the home—a resident they both know. He doesn't tell me much about his life here, but I think he'd mention it if a close friend died.

I'm so stunned it's a second before I notice my father pushing the woman's hand away from his face. He glances to the left, then right, before returning his gaze to the old lady. No one seems to be paying attention, though she sounds like a frantic crow as she rasps out the litany "murderer, murderer."

I reach a protective arm around my dad's shoulders, which rise and fall as he struggles to catch his breath. His health is good for an eighty-five year old but he has asthma and I'm afraid he'll start wheezing. After what feels like hours, but could only have been a minute or two, a male nursing assistant in a crisp white uniform comes over and takes the old woman's elbow. He guides her across the porch; she continues to mumble *"rotseyekh, rotseyekh."* I clasp my father's hand, which is cold and clammy, and hold it until his breathing returns to normal.

"Who is that?" I ask, surprised by my father's willingness to let me comfort him. Normally, my father would sooner die than let me be his protector.

"Nobody you need to know." He pushes my arm away and starts hacking. It's the cough he gets when he's upset or angry, a series of snorts that start in his nose and gets trapped at the back of his throat in a repetitious *"ung, ung, ung."* His shoulders shake and his hands grip the sides of his chair.

I'm sweating from the tension as much as the heat and when I wipe the back of my neck, my hand comes away soaked. Being careful to avoid her gaze, I watch the old lady as the nursing assistant eases her into a chair at the far end of the porch. She looks much like every elderly woman at the home, tiny and fragile as a newborn hatchling. When she leans to the left to let the assistant drape a lightweight sweater across her shoulders, I catch a glimpse of the sparse white hair that covers a balding pink spot at the crown of her head. The passion's drained out of her, and she resembles a deflated pastel balloon. Once the assistant leaves, the old lady sits alone staring straight ahead, red lipstick and expectation splashed across her wrinkled face.

"You might as well tell me who she is," I say once my father stops coughing and I can see he hasn't ruptured anything. "It's obvious she knows you."

"The old broads here think they know everyone. Probably thinks I'm her dead husband."

Or an old boyfriend—given his past.

I send my father a menacing glare, the one that frightened my sons into admitting when they'd missed their curfews or forgotten to do their homework.

"You're a pain in the ass," he says, crossing his arms.

"I'm not leaving until you tell me."

He looks away, then back, and compresses his lips.

"Yeah, I know her," he admits. "Florence Karpowsky. She just moved into the Alzheimer wing. Her *putz* of a husband screwed me over years ago."

My father's choice of words is less than ideal. Growing up, my friends thought his colorful language—not to mention unusual name—was a hoot. I was embarrassed and tried to keep them away from him.

I wait for Tootsie to continue. My father tells stories in his own way and in his own time. These days, they come out in dribs and drabs, bubbling up from somewhere deep in his mind like a pocket of air rising through a pot of simmering *cholent*.

"You heard of Florence Karpowsky? The fancy society lady?"

I shrug and he looks at me like I'm stupid.

"They named a wing of this place for her husband. The old broad's so senile, I'm surprised she recognized me." He gazes at me out of the corner of his eye and snorts. "She probably doesn't recognize herself. Which is a good thing. You wouldn't know it to look at her, but she was a beauty in her day. Red hair and one of those, what do you call it, pinkish complexions. She was a little zaftig, but that was fine. We liked a little meat on the girls then. And nice. My old buddy, Fat Louie, grabbed her up the minute she moved to Miami."

He mutters something in Yiddish. I don't speak the language, but from the way he curls his lip and spits out the words, I figure Louie's persona non grata.

I remind my father for maybe the billionth time that I don't speak Yiddish and he switches back to English. "Louie saved my life on Utah Beach. You know that story."

"I knew you were shot, but you never told me who saved you."

He stares at me incredulously. "You must have forgot. We went through basic training together, got sent overseas together. Fat Louie and I were together on D-day. I made it off the assault boat and on to shore but got a bullet in my gut before I'd gone five yards." He starts to lift the front of his polo but thinks better of it.

"I can't believe you don't know this." He raises his eyes heavenward as though God can explain his oversight. "Louie crawled up the beach next to me and stayed at my side. I thought I was done for. Louie kept yelling for a medic until one showed up and shot me full of morphine. I owe my life to him. I got shipped back to a hospital in England to recuperate then finished out the war pushing pencils at a base post office in France. Louie fought in Europe."

He stops and glances at his watch. His eyes are red. "Jeeze, it's getting late." He grabs the chair arms as though to rise. "I'm heading upstairs."

"But you haven't finished the story."

"It's ancient history."

"Not for her," I say, looking at Mrs. Karpowsky.

We glare at each other for a half minute before my father lifts his hands, palms up, in a gesture of surrender.

"You don't give up, do you? But I got to go upstairs soon. Okay, I don't see Fat Louie for months after I'm shot. But when it comes time for our discharge, I send a letter to his parents' home in New Jersey, asking Louie to visit me in Miami Beach.

"My father—your grandpa Leo—retired there during the war, bought a couple apartment buildings. I figured we'd have a nice place to stay, take our time finding jobs. I'd been to Miami Beach. The girls there were something else."

He gets that sly look that means he's going to divulge something I don't need to know about his sex life.

"So why'd the lady call you a murderer?" I break in.

"Hold your horses. I'm getting there. You know what a wise guy your Uncle Moe was. He was discharged from the army a few months before me and landed himself a job running numbers. An operation out of Havana. Some big shot got it going in Miami. Bolita. You heard of it?"

I shrug. It's not the first time he's suggested Uncle Moe was dishonest. But he never said his brother, who was also his business partner, ran numbers. My Uncle Moe died when I was eight, but I remember the laughter that surrounded him when our families got together. It's hard to imagine him a hoodlum.

"By the time we get to Miami," my father continues, "Moe's bought himself an Oldsmobile and has his own bachelor pad. Louie and I spend a few weeks working on our tans. A month after Louie arrives, though, your grandfather lets us know he's not supporting a couple of moochers. We pick up the newspaper and study the want ads, but most of the jobs seem tame after what we've been through. Then one Saturday, we're at a bar and Moe suggests we pay a visit to his boss, this Murray Landauer. Says the money's a lot better than what we'd make as desk jockeys and Landauer's hiring. Moe is pretty closemouthed about what he does for a living but assures us it's all above board. We take him up on his offer and he sets an appointment for the next Tuesday.

"What a day *that* was. Moe takes us to the Sands Hotel. We walk through this fabulous lobby, everything elegant—marble floors, crystal chandeliers, mirrors on all the walls—and meet Landauer to work things out. He's at this little cabana room off to the side of the pool sitting at a concrete table covered with chunks of colored tile. I guess he's feeling generous because Moe gets a promotion, doing who knows what. Louie and I get routes in Overtown—it was a hopping Negro neighborhood then—picking up cash and receipts from the shopkeepers who took bets from their customers. Landauer says if we want to work together, fine by him."

I have a hard time picturing my father and uncle meeting with a gangster at a Miami Beach hotel. When I was a kid, Tootsie talked about taking my mother to fancy Miami Beach restaurants and nightclubs when they were dating in the 1940s. I pictured them as Fred Astaire and Ginger Rogers. He never said anything about picking up bets in Overtown.

"So you and Louie . . ."

"Will you let me talk?"

I nod.

"Everything's great for a year or so. Louie and I are making enough moolah to hit the clubs, take girls to the hotels for the big bands. Count Basie. Tommy Dorsey. You name it. Everyone who was anyone played Miami Beach. Louie met Florence that year at the Five O'clock Club on Collins and they were married three months later. Louie was a real sport, throwing money around on dames, so I was surprised to see him settle down. I met your mother, may she rest in peace, a few months later. He was the best man at my wedding and vice versa."

He lifts a hip off the chair and wrests a neatly-folded white handkerchief from his rear pocket before dropping back in the seat. I wait for him to blow his nose and collect himself. Lately, he seems to tear up at the merest mention of my mother. I suspect it's old age but hope it's also regret at how he treated her. Though my parents were separated at the time, he seemed to grieve as much as my sister and I did when our mother passed away.

"About three months after your mother and I were married," he says, "I get a call from Fat Louie. 'Toots,' he says 'I got an idea. You know how some of them businesses in Colored Town are from Brooklyn? Well, these guys are used to paying protection. But no one's collecting it here. You want to do them a favor?"

I cringe at the term, Colored Town, but don't bother to correct him. At eighty-five, he's not about to change his ways.

"Louie'd mentioned it before, but just joking around," my father continues. "So I decide to play along. Louie says we'll let them know, friendly-like, that we'll take care of them. Give them a price. See if they bite.

"I didn't like the sound of that. But I figure he knows what he's doing. Louie had a way with people, kibitzed with them and got what he wanted. He was a short guy with a solid barrel chest that made him look fat. And always with the big smile on his face and slicked-back hair. The kind of guy who cared how he looked. I'd hang back, keep my trap shut. I knew when to turn on the scowl. And I was in shape then. Not like now."

He pats his stomach, which has softened from a solid beer gut to a less than impressive mound of flab, then punches me in the arm. "Didn't know your old man was such a tough guy, did you?"

I laugh. It's hard to picture my father a tough guy. He's tall but always moved with a soft fluidity that suggested a lack of muscle tone. We lived in Coral Gables, suburbia itself, and as with all my friend's dads, he left for work in a suit and tie and came home expecting dinner. He was the joker, the soft touch among our parents. All this talk of running numbers and providing protection makes me uncomfortable, as though I'm talking to a stranger disguised as my father. The man he describes, this tough guy, has nothing to do with the dad who took the family and dog to the beach every Sunday.

"Louie, the hustler, doubled our income in three months, which was great by me. He kept the tote sheet. The guys who took the bets—the restaurant and bar and grocery store owners—would turn their receipts in to Louie, and we'd run them over to the counting house on Saturdays before the lottery number was announced. I let Louie handle the money. He was better at keeping track of it than I was. Plus he had a good memory. Always knew which counting house we were using that week."

My father, who's not exactly gifted in the manners department, leans across me to stare at Florence Karpowsky. "A great big wing of the nursing home named for her husband the big shot and she sits there like a bump on a log. Damn shame." He settles back in his seat. Mrs. Karpowsky hasn't moved a muscle. The expectation's gone from her face, leaving only a slash of smeared lipstick.

"I got to hit the sack," he says. "I'm beat."

My father's cheeks are flushed and I realize how much this story has upset him. But if I let him go, I'll never hear the story.

"Come on, Dad. You can't stop now. You still haven't told me why Mrs. Karpowsky got so worked up."

"She wasn't so worked up."

"She called you a murderer, for God's sake."

"She's in la-la land."

"All right." I rise. "Call me when you're ready to finish your story. I'll see you then."

"You are something else." He glares at me, then nods. "All right, I'll finish."

I return to my seat.

"It had to be December because I was wearing one of those bomber jackets the air corps guys were coming home with. It was a Saturday afternoon. Fat Louie and I'd just gotten out of the car and were heading toward the counting house to turn in our dough when the boss, Mr. Landauer, comes at us with this gigantic Yid.

" 'Youse guys, give your tote sheets and money to Hymie here,' he says, 'and come with me.' "

I have to laugh. My father sounds like a gangster in a forties movie.

"You think that's funny? I almost shit my pants."

"Sorry." I'm shocked. He never used that expression before.

He shakes his head. "Landauer's so furious he's turning red but I don't know why or what he's going to do about it. Usually we enter through the front door of this rundown wooden house and hand the money off to two broads at the kitchen table. That day, we hand our envelopes to the big Yid and follow Landauer around the side of the house, past a climed out pool, and onto the back porch.

"The minute I step inside the house, POW, a fist slams into my nose. Blood drips down my face and onto my jacket. Before I can figure out what's going on, another bastard delivers a blow to my gut. Turns out Mr. Landauer's got two goons waiting. The whole time they're pummeling us and bouncing us off the furniture, Landauer's screaming about how we double-crossed him and he's going to kill us. The rest I don't know. I must have passed out. When I wake up at home, your mother's crying and Moe's standing over me, muttering about what an asshole I am."

The anger and fear on his face frighten me and his hands, which grasp the arms of his chair, tremble. My head starts to throb as I realize how upset I am at the idea of my father being beaten, even decades ago. I'm not sure I want to hear more, but curiosity gets the better of me. "What'd you do?"

He shakes his head. "I don't know what to do. Once I can breathe and sit up, I call Fat Louie. He's as messed up as I am, says he has a busted lip, maybe a broken nose. Tells me it's the Christmas season and people are spending on their kids, not the numbers. But he's already got a plan to pay back the two thousand bucks Landauer claims we owe. He wants to confess to the protection racket, which Landauer doesn't know about, and pay Landauer off with our earnings. I don't like it. But I don't have any better ideas so tell him to go ahead."

I'm so wrapped up in the story that my stomach contracts at the thought of his meeting Landauer again.

"Weren't you scared?"

"You bet. But Landauer wasn't the type of man you could hide from. He'd find out sooner or later. So the next day, Louie and me show up at the Sands and find Landauer at his cabana. He's there with his wife and kids, doing the family shtick, and motions us to the bar. It's a gorgeous day. Everyone's in bathing suits except us two schmucks. Landauer's in this cabana outfit, polka-dot shorts and matching shirt, and we're in black suits, sitting at a tiki bar, *shvitzing* like pigs and begging Landauer's forgiveness."

"Was he surprised to see you?"

"Didn't seem like it. Though I think he's going to punch Louie one when Louie tells him about our protection racket. But he agrees to the payoff. We work three more months, deliver the protection money to Landauer. A week after we're square, Landauer gives us the boot."

By this time, it's dark out. Yellow bug lights in black metal fixtures throw urine-tinted rays over the building's front porch.

The bulbs are supposed to keep bugs away but mosquitoes circle my ankles and I reach down to scratch. Steam condensing in the night air forms a tar-scented fog that hovers over the parking lot. Two residents rise from their lawn chairs and shuffle inside. Tootsie's quiet and, when I turn to him, his shoulders are shaking. At first I think he's laughing. Then he brings the handkerchief to his face.

"Dad, are you okay?" I put a hand on his shoulder. I've never felt this mixture of tenderness and contempt for him before and it frightens me. It's unsettling to realize the man I envisioned as a tower of strength was so vulnerable.

He takes a few deep breaths and lets them out in long sighs. "Becks, darling, I swear to God, I didn't know. Louie saved my life, he was my best friend. I loved him like a brother." He's pleading but I don't understand why.

"What happened?"

He hangs his head and stares down at his lap, studying it like a chessboard. "A few months after Landauer fires us, Florence shows up at the house." He nods toward Mrs. Karpowsky "She was a fireball then, a real redhead. She's banging at the door, screaming like a crazy person. You never heard a lady use such language. When I open the door, she beats my chest with her fists. Finally, I grab her hands and force her into a chair. Your mother makes her a cup of tea. When she settles down, she tells us what happened."

He shakes his head. "I should have known." He sobs suddenly, loudly. It's a high-pitched gasp that cuts through the humid night air and draws the attention of a nurse who leans against the porch's wrought iron railing, having a smoke. I motion that everything's fine.

"Dad, it's okay," I whisper and put my arm around his shoulders. I wait for him to collect himself. I don't how to respond. Can this be *my* father, the gentle man who refused to spank my sister and me no matter how badly we behaved? He never mentioned any of this—his friend Louie or gangster connections—before. I can see where his story's going and fight the urge to cut him off. It's like easing on the brakes as I approach a fatal highway collision. I don't want to look but I can't tear my eyes from the dreadful scene.

"Florence says that the night before, when Louie doesn't come home, she calls the police. The cops tell her it's too early to file a missing person's report so nothing happens. The next afternoon, same day she comes to us, she says a fisherman found Louie's body floating in Biscayne Bay. He'd been shot through the chest. When she tells me this, I run into the bathroom and throw up. This is my best buddy. The guy saved my life and survived the allied invasion. To end up like that?"

My father takes a deep breath and holds his fist to his chest. I reach for his hand but he pushes it away.

"Florence thought I ratted on Louie. She'd never look at me after that. I don't blame her." He raises his head, then drops it in his hands. "Later, I heard Landauer found out Louie had double-crossed him. He'd held on to the cash and receipts he'd collected from our customers. Landauer ordered Louie's murder." He takes a deep breath. "Thank God Florence was a good-looking dame. She didn't stay single long. Married Karpowsky a year later, had kids with him. He did well, spread his money around town. She was okay."

"Did you get another job?"

"I was fine."

"So you left the mob?"

My father shrugs. "I wouldn't call it that. But yes. More or less."

I raise an eyebrow. "You stuck around after your partner was killed?"

"None of your business."

"What's that supposed to mean?"

"It means what it means. I stuck around a little longer. Got out. And started my own business with your Uncle Moe."

"Did Uncle Mo . . . ?"

"Enough already with the questions," my father interrupts. "I'm beat."

"But Dad, you can't just drop that on me."

"I said enough." He gets a familiar set to his jaw, the lines on either side of his chin etching out a square of resolution, and I know he's through talking. He raises himself from the chair, an arduous task that involves leaning forward with his hands braced on the arms, pushing off and waiting for gravity to propel him forward. On other nights, I'd give him a hand. Tonight I don't. I'm too appalled at what he's told me.

My father a hoodlum? A numbers runner? It's an outrageous concept. I knew he'd gone into the restaurant supply business with Uncle Moe after my sister was born. I never considered what he did for a living before that.

I rise and glance to my left. An aide is helping Mrs. Karpowsky stand and position herself in front of the walker. We wait as she approaches, each step an agony of effort. A fine dusting of powder covers her pink-skinned cheeks and, as she nears us, I catch a hint of past beauty in the curve of her chin. I feel a pang of pity for the elderly woman. How horrible it must have been to learn her husband was murdered? Yet she moved on with her life. My problems with Daniel pale in comparison. Tootsie grips my elbow as she passes. Mrs. Karpowsky ignores us.

Once she's inside, we follow her into the air conditioned lobby. I tell my father I've got to get up early tomorrow to start research for a Rosh Hashanah food article that's due in three weeks. It's a pain because it means a return trip to Miami to visit the historical museum. After accepting his offer to make me dinner the following Sunday, I kiss him good night.

I return to my car and sit with the engine idling and the air conditioner blowing full blast. I consider what my father told me. It's hard to imagine him a hoodlum, an errand boy for that gangster Landauer.

I try out the image of my dad in a striped suit and fedora hanging out with tough-looking men with heavy New York accents. He loved those characters in the gangster movies he took me to as a child. But the image is too absurd, too Hollywood to fit Tootsie. It reminds me of when I was a kid and studied the silver-framed photo my father gave my mother when they were dating. Tootsie had a full head of thick black hair and his lips curved into the dreamy smile of a forties movie idol. I wondered how that good-looking man could be my dad.

Now I'm stuck with this new image. A numbers runner. A criminal who made a living preying on poor people's dreams. It doesn't jive. That isn't the dad I knew. The father who brought me pretty dolls whenever he traveled. The cantankerous *alter cocker* with the dumb jokes.

As I pull out of my parking space and leave the grounds of the Schmuel Bernstein, I try to figure out why he decided to tell me now. Sure, I pressed him for information about Mrs. Karpowsky. But maybe he feels the need to confess before he grows too old to remember. On the other hand, he could be lying, trying to impress me. It wouldn't be the first time. Over the past few months, he's mentioned old girlfriends and bragged about business deals. Some of the stories are preposterous, involving huge sums of money. His story about Fat Louie sounds just as over the top.

I'm not sure if I believe my father. And if what he says *is* true, I have a feeling he hasn't told me the whole story. I resolve to check it out for myself.

The road's pitch dark and I can barely read the clock in my old Mercedes. It's almost nine and I'm exhausted. I head up I-95 to Boca Raton. The highway's empty so the drive goes quickly. I'm in Boca Raton in less than forty five minutes. But I'm so lost in thought I miss my exit and have to backtrack.

4

Tootsie

Becks' shoulders slump as she walks to her car and I realize I should have kept my mouth shut. My throat tightens as I realize how hard she's taking this. But running into Florence after all these years threw me for a loop. I should have known the old broad would show up at the Schmuel Bernstein. Her big shot husband's name is plastered on practically every building on campus. Even so, I thought I'd have a heart attack when she accused me of murder.

Watching Becks get in her car, I realize that I've been waiting for the shit to hit the fan. I shouldn't have told her sister about my past. I can't imagine where I got the stupid idea that telling Esther what I'd done would make her feel better about the embezzling charges against Bruce. Which, I might add, turned out to be bullshit. Esther's like her mother—always judging and letting me know when I don't live up to *her* standards. I never thought she'd stop talking to me.

Becks is different—more realistic and understanding. At least since we started talking again. Esther promised not to tell Becks, but who knows what'll happen. I don't want to lose my youngest daughter too.

There's nothing I can do about it tonight so I head upstairs to the card room, figuring a couple hands of poker will take my mind off my problems. All that's left of the regular Sunday night game, though, is a lousy folding table and a deck of cards. Damn shame. I could use the company. The television's still on and I try to catch the last few minutes of the Marlins against the Reds. The Marlins are losing.

I drop into a chair and shuffle the cards, but my mind keeps returning to the anger on Florence's face. I wonder how much she knows. Or remembers. Growing old had to be tough for a beauty like Flo. I wouldn't have recognized her if she hadn't come up to me. I haven't seen her since Bernice was pregnant with Esther.

A familiar pain—the doctor tells me it's heartburn—constricts my chest at the memory. A few weeks after Landauer canned me, Bernice announced she was expecting. I should have been thrilled. We'd been trying to have a baby. But I wasn't making enough to support a family. Fortunately, Moe used his connections to land me a job as a bouncer at the Deauville. It didn't pay much, but what choice did I have? I hated it when Bernice returned to her job at Woolworths. She said she didn't mind but I didn't believe her—especially knowing her friends were gossiping about how she *had* to go back to work.

To top it all off, a month after I started at the Deauville, Fat Louie and Florence came sauntering into the restaurant where I worked, Louie looking like a big shot millionaire in his tux and Florence flashing a diamond bracelet. I wasn't supposed to fraternize with the customers. But once Louie and Florence had settled in and were waving their martinis around, I strolled over, casual-like.

Louie's eyes narrowed but he kept his cool. We hadn't seen each other since Landauer canned us. We'd been through enough bad times, I figured, why go looking for more?

"Louie," I said, "you're looking good. I guess things turned out okay for you after all, huh?" I made no secret of eyeing Florence's bracelet.

She had the decency to blush but Louie smiled and nodded his head like one of them Hawaiian bobble dolls. He must have thought I was a schmuck.

"You got a job right away." I said. "That's great. How about giving me a piece of that action?"

Louie laughed like I'd made a big joke, which I clearly hadn't. "Got lucky," he said. "Got a great deal on a restaurant. It's turning into one of the hottest joints in town. You know it, the Blue Smoke."

I scratched my head like I was stumped. I knew the Blue Smoke all right. Me and Louie shook the owners down for protection. The joint went out of business a month before Landauer let us go. No way Louie was buying diamond bracelets with what he took in at that shit hole.

"Well, good to see you," I said when I saw the boss moving in my direction.

"Keep in touch," Florence said. "My love to Bernice."

Yeah, right, I thought. Some friend you are.

It killed me, that son of a bitch showing up at the club where I'm busting my ass. And Florence wearing diamonds while my Bernice is on her feet all day. I don't have to be a genius to figure something doesn't add up.

The next day I called Moe and told him about running into Louie and my suspicions over his newfound wealth. Moe offered to set up a meeting with Landauer to go through the receipts from the period before Louie and I were given the boot. By this time, I figured Landauer had some doubts about whether the two of us were cheating. If he knew we were, we'd have ended up in the hospital with busted knee caps.

For once God was smiling on me. Moe convinced Landauer to let me go through some old records. Turned out the old gangster had held on to the receipts from the six weeks before he sacked us and was willing to let me check them out.

I was plenty nervous going to Landauer's office, a crappy storefront on Collins Avenue where he kept a metal desk and a wall of file cabinets—I guess to look legit. Who knew what he'd have waiting for me? But after running into Louie at the restaurant, I had to find out what he was up to. One of the girls who handled the money met me at the office and went over the receipts with me. And sure enough, Louie hadn't bothered to hand in five thousand bucks we'd collected before getting the sack. That son of a bitch, Louie, held on to the money, screwing me *and* Landauer.

Moe agreed to join me to break the news to Landauer. And no surprise, the old gangster went ape, rising from behind his desk to yell at Moe and me. His face went bright red and I thought he'd have a stroke. Then he tells us we brought Louie into the operation, we've got to take him out.

The bile rises in my throat as my chest burns. I toss the deck on the table and leave the card room. On the elevator ride to my floor, I picture Becks, her eyes wide as she presses me to tell her what happened fifty years ago. I told her more than I should. It's painful enough recalling those days—never mind repeating what happened to her.

Inside the apartment, I go to the kitchen and down an antacid with a glass of milk. I finish it off with one of the sleeping pills I've been hoarding for those nights when the nightmares return. I always end up wide awake with the shakes, unable to fall back to sleep. This is certain to be one of those nights. A sleeping pill. That's what I need. For a few hours at least, my memories will disappear.

5

It's Monday morning and I'm running late, thanks to heavy traffic on I-95. The fifty-mile drive from Boca Raton to Miami usually takes an hour. Today, it takes an hour and a half. When I called the historical museum last Friday, the librarian I spoke with ordered me to be there by eleven. By the time I find the parking garage, circle the ramp to the top floor, and squeeze in between a black Hummer and a red Cadillac, it's eleven thirty. I race down the stairs, stepping gingerly around a homeless man snoring beneath layers of newspaper on the second floor landing.

My chest contracts as I realize that the last time I came here was when Daniel and I brought Gabe and Josh to the art museum. The boys made no secret of the fact they'd rather stay home, but Daniel and I insisted. Gabe followed us around the whole time whining that he was bored. Josh plopped on a bench in the first room we entered and said he was too tired to budge. After fifteen minutes, I gave up and told the boys to wait outside. By the time Daniel and I joined them a half hour later, Josh had mustered enough energy to kick a beer can around the plaza. Gabe sat on the ground watching his brother.

That was five years ago. The cultural center is still a beautiful complex, with large Mediterranean-style buildings of cream, fossilized limestone and orange barrel-tiled roofing. As I cross the bridge that links the parking tower to the cultural center where the museum's located, I glance through the ornate wrought iron railing to the street fourteen feet below. It's still packed with small shops selling cheap electronics and Cuban food. The open-air plaza that connects the three buildings is dotted with black metal tables and chairs where unshaven men and women in dull baggy clothing chat and smoke. Years ago, the plaza held a health food kiosk and the chairs were filled with stylishly-dressed business people. But I'm not surprised. These days, the homeless are as much a part of South Florida's cultural landscape as Miami Beach's art deco district.

But I'm not here to solve South Florida's social problems. I've made this trip in search of recipes. Rosh Hashanah is three weeks away and I've promised my editor something unique for the High Holiday spread by the end of next week. We both agree it's enough already with the brisket prepared fifteen different ways. I'm on a mission to learn what Miami's original Jewish settlers prepared for the holidays. There is, of course, more to this than meets the palate. I'm growing impatient with the short restaurant reviews he's assigned me of late. I know I can write better than that. It's time to prove my culinary writing skills with a front-page story.

When I enter the museum, it's easy to spot the librarian I've arranged to meet. She *has* to be the petite woman waiting in the lobby with her arms crossed and her lips pressed into a pencil-thin line. The narrow gold bar on her lapel reads "Mrs. Dupree." I feel like a giant next to this Thumbelina of a librarian. Slim and no more than four feet nine, she wears a tailored tweed suit that might have been stitched together for a child-sized doll. Tiny pleated skirt, petite white blouse with a delicate lace collar, and a miniature suit jacket.

After a quick nod and handshake but no acknowledgment of my apology for being late, she leads me through double glass doors labeled "Archives." The clicking of her patent leather heels stops so abruptly in front of a small wooden desk that I almost rear-end her. A single wooden chair is pushed under the desk. We remain standing.

"I found what you want, but be careful. Don't smudge the pages," she says, wagging a finger in my direction before lifting a book from the stack she's set out on the desk for me. The tome is bound in faded green buckram and splotched with grease marks.

"And, whatever you do, don't rip the pages. They're fragile."

I find her remarks insulting, but nod politely and reach for the book.

She retracts it and purses her lips.

"You may use the copier in the back room, but don't press the spines too firmly," she continues. "The bindings are old and delicate."

She gives me a once-over, head tilted, eyes slit. I'm tempted to inform her that I do know how to handle books, yet feel an unreasonable surge of guilt, as though she suspects I'm the type of person who tears recipes out of magazines in doctors' offices. Which, in fact, I am.

"If you have questions, call me."

That sounds like a sign-off, so I reach toward the books she's piled on the table. But she's not through yet. She inserts her tiny frame between me and the table. "You do understand that you may not remove anything from this room without my permission." This time, there's a definite challenge in her voice.

"Yes, ma'am," I say. I'm fifty years old, for crying out loud. Why does this little tyrant make me feel so guilty?

With a brisk nod, she turns and marches off.

I take a minute to look around the room. It's long and narrow and a series of wooden tables run down the center. Every table, except the one at which I'm working, is mounded with books and maps, newspapers and magazines. In contrast to the librarian, who is tidiness and efficiency personified, the place is a massive and disorganized collection of . . . who knows what. The detritus of dead Floridian's lives? I assume there's some order to the books, magazines, yellowed newspapers, and albums crammed into metal cases mounted along both sides of the room. I'm tempted to poke around before I get started on the cookbooks. But I don't want to get caught going through *her* things. So I sit down with the stack she left me.

In the last week or so, I've been considering what to do with myself, where to go with my career. With Daniel and the boys gone, I have more time on my hands. I'm trying to be positive and view this as an opportunity to focus on myself. But I'm not kidding anyone. I'm rattling around in a big house and need something that'll get me out in the world. Friends have been great about meeting me for lunch and Aviva and Noah, the couple Daniel and I spent most Saturday nights with, invited me out to dinner last weekend.

I've been considering pulling together a cookbook since I started my food columns two years ago. I'd like to focus on Jewish cooking, including my mother's recipes. This might be the project I need to get my mind off Daniel. I've already been through my own files for ideas. This morning, I hope to gather a few recipes for my Rosh Hashanah article as well as my book. It'll give me a goal to work toward and, with luck, help me become more financially independent. Daniel's been generous so far, giving me enough money to run the house, but that won't last forever.

The librarian's collection is disappointing. *The Settlement Cookbook* is the same my mother used and I've already tried most of the recipes. It was written at the turn of the nineteenth century to raise funds for East European Jews migrating to Milwaukee and includes basic recipes for steak, chicken, and the like. But it's too American. Mrs. Dupree included five charity cookbooks by the National Council of Jewish Women and Hadassah, but these date back only to the 1970s.

The most valuable find is a stack of recipes assembled by a group of Jewbans, Cuban Jews who moved to Florida, most after Fidel Castro's revolution. The yellowing pages are stapled together to form a small booklet and many look promising, certainly more exotic than the bland Ashkenazi matzo balls and gefilte fish on which I was reared. The oldest item on the pile, a booklet entitled *Crisco Recipes for the Jewish Housewife*, is written in English and Yiddish and dates back to 1930. I smile at the idea of immigrant women—in babushkas and flowered aprons—debating what to do with this big metal can of vegetable shortening.

I take the Jewban collection back to the room Mrs. Dupree indicated and copy three recipes, dropping three dimes into the rusted Maxwell House coffee can on a table by the copier. It hasn't been a productive morning and I'm anxious to head across the plaza to the library to check their cookbooks. But I don't want to leave without thanking the librarian and informing her page thirty-five of *The Settlement Cookbook* was ripped before I touched it. The problem is, I have no idea where to find her. I decide to nose through the archives and leave if she doesn't return in fifteen minutes.

After making sure that the spines of my cookbooks are as perfectly aligned as Mrs. Dupree left them, I wander over to the nearest bookcase. Each shelf is labeled with a tiny handwritten sticker. The top two shelves contain maps and books on the Miami River and the two below are packed with similar materials on Biscayne Bay. I make my way down the wall, leafing through collections on Florida's Tequesta, Seminole, and Miccosukee tribes.

I've given up on the likelihood of Mrs. Dupree's imminent return and am ready to leave when I spot a smudged label at the bottom of a shelf. I have to squat to read it. "Miami crime." That's intriguing. Not a topic I'd expect to find in a museum celebrating

South Florida history. Mrs. Dupree still hasn't returned so I poke around for information about the 1940s, when my dad's story about Fat Louie took place. The documents don't seem to be in any special order and, after leafing through a few magazines, I pull out a book about Murph the Surf, which sounds like a reasonable name for a gangster. But the book's about a jewel thief and murderer. I pick up a few books about rum runners and cocaine cowboys, but find nothing about gangsters.

I'm about to give up when I spot a large photo album bound in forest-green tooled leather. It looks promising so I bring it to the desk and prop it on my lap. There are no identifying signs on the outside, which is odd given the amount of work that obviously went into assembling the book. It's filled with newspaper clippings, arranged chronologically, about the Kefauver investigation into organized crime in Miami. I'd heard about the investigation, but didn't know much about it. The articles date from 1950 to 1951.

It's pretty scandalous stuff, though dry at times, and most of the articles cover testimony about racketeering and gambling dens. I get a thrill when I recognize the names of characters I've heard about from gangster movies — Meyer Lansky, Joe Adonis. Then, as I'm reading an account of a hearing, the name of one of the men called to testify catches my eye. I read the sentence twice before it registers and stand so abruptly the album topples onto the floor. Newspaper clippings scatter all over the ground and I drop to my knees to gather them.

I'm breathing heavily, as much from shock as the effort of crawling around on the ground to collect papers, when a pair of tiny black pumps appear on the floor in front of me. I look up. But not far. The tiny librarian scowls down at me, hands resting on her narrow hips.

I rock back on my heels and stare at her.

I should apologize.

Tell her I was killing time while waiting for her to return.

Thank her for letting me use the archive.

There's a lot I could say.

But the words that escape my mouth are, "Holy cow, it's Uncle Moe."

6

The old man's full of piss and vinegar tonight. When I arrive at his apartment for Sunday dinner, he's standing with the door open, squirming like a kid with a secret. I figure he's been sitting by the window for a half hour, watching for the so-called "classic" Mercedes my husband Daniel left behind when I threw him out. Unlike his Volkswagen, which spends its life in the shop, the Mercedes Daniel bought secondhand twenty-five years ago refuses to die.

I called Tootsie Monday after getting home from the library and he told me I was nuts. It couldn't have been his brother in the article. Sure, Moe had friends in the mob. But by the time Kefauver held his hearings in the early fifties, Moe and Tootsie were running a legitimate restaurant supply business. And didn't I have anything better to do with my life than read about dead criminals?

"I'm not mistaken. I saw his name, clear as could be," I insist. "It said he testified about this outfit, S and G, that ran bookie operations."

"And what did your uncle have to say about S and G?"

"Not much. Just that he'd heard of the group and thought they were legitimate businessmen. That he'd met with members of the company at various hotels to discuss their restaurant supply needs."

"I don't remember anything about that. But we did business with a lot of parties. If the newspaper says your Uncle Moe testified, it may be true. He was the big shot in the family. He didn't tell me everything."

I'm not satisfied with his explanation but let it drop. My Uncle Moe died years ago, and neither my father nor I are talking to his son, Zvi, who would've been too young to know what was going on at the time. I tried to explain to my dad how shocked I was to read about Uncle Moe's appearance before a committee investigating organized crime—especially after learning of his own ties to the Jewish mob. The old man kept mute. I'm pretty sure he knows more than he's telling me. Lying in bed at night these days, unable to sleep, I sometimes feel as though I'm spinning off into a strange world. First, Daniel betrays me, then I learn my father and uncle may be gangsters. No one seems to be who I thought they were.

Tonight we're having the stuffed cabbage my father bought at Epicure, a gourmet grocery across the causeway from the Schmuel Bernstein. Back in the fifties, when Miami Beach was a refuge for retired Jews, everyone went there for their borscht, chopped liver, and matzo balls. Straight from the shtetl, the Old World, my father claims. The Epicure still caters to the old Jews. But they also stock gourmet cheeses and mineral water for the skinny models and what my father calls *feygeles*—slang for gay men.

Stuffed cabbage is a big deal for Tootsie. He asks me to make it at least once a month since my mom passed away. This week, when I again remind my father I don't make Mom's recipe, he acts like I'm holding out. "A balebosta like you. A big shot food writer. You're running her noodle pudding and chicken soup recipes in the newspaper. And you can't come up with her stuffed cabbage?"

Maybe he hears me shrug over the phone or tires of riding my rear. "Okay," he concedes, "Sadie Goldfarb's daughter, Mavis, brought us to The Epicure Wednesday and I filled the freezer with cabbage rolls. I can spare a few for my favorite daughter."

That's what he calls me when he wants a favor. It's also what he calls my sister, Esther, on the rare occasions she phones or visits.

When I got off the elevator on my dad's floor, I was accosted by the rancid odor of several generations of boiled beef and cabbage. But once I step inside his apartment, I'm greeted with the pungent aroma of simmering tomatoes and vinegar. Tootsie turns down the heat on the stove and gives me a kiss, then follows me into the living room where I plop on the couch.

He plants himself in front of me and shifts from foot to foot, rocking like a dinghy on rough seas. "You notice anything different?"

I glance around the small room. The swivel chairs are covered with faded blue sheets. Back issues of the *Forward,* a Jewish newspaper, are strewn across the cocktail table and couch. The bulletin board next to the kitchen, normally plastered with colorful ads for early bird specials, is covered with black-and-white photos. I can't make out the images from where I'm sitting.

"I don't see anything," I say, looking straight at my father. I reach for the newspaper lying on the couch beside me. "Should I?"

He walks over to the bulletin board and taps its edge. "You know who this is?"

I get up, grunting, making a big show of the effort it takes, and walk to the board. My stomach contracts. An attractive thirtyish woman stands on a boat dock in one photo, leans against a market stall of straw hats in another, waves from the passenger seat of a 1950s convertible in a third.

And she's *not* my mother.

Her skin's fairly light but her features—the fullness of her lips, the curl of her hair—suggest African blood. A snapshot in the middle of the display shows my father with his arm around the woman in a banquette. I recognize the restaurant in which they're sitting as a once-famous Bahamian nightclub. When my father brought us to Nassau the summer after I finished sixth grade, we had dinner there and I admired the giant jeweled elephant statues that stared at us from shelves around the club. My father—who always used the term *schvartze*, a derogatory Yiddish word for blacks, when he talked about the truck drivers he employed—made a big show of his friendship with the owner, having me shake hands with the darkest man I'd ever seen. I felt intimidated by the man, whose deep laugh and large frame filled the nightclub, and was surprised by the gentleness and warmth of his handshake.

When I turn to my father, I catch a nasty glimmer in his eyes, a hint of wiseass in the curl of his lip. I wonder if he put the pictures out to brag of his prowess or get my goat. It's a game he plays, daring me to react. I want to snarl, but resist the urge. I look back at the photos and ball my fists, pumping them open and closed. This time he's gone too far. I walk to the bathroom and slam the door. When I'm through splashing water to relieve the heat flushing my cheeks, I look in the mirror.

And there she is, again. My mother. It's uncanny how much I look like she did at the same age.

As a teenager, all I felt for my mother was contempt. I'm not proud of it, but when you're young, the world is black and white and you're unwilling to dwell in the subtle grays and off-whites that make life bearable. If your husband cheats, you leave him. I never thought about the fact that my mother was married at twenty-one and a mother of two by twenty-four. And a woman who spent her life keeping house, raising children and playing tennis is ill prepared to face the working world. I often heard my mother and her friends speak in the hushed tones they used in discussing a friend's cancer diagnosis when they talked about Bunny, who returned to work after her husband died. A working mother was someone to be pitied.

She and my father fought late into the night, sending me scurrying for the comfort of my sister's bed when I was little.

When we were in our early teens, Mom would call us into her room, sit us down, and solemnly announce she was leaving my father. Esther would get upset, which bugged me no end me because we'd been through this so many times and our mom always stayed. I'd shrug, say go ahead, makes sense to me. Then my mother would glare at me, waiting, and I'd squirm under the pressure of her desperate need for sympathy.

It seems crazy now. I resented my father for cheating on my mother. And my mother for putting up with him while pressuring Esther and me to take sides. The older I get, the more I realize what a lasting effect my parents' relationship had on me. I had a hard time trusting boys, worried that the boyfriends I dated saw other girls. Daniel proposed three times before I felt confident enough of his love to accept.

"Becks, you okay?" My father bangs on the bathroom door. "I'm reheating the stuffed cabbage."

I splash more water on my face before coming out. He's in the kitchen, adjusting the heat under an open pan. "Let me tell you a little story before we eat," I say. "Let's sit down?"

When he hesitates, I take his arm and propel him toward a kitchen chair. He looks confused but sits and I join him.

"You remember the Boopsies?" I ask, referring to what my mother and her girlfriends called their little circle. It consisted of four couples from the neighborhood who dined at one another's homes on Saturday nights.

He nods.

"There was this one night, I was nine, when mom took Esther and me to meet them at Burger King. You," I take a few seconds to emphasize the word, "were in Nassau. On business."

He raises an eyebrow but I continue.

"I figured it was just another night without Dad, which was okay with me because we got to eat at Burger King. Mom seemed nervous all day and yelled at me twice to do my homework. Usually she wouldn't take us out if we didn't have our homework done, so I was surprised when she told me and Esther to get in the car."

I stop a second to collect my thoughts

"When we got to Burger King, Aunt Lacey and Aunt Bunny were at a table, eating. Mom got Esther and me hamburgers and made us sit at a separate table with the kids."

My father smiles, probably remembering how I resented being relegated to the children's table.

"So I was sitting there, fighting with Robbie, when I looked up. Aunt Lacey had her arm around Mom's shoulders and Mom was crying. I got scared and thought something happened to you. I jumped up and started toward Mom but Esther grabbed my arm and told me Mom didn't want us to hear."

"Do you really need to tell me this?" my father breaks in.

"Fair is fair. I'll listen to your story about that lady," I nod toward the bulletin board, "but I get to talk too."

He shakes his head and sits back, staring through the glass sliding doors toward the concrete slab patio. The only furniture out there is a weather-beaten wicker chair that my parents kept in their bedroom for thirty years. The legs have unraveled and the once-pink cushion is white from exposure.

"Mom and Aunt Lacy left the restaurant and sat in Mom's car but it was too dark for me to see them in the parking lot. You remember what a troublemaker Robbie was?"

My father nods without meeting my gaze.

"He saw me staring out the window and told me he heard Aunt Lacey talking on the phone with Mom that afternoon. She sent him out of the room, but he listened at the door and heard his mother say you had a black girlfriend and child in Nassau."

My father rises and walks into the kitchen. I stop talking as he gets the flatware from the drawer, then returns and slams forks and knives onto the placemats. His eyes are red and I suppress a pang of guilt.

"I punched Robbie so hard his nose bled," I continue after my father is seated. "Aunt Bunny dragged me off of him and sent Esther to the car to get Mom and Aunt Lacey. We left before the bleeding stopped.

"Later, in the car, I told Mom why I hit Robbie. I asked her four or five times if it was true before she answered. Know what she said?" I wait a second. "She said that you loved me and Esther and that's what mattered."

I don't know what to expect from my father. Contrition? Maybe shame? I wouldn't be surprised if he grew angry. Instead, he shakes his head and looks at me with pity.

"Your mother was right."

I raise an eyebrow.

"Sure, I cheated. But it didn't mean a thing and your mother knew it. I loved her and I loved both of you kids. She," he nods toward the bulletin board, "had nothing to do with my girls at home. A man travels a lot, he gets lonely. And I don't have another family, white or black." He laughs. "Why make such a big deal?"

I stare at him, too outraged to speak. He has no idea what I'm trying to tell him. I've wasted the last half hour explaining something he's incapable of understanding. Is he unaware of the pain he caused? Or in denial? Maybe he doesn't care.

"But you were gone so often and for so long. You can see how Robbie came up with that idea." I know my question is feeble and beside the point, but I ask anyway.

"Robbie was an idiot. Probably still is. I had a family to support and I did what I had to. If that meant a week or two in the Bahamas every month, so be it." He hesitates, looks toward the bulletin board. "It's not like I had a choice."

"What's that supposed to mean?"

He glares at me. "It means that you and your mother and sister lived very well and you have me to thank."

His face takes on a closed look and the angry set to his jaw signals the conversation is over. I'm furious but realize there's no point in arguing. If he feels no remorse for cheating on my mother, how can I expect his sympathy over Daniel's betrayal? Further discussion will lead to an argument. I don't want that. Right now, I need my father. Friends are one thing but with the kids away at college and Daniel gone, I desperately need the comfort of family.

I walk to the bulletin board and examine the photo of my father and his girlfriend in the banquette. Tootsie looks proud of the attractive woman around whose shoulder his arm is draped. I search for the slightest sign of contrition in his expression. There is none.

"You know what?" I say. "My appetite seems to be gone. I'm going to skip dinner. You enjoy the stuffed cabbage."

I grab my purse and step into the kitchen on my way out, leaning over the stove to sniff the sweet and sour scent of cabbage, raisins, and meat rising in heady waves from the pot. Unless my nose misleads me, The Epicure uses a hint more vinegar than my mother did. The pungent aroma recalls the smell I often came home to on Friday afternoons. It meant Dad was flying back from a business trip.

Driving home on I-95, I try to figure out why I've waited forty years to tell my father this story. I think it's because even as a child, I knew he wouldn't change. He saw no reason to. When I was a teenager and lashed out at him for hurting my mother, he told me to mind my own business. He didn't understand it *was* my business—and Esther's. We witnessed our mother's anguish. She turned to us for the love and companionship Tootsie wouldn't provide. It was too great a burden for a child and I grew up resenting her for demanding more affection and loyalty than I could offer.

I'd hate it if Josh and Gabe felt they had to choose between Daniel and me. They're already upset enough. When I called the boys last Monday and told them Daniel had moved out, Josh sounded near tears and begged for more details. I told him about Dawn without mentioning her age. Gabe isn't much good at feelings. His "that's too bad" was roughly the same reaction he had a few weeks earlier when I told him I'd cut my hand and gone to the emergency room for stitches. He'll process the information his own way.

Daniel's called every day since I threw him out. The first few times I listened to his apologies and pleas, but told him I wasn't ready. I'm too angry and hurt to face him—and the pain seems to be worsening with time. Now I don't answer his calls. Alone in bed at night, I picture him and Dawn on the sofa in Daniel's office or sneaking into her apartment after work. I imagine him comparing her flat stomach and firm breasts to my older, looser-skinned body. Most nights, I become so enraged and embarrassed that I have to get up and walk around. Daniel insists his affair is over, but I don't believe him. Why should I trust anything he says?

When I get home from my father's, I open the plastic container of stuffed cabbage I left on the counter to defrost that afternoon. Josh and Gabe are coming into town tomorrow to make sure I'm surviving the breakup. Grandma's stuffed cabbage is one of their favorites, as it is my father's. But it's a lot of work and, because of how my father treated my mother, I won't make it for him. When I open the container to check if it's defrosted, the odor nauseates me. I pour it down the disposal and listen as the metal blades shred the chopped meat and cabbage.

7

Tootsie

The garbage disposal churns to a halt as I flip the switch above the sink. Epicure's stuffed cabbage is good but it leaves a funny aftertaste and the prospect of eating it a second night turns my stomach. I fill the pot with warm water and leave it in the sink. Then I collapse on the couch and prop my feet on the cocktail table.

That Becks is something else. Smart. But a pain in the ass. I never should have opened my trap about Fat Louie. Now she's poking into my past. Like she has nothing else to do. Better she should work on her marriage. The dark shadows around her eyes make her look like a sick raccoon. And her rat's nest of a hairdo—I was tempted to offer to pay for a beauty parlor visit.

The article about the Kefauver investigation—how did she find it? I never saw it but I sure as hell remember what a wreck Moe was when he returned to the store after testifying. He shook life a leaf. Even the secretaries picked up on his panic.

"Dammit, Tootsie. They know," he said, slamming the door to our office and dropping into his chair. "Someone's feeding the feds information."

He'd stopped by a bar on the way to the office and his breath stank of Scotch.

"Did anyone mention Louie?" I asked.

"It didn't come up. But the deals with the Colonial and the Sands did. The committee knows something's up. They wanted to know why *we* got the contracts to outfit the restaurants."

"You held to our story, right?"

Moe nodded.

"The restaurants called *us*. We did what any business would do."

"You think they're buying it?"

"Absolutely. We sent out bids. That's it. If the restaurant owners wanted to pay a little more than our competitors were asking, so what? We're good businessmen. Deliver on time. Provide reliable service. Nothing wrong with paying a little extra for that."

Moe tied one on that night and came in hung over the next morning. A dumb thing to do, but that was Moe. Always ready to go out with his friends. Who knew how we survived with him drinking and shooting off his mouth? We were lucky. After one day of testimony, the committee left Moe alone.

Shaken by the memory, I rise from the couch and return to the kitchen, where I scour the pot and set it on the counter. If only I could make Becks understand how things were back then. When men were *expected* to have affairs. And when you had to be tough to support a family. I worked damn hard. And if I had a woman on the side, so what? I deserved it. I didn't have the advantages Becks and Esther had—a house in the suburbs and a father who could send me to college. Surviving in the business world meant compromising and dealing with whoever had the power to make or break you. Legitimate or not. She's never known the tough demands life can make, never had to face the darker side of human nature.

After all I've done for my family, she should have the decency to back off when I ask her. I've worked hard, and done a few things I regret, to give her and her sister a good life. But convincing her of that is going to be tough.

8

I love grocery shopping in the early morning, when the tomatoes are piled in glossy red pyramids and the kale, romaine, and red leaf lettuce sparkle like dewy spider webs from their first-of-the-day showers. Other than the roll of trolleys and the rip of cardboard boxes by clerks stocking shelves, the store is silent. I can be in and out in a few minutes and don't have to maneuver around pokey shoppers or make small talk with acquaintances.

This particular Monday morning is different. I haven't had a chance to shop all weekend and Josh and Gabe are due in at noon. As I'm racing around the produce section to pick up ingredients for a Niçoise salad, a familiar cough whips me around.

I do a double take. It's Daniel. He's picking through the organic broccoli, looking sheepish and grasping a bag of apples. They're sour apples, the kind he hates, but I don't tell him that. I suspect he's here because he knows it's where I shop. After weeks of dodging his calls, I have to face him.

I search for an escape route but a produce clerk arranging eggplant blocks my exit. I'd feel silly pushing her aside, then bolting like an Olympic sprinter. I try to control my breathing and smile.

It's the first time we've come face-to-face since Daniel left. I'm wearing torn jogging shorts and haven't washed my hair in three days. He looks crisp and professional in khakis and a blue button-down shirt. Both are neatly ironed. If he's moved in with Dawn, she's taking good care of his wardrobe.

"Becks. What a surprise!" he says in what sounds like a well-rehearsed line. "I needed some fruit for the office so stopped by. How are you?"

"I'm fine," I say, looking around for his basket or cart. There isn't one. "Are you cooking now?"

He laughs. "Yeah. Frozen dinners. I've moved into the Carlisle Apartments and have a kitchen you'd love. But mostly I eat out."

The Carlisle is a haven for over fifty singles and it's hard to picture Daniel in its world of hot tubs and cocktail parties. Even so, I feel a stab of jealousy at the thought of attractive single women bringing him casseroles. Then, as though to prevent me from feeling sorry for him, he adds "There are terrific diners in East Boca and I've become an expert on the local pizza joints."

Daniel's pants hang loosely around his waist and his shirt bunches over his belt. He's lost a few pounds. Dawn may be gorgeous, but she's a lousy cook. Or he's telling the truth about living alone. His apartment is a mile from our home, close to his office, and I wonder if he's been driving by the house, keeping tabs on me. He knows I don't shop every day, so that would explain how he "ran into" me here this morning.

I pick up two ears of corn and put them back. He turns toward the broccoli, takes a bunch, and stuffs them in his bag of apples.

The clerk must sense our unease because she eyes us, then abandons her eggplant for the tomatoes on the far side of the produce section.

"The apartment's nice," Daniel says, breaking the silence. "I rented some black leather couches and a wood kitchen table, just like at home."

I picture Daniel at a furniture store, struggling to pull together a bachelor pad. It sounds like he's trying to re-create the decor of our home and I feel sad, realizing how homesick he must be.

"Becks. I came here to talk to you."

I refuse to meet his gaze. "About what?"

"Getting together. I've been patient and a good sport. Whatever you needed was fine with me."

I know he's talking about money. He *has* been generous. But that doesn't make up for his betrayal.

"What about Dawn?" I say. "What's *she* supposed to do?"

"There is no Dawn. I told you it was over."

"She must have been devastated."

He folds his arms across his chest. "You need to let it go. I did something awful and I'm sorry. But we can get on with our life. I love you and I think you love me. We have too much history to walk away from. And we have the kids. They're upset."

"Of course they are." I let my voice rise. "Their father had an affair with a girl their age. Their mother is alone for the first time in her life. But they'll be fine. No thanks to you." I reach for my cart. "I don't want to have this conversation. I can't let it go. I don't know that I ever will."

I walk away with as much dignity as I can muster in shorts that bunch between my thighs and a grocery cart that squeaks like a trapped mouse. When I pull into line for a register, he's standing with the plastic produce bag at his side.

Yeah. I feel the tiniest bit sorry for him. But mostly I hope he enjoys his sour apples.

9

It's Friday morning and I've come to the conclusion that if I read another recipe for matzo ball soup, I'll be sick. I've been through more than fifty cookbooks and internet searches and come up with nothing. You can prepare matzo balls with chicken fat or vegetable oil. Leave them in the refrigerator for twenty minutes or overnight. Add leeks or flanken to flavor the broth. It's old news to me. You'd think that after centuries of making the golf ball-sized dumplings, somebody would come up with a new spin.

Tradition.

I don't think my editor's going to accept that excuse. My article's due in a week and I spent so much time with my sons during their visit that I'm behind on my work. Gabe drove up from Miami Monday morning, picking Josh up from the Ft. Lauderdale airport. It was the first time I saw either of them since Daniel's and my split. I'd hoped they could stay through Saturday and Sunday, but both had plans—a fraternity party for Josh and a paper for Gabe.

They asked about the breakup as soon as they entered the house, hugging me and asking if I was okay. Daniel and I have raised great boys. Both offered to run errands and do repairs around the house. Over lunch Monday, Josh admitted he was horrified by his father's affair. When he asked if I'd take Daniel back, I shrugged and told him it was too early to tell. Why cause the boys more worry?

We spent a few days relaxing around the house, hanging out at the mall and eating at their favorite burger restaurant. The boys slept late every morning, leaving me time to bake them chocolate chip cookies to take back to school.

Though upset with their father, they agreed to join him for breakfast Wednesday. When they got home. Josh told me his father made a point of telling them Dawn no longer worked for him. I should have been relieved, but didn't feel much of anything. Dawn's disappearance from Daniel's life does nothing to ease the sting of his betrayal. Naturally, I didn't go into that with Josh or Gabe.

I threw together a barbecue Wednesday night and Tootsie surprised me by agreeing to come—something he rarely does. Josh drove down to Miami to get him and it was nice being with family. But the table felt incomplete, a chessboard missing its king, without Daniel and his silly jokes.

"So how're you boys taking the split?" Tootsie asked once we were seated at the picnic table on the back patio. Josh, who's become quite a cook since leaving for college, brought the London broil he'd grilled to the table.

Gabe exchanged a glance with his brother. "Okay, I guess."

"Your mom tell you what happened?"

"About Dad cheating?"

"What else? Maybe you boys can talk some sense into her."

"Dad, will you drop it?" I was tossing the salad and sent a few lettuce leaves flying onto the table.

Tootsie ignored me. "What your father did was stupid. But your mother's stubborn. She won't listen to me when I tell her to get over it. Maybe she'll listen to you."

Josh winced. "That's kind of up to Mom and Dad, isn't it?"

I wanted to hug him. He sounded so mature.

"It affects you too."

Josh shrugged and slid several slices of steak, pink in the center and cut perfectly across the grain, onto Tootsie's plate.

"We're fine." He set his jaw in a line that was so similar to my father's expression of anger that I wanted to laugh. Tootsie let the subject go.

At any rate, this morning I call a dozen synagogues looking for Rosh Hashanah recipes that date back to Florida's pioneer days. They have plenty of cookbooks in their libraries and sisterhood stores. But nothing historic. Or what I'd call historic.

One of the younger librarians I phone ticks me off.

"You called the right place," she says after I explain I'm seeking holiday recipes by early settlers. "Temple Shalom has the best Jewish cookery collection in town and I'm sure we have recipes from early settlers. Let me put you on hold while I look."

I wait, envisioning her thumbing through a series of ragged tomes, their bindings barely intact, as she searches for a yellowed scrapbook of treasured recipes.

When she returns to the phone, her voice is bright with excitement. "I think I have what you're looking for. It's a sisterhood cookbook dating back to the midcentury. Here. It says nineteen sixty. You should find some historic recipes in this."

I don't tell her that's the year I was born. Or slam the phone into the receiver. Instead, with my usual ladylike restraint, I say thanks, I'll get back to you. Then I glance in the mirror on the wall in the dining room, now my office, to reassure myself I'm *not* an early Jewish settler.

Well, maybe I am.

So I've driven back to the cultural center, this time to search the library's cookbooks and, to be honest, look further into my father's past. I was too shocked to go to the library after my visit to the museum a week earlier. But the main library has an impressive collection of books and documents on Florida. I figure if I can't find the recipes I need here, I might as well accept that any records of what my foremothers cooked were swept away in a hurricane.

The garage's stairwell is free of sleeping men today, although a dozen characters in shabby clothing slouch at the black metal tables and chairs on the plaza. Most are middle-aged or younger and show signs of sleeping rough. When a gray-bearded man approaches me for a handout, I give him a five. Living outdoors has to be tough on older people and I briefly catch his gaze before he mumbles his thanks.

It's late August and the air's sticky with humidity, but at nine in the morning the sun is too low on the horizon to cast its heat on the open plaza. It'll be unbearable in a few hours when Miami's furnace sun scorches its red and yellow tiles. I assume most of the people in the plaza will escape the heat under highway overpasses, where I've seen cardboard shelters.

The hushed sanctuary of the air conditioned library is a welcome relief from the humidity and I take my time mounting the gracefully-banistered wood and metal stairs to the second floor. Upstairs, the room that houses the Florida collection is cool and faintly lit by overhead chandeliers. I pass five long tables on which small lamps throw soft yellow light, and wonder if the men sitting there, some reading and some snoozing, come to this room to escape the heat. Rows of metal shelving stocked with books extend almost fifty feet from the wooden tables to the room's windows.

I haven't been here in years so I start by approaching the librarians at the wood-paneled enclosure in the middle of the room. A tall man in khakis and a dress shirt looks up as I draw near. He's almost completely gray and has a full, neatly-trimmed salt-and-pepper beard and moustache. Thick glasses distort his eyes into large orbs. I assume he's a retiree, a senior citizen who volunteers at the library. But the sound of his "can I help you" stops me. He speaks with the deep timbre of a much younger man and I stare at him a second, experiencing an odd sensation. It's as though a masked man has removed his disguise—his beard and thick glasses—to reveal the same face, but much younger.

It doesn't take him long to catch on to what I need. He pulls a set of keys from the drawer and leads me to an enclosed room where the library keeps its rare book collection. I've always wanted to enter the library's Fort Knox, to see books that are so valuable, so precious, they're worth locking away. When the door to the small room clicks behind us, the bearded librarian pulls out three scrapbooks and a leather-bound tome. He lays them on an antique wooden table and announces he'll check back in half an hour. Then he pulls the door shut.

Although the books that fill the walls are sequestered behind glass, the room emits a musty scent and I imagine each of the well-worn volumes releasing an aroma as distinct as that of an aged wine in a well-stocked cellar. I feel remarkably at peace in this inner sanctum with its carved wooden table and shelves of rare books and wander for a few minutes, glancing into the cases. None of the titles are familiar but there's a sense of sacredness to the room. Perhaps it's because these books are a testimony to the past, to the permanence of the written word and the value humans place on the preservation of knowledge. I settle into a chair, don a pair of white cheesecloth gloves from the box on the table, and begin my search.

This time I'm lucky. The recipes I find for baked, boiled, and stewed fish are unlike anything I've seen before. The most appealing come from a small brown scrapbook with recipes written in a delicate, spidery penmanship. I squint to read the small, faded words. I'll need to do a bit more research to identify some of the ingredients, but it'll be worth the effort for something so rare. I'm surprised by the number of recipes that involve fish, then recall that's what was available in South Florida in the nineteenth and early twentieth centuries when the region was being settled.

I've just finished jotting down the third recipe, this one for a kosher fish stew, when the librarian returns. I can tell from his placid smile that he knows I've found what I'm seeking. I gather up my notes and precede him out the door.

I'm about to ask the librarian if he has any books or ideas about researching criminal activities in Miami during the 1940s when I notice a stack of small boxes on a shelving cart outside the librarian's station. They're containers of microfilm. I haven't seen those since I began searching the internet years ago. The uppermost box is labeled *Miami News, 1950*.

I turn to the librarian. "You can read the paper that far back?"

He reassures me I can. "But there's no good way to search it," he adds, "so you need some idea about when the story you want appeared."

I think back to the conversation I had with my father about Fat Louie and to the Kefauver articles I found in the museum. I know it's a long shot and that it'll mean hunching over the microfilm machine for hours, but curiosity gets the better of me. I ask for the *Miami News* from 1948 to 1949. If my uncle testified at the hearings in 1951 and World War II ended in 1945, those would be likely years to find articles on him and, maybe, my dad. I make a trip to the ladies room, then settle in front of a microfilm machine with ten boxes of film.

My stomach is grumbling and my eyes ache but, two hours in, I'm no better off than when I started. It's taking longer than it should to scroll through the blurred images of articles published more than a half century earlier; I can't resist reading the occasional story. Nineteen forty-eight, it seems, was particularly eventful. Mahatma Gandhi was assassinated and Israel declared its independence from Great Britain.

I move on, finding an interesting piece about movie studios blacklisting Dorothy Parker for her left-leaning politics, then realize I'm nearing the end of my final microfilm roll. I'm disappointed at finding nothing, but relieved to be ending my search. Then a familiar name flashes across the screen. I back up the roll until I find it again. Abe Kravitz. I smile. Abe was one of my father's best friends, but I haven't heard his name in decades. He was a skinny guy, always in motion, with too much energy to stay seated for long. He and his wife, Betsy, were regulars at our home. The two never had children but were among the close family friends who attended my sister's and my birthday parties. I knew Abe did business with my dad, but never knew what it was. At some point, I realize as I fiddle with the microfilm machine, he stopped coming to the house. I can't remember why.

The article is three paragraphs long but it takes a few minutes to enlarge the type and focus well enough to read. The article reports that Abe was convicted for selling stolen goods to restaurants and bars on Miami Beach. He was sentenced to five years. I do the math. He was out of prison by the time I was born. I glance around, wishing there was someone I could tell. Abe a thief? It sounds crazy. But so did my father's story about Fat Louie. I press a button to copy the article and stuff it in my purse to show my father. If I confront him with it, he may be willing to tell me about his past. I return the microfilm to the book cart.

On my way out of the library, I swing by the free computers and log in to my email account. Nothing important. I decide to do a search on Abe Kravitz. The odds are good he's long gone and the best I can hope for is an obit. After a bit of surfing, I learn Betsy passed away two years earlier. But Abe is still around. In fact, he lives in Harbour Villas in Boca Raton, fifteen minutes from my house. A short click to anywho.com and I've got his phone number. It's only three, so I decide to call from the car and ask to stop by. Maybe he'll tell me something about my father's past.

Abe sounds delighted to hear from me and says come over. I don't mention how I came across his name. Or bother him with my father's cockamamie gangster tale. I don't need another *alter cocker* angry with me.

An hour later, I'm idling in line behind the Harbor Villas guardhouse, a rickety white shack inside of which sits an elderly man in a burgundy toupee. When it's my turn to enter, he scrutinizes me, letting his gaze run up and down my face and peering into the car before he asks for identification. I suppress a laugh as he squints at the front, then back, of my driver's license. Satisfied I'm not a middle-aged suburban terrorist hell-bent on taking out elderly Jews, he returns it to me. The arm of the gate rises and I enter a maze of low-slung, two-story buildings painted the same mind-numbing white as the guardhouse.

Harbour Villas is a concrete Mecca where retired northerners move to spend their golden years in the land of sunshine, palm trees, and early bird specials. I'd never been inside but heard its residents love it. Always something to do. Singing, dancing, bingo, canasta, mahjong. And bus service to the mall, the grocery store, and the doctor's office. Including Daniel's oncology practice.

It takes fifteen minutes to find Abe's apartment and park my car. Each building is an identical two-story cement structure with glass-jalousied windows and doors that open to a narrow walkway. When I make it up the exterior steps to his apartment, it's almost six. Although the apartments open to an outdoor corridor, the walkway smells of cat urine. I hear the faded roar of a television behind Abe's door and hope I'm not interrupting dinner.

I knock and wait a minute. When Abe opens the door, he holds a cane in his left hand but greets me with a powerful handshake. "What's it been? Twenty, thirty years?" he says, appraising my appearance like a butcher examining a side of beef. I half expect him to guess my weight.

"At least thirty," I answer as he steps back to let me in. "You're looking well. It's nice to see you in good health."

The apartment's larger than I expect. The kitchen is no more than a single wall of appliances and cabinets with a dinette, but the living area is as big as my family room. A white leather couch occupies one wall. To its left sits a matching recliner and end table. Opposite the chair is a large-screen television, tuned to a football game with the sound off. The only object that distinguishes the apartment as Abe's is an eight-by-ten studio shot of Abe and Betsy in their fifties on the end table. Otherwise the apartment feels as cold and impersonal as a budget motel lobby.

Abe hasn't changed much, though I suppose he always looked old to me. His hair is completely silver, but he still has a full mane that he's brushed back and left long at his nape. He flashes a familiar crooked grin when he sees me studying the photo. "Love of my life," he says, easing himself into the recliner. "Passed away two years ago next month."

I settle into the couch, offer my condolences.

We make small talk. "How's your dad? Any kids? What're you up to these days?" I tell him I've got two sons in college and that I write for a newspaper.

"I heard your Uncle Moe died young, what was he, thirty-five? A damn shame. You see your cousin much?" He watches me closely as he asks these questions and I assume he's being tactful.

My uncle had a heart attack when I was eight and his son, Zvi, twelve. At that point, I wasn't old enough to grieve for him. Which isn't to say I didn't love him—but I was too young to understand what death meant. He did magic tricks for Esther and me, pulling quarters from behind our ears and teaching us card tricks we'd show off to our friends. I felt sorrow for Zvi, who was much nicer to me than Esther was. He worshipped his father and spent the week after Uncle Moe's death holed up in his bedroom

My father was so devastated he closed his business for two weeks and disappeared into his study. Esther and I were frightened by the sobs and moans coming from behind his locked door but our mother assured us he was fine, that it was his way of grieving.

"I hardly ever see him," I tell Abe. "We used to do all the holidays together but that stopped after Uncle Moe died."

"Well, how about that?" He sounds almost satisfied by my answer. Then he adds, "I'm sorry to hear it. It must have been hard for your cousin and aunt to see the happiness your family shared.

"What about your husband?" Abe says, changing the subject. "Did you keep your original model?"

I laugh and tell him I'm married to a doctor named Daniel Ruchinsky. At that, his eyes light up. "*The* Dr. Ruchinsky?" he asks, leaning forward. "The oncologist on Eighteenth Street."

I nod and decide against mentioning our separation. "You know him?"

"Who doesn't?" He laughs. "At my age, everything's a scare. You feel a bump on your leg. It's cancer. Your appetite is gone. It's cancer. The one time I had cancer, your husband saved my life."

I often went to Daniel's office to help with hiring and paperwork, but didn't get to know his patients. "I'm glad to hear that," I say, though Daniel is the last person I want to discuss.

"It was last August. My internist noticed my white blood count was low and sent me to your husband. One, two, three, he's got me in the hospital, on chemotherapy, and after a few months, I'm back to myself. Without Dr. Ruchinsky's help, who knows?" He leans back in his seat and waves a hand in the air as though to indicate his apartment or his life or maybe the football game. "Bought me a few more years."

Our conversation moves to the past, and Abe tells me stories about excursions to the horse track and jai alai with my father and uncle. About dinner parties when the men were first married, Hanukkah celebrations after my sister and I were born. When we run out of chit chat, Abe cocks his head and flashes his crooked smile. "So what brings you here after all these years?"

I've been anticipating this question but still don't know how to respond. On the drive over, I considered whether to show him the article or bring up what my father told me about Fat Louie. I know Abe goes back far enough with my father and uncle to tell me about their involvement with the Jewish syndicate. Whether he's willing to share that information may be another story. I pull the article out of my purse and place it facedown on my lap. I try not to fiddle with it as I talk.

"A few weeks ago, my father told me a strange story. I don't know whether he was making it up, but he seemed upset. It was about gangsters he knew in the nineteen forties and a job he got through Uncle Moe."

When I look up, Abe's good-humored smile is gone, replaced by a scowl. He sits back with his arms crossed.

"I don't know how much of it is true," I continue. "Or if any of it is. He's getting on in years and he likes to test me, to see how I'll react to the outrageous things he says. I think that's what he's doing. But maybe not."

Abe's face darkens and his eyebrows crease to form a single line across his forehead. I'm alarmed by his reaction, but keep going.

"He told me this story about a friend named Fat Louie who crossed the mob. Dad says the guy ended up in Biscayne Bay." I don't know how much my father told Abe, and I don't want to give anything away that I shouldn't.

Abe's been so still and quiet that I'm surprised when he leans in toward me. He grasps the wooden handle on his recliner and jerks it up, returning his chair to an upright position. Then he rises. His hand, as he reaches for his cane, trembles.

"So why come to me?" Abe speaks in a deep voice. The warm avuncular man who greeted me ten minutes earlier has turned into a frightening stranger. He sounds deliberate and sinister, and the fierce glare he directs at me makes clear he'll accept nothing short of the truth.

I glance at the clipping on my lap, then at Abe. I cover the paper with my purse.

"What've you got there?" he demands, extending his free hand.

"It's nothing. I was just—"

"Give me the damn thing."

I debate a second, then hand it over. As Abe reads, the blood drains from his face. He looks up and his eyes narrow into a thunderous glare.

When he finally speaks, his words come out like a metal rasp drawn across rusted steel. Each word emerges distinct and sharp, repetitive blows to the gut. "Get. Out. Of. My. House," he says, jabbing a finger in my face. "And. Never. Come. Back."

I'm terrified he'll hit me or have a heart attack. I slink backward toward the door.

As I pull it open, he steps forward and presses his face into mine. His breath reeks of tobacco and mint.

"And tell your father to go to hell."

I'm so upset I don't remember leaving Harbour Villas or pulling up to my house. The violence of Abe's reaction left me stunned and frightened. What did my father do to provoke such hatred? My image of Tootsie, already shaken, is teetering on the brink of disbelief. What is he hiding? Did my mother know? I keep getting hit with these bombshells. First, Daniel cheats on me, which is the last thing I'd expect. Then Tootsie turns out to be a gangster with a past that's so horrendous he can't discuss it. It undermines me, makes me fearful about what my friends, even Josh and Gabe, may be hiding. Who else is lying to me?

I sit in the car, engine off, in the dark garage. What should I do next? My first instinct is to call Tootsie and tell him about my meeting with Abe. But that conversation is better held face-to-face. On the phone, it'll be easy for him to blow off my questions and claim Abe is demented. He tried that with Mrs. Karpowsky. I need to take him by surprise in a relaxed setting when he's in the mood to talk. I leave the car and let myself into the kitchen. The answering machine blinks; another call from Daniel. I ignore it. I resolve to question my dad. Really question him.

And hope he'll tell me the truth.

10

My kitchen looks like a farmers' market, the counters heaped with red bell peppers, carrots, scallions, potatoes, garlic, and mahi-mahi. The water's just reached a boil and I'm about to throw everything into the stockpot when the phone rings. It's my father, insisting I drive him to the mall to buy white trousers. It's the Sunday morning after my meeting with Abe and I'm in no mood to take Tootsie shopping. Especially since he wants to be there when the stores open at noon.

I try to put him off. "Can't it wait? I need to test a recipe for my Rosh Hashanah article while everything's fresh. Let's go next weekend."

"You have all day tomorrow to cook," he says, generously rearranging my schedule. "I want the pants for a party Tuesday night and I might need to get them altered. If you can't take me, I'll drive myself."

I take that for what it is—a threat. The last thing I need is Tootsie careening down Dixie Highway in his ancient Lincoln Town Car. The last time he did that, he took the rear fender off a Maserati. I agree to pick him up in an hour and start shoving food into the refrigerator. My stew will have to wait.

The old man makes no secret about considering me his chauffeur and valet. In the last few years in particular, as his driving has worsened, I've put up with it. My sister, Esther, says I'm a doormat for squiring him around. Then again, she won't even talk to him. She says it's because he treated my mother badly and made no effort to hide his affairs. I explain to Esther that, sure I resent Dad, but he's still our father. The only parent we have.

He's not an easy person to love and there are times I'm tempted to cut him off. But he has moments of charm and humor and I treasure those.

What I haven't spelled out to Esther is that, more than anything else, I don't want to live with regret. After he's gone, I want to know I've been the best daughter I could be. Even if that means overlooking his faults.

I throw on the same jeans and shirt I wore Saturday and head down to Miami to pick up Tootsie. He chatters the entire drive to the mall. The Schmuel Bernstein is having a dinner dance at the Eden Roc Tuesday night, he says, and it's hosted by the Karpowsky Family Foundation.

I'd Googled the Karpowsky Foundation a few weeks earlier after noticing the name on at least half the buildings on the Schmuel Bernstein campus. Mrs. Karpowsky's late husband, Ira, made his fortune manufacturing Sheetrock and set up an endowment to build and maintain housing and medical facilities at the home. He also left a substantial fund for entertaining residents that stipulated a dinner dance be held in his memory every other year. It's ironic that the family of the woman who accused my father of murder is hosting him for an expensive dinner. I don't mention that. Tootsie's revved about the affair and determined to show up in new white trousers.

"Maybe we should look at rental tuxedos," I suggest as I pull into a parking spot.

"When did you become Miss Emily Post?"

"I'm just saying. People will dress up."

"I happen to have good fashion sense," he says, unbuckling his seat belt. "I bought a beautiful shirt from Costco that'll be perfect with white pants and the white loafers your mother got me."

I don't know which dismays me more, the fact that he's hanging on to shoes my mother bought fifteen years earlier, before she left him, or that he's turning into a caricature of an elderly Florida tourist—white shoes, white pants and, no doubt, a white belt.

There's no point arguing so I step out of the car and follow him into Macy's. The heady scent of expensive perfume puts me in a spending mood as we walk past the glittering glass makeup counters to reach the men's department. I need a dress for a bar mitzvah in two weeks, but resist the urge to take a side trip to the women's department.

Maybe it's because a cool breeze is replacing the oppressive heat of the past month and everyone wants to be outside, but the men's department is deserted except for the saleslady folding shirts at the checkout counter. My father pulls five pairs of white pants off the first rack we come to without gazing at the tags. "Size don't mean nothing no more," he says when I object. "I'll try them on until something fits."

Daniel does most of his shopping at Costco so I don't know my way around Macy's men's department. My husband's no clotheshorse, but he looked particularly shabby when he stopped by Wednesday night for more shirts. He still calls every day and I still ignore him. Thursday, he emailed me about seeing a marriage counselor. I wrote back that he's welcome to consult a therapist about his cheating. As far as I'm concerned, that's our only problem. I know I'm hiding, avoiding any steps toward moving on in our relationship, but I don't have the strength yet to deal with the future.

I follow my father to the men's dressing room and stand at the entrance so Tootsie can model his pants. This is the first chance I've had to mention my visit to Abe's.

"I saw an old friend of yours Wednesday," I yell into the general emptiness of the dressing rooms. "You remember Abe Kravitz?"

I hear a rustle of clothing, then the jingle of coins.

"You hear me?" I ask after a few minutes.

"Yeah, I heard you."

"Do the pants fit?"

"The first pair's too big."

"So what do you think? Of seeing Abe?"

"What am I supposed to think?"

"He seems fine. His wife died a few years back."

"Good for her."

My father steps out of his dressing room. The pants drape around his ankles and over his shoes and fit too snugly across the stomach. I shake my head and he returns to the room.

A few minutes later, the saleslady enters the changing area and dashes from room to room snapping up discarded clothing. Once she's out of earshot, I speak up again. "I came across a newspaper article about Abe while doing research last week. Did you know he went to jail for selling stolen goods?"

"What about it?"

"You tell me."

"There's nothing to tell. That was before we met."

"I decided to pay Abe a visit. I thought it'd be fun after all these years."

My father sticks his head out of the dressing room door. "You're full of crap." Then he ducks back in. "What's with you, Doll? I tell you a little story and, before I know it, you're all over me and everyone in town with these stupid questions. No one cares anymore. Everyone's dead. Or should be."

"Not Abe."

"What's that supposed to mean?"

"He was friendly at first, talking about good times with you and Uncle Moe." I don't mention I was pumping Abe for information about Fat Louie. "When I showed him the article, he went ape."

"What'd you expect? It's none of your business."

"Maybe not. What I don't get is why he got mad at *you*. He said to tell you to go to hell."

Tootsie doesn't answer. Instead, he leaves the dressing room in a pair of pants clearly made for a giant. I shake my head yet again and he returns to the room.

My father is right about the pants. The fifth pair he tries fit. After the saleslady rings us up, we head to the food court for lunch.

"What happened between you and Abe?" I ask after we're settled at a table with our trapezoidal orange trays. The seating area is surrounded by delicatessens, Chinese takeout joints, and fast food outlets. I have to lean in so my father can hear me over the chatter and clinking of trays. "He used to come over all the time. Then he disappeared."

"You are a pain in the ass, Becks," my father says, tucking a napkin under his chin. "Do you promise to leave him alone if I tell you?"

I shrug.

"You can't let things drop, can you? Maybe this'll convince you. Abe was a hoodlum. I knew he had a hand in the rackets and did time, but everyone had something not quite kosher going then. It was no big deal. By the time we met him, Abe was in the electronics business. At least that's what he called it."

"We?"

"Your Uncle Moe and me. When we first started the restaurant supply business, we bought our refrigerators from Abe. He had the best prices in town. Nobody could compete. Of course, I should have figured it out."

"Figured out what?"

He rubs his thumb against his fingers, making the sign for cash.

"The stuff was hot?"

"You bet." He reaches across the table and taps me on the forehead. "Smart girl. One day, two cops stop by. Tell us someone's been holding up trucks heading south on U.S. 1 with restaurant equipment. Ovens. Refrigerators. You name it. The police have serial numbers for a few dozen stolen items and leave us a list. If any of it shows up, we should call them."

"Did you have any of the stuff?"

"Sure we did. But we're not about to report it. We know what refrigerators cost. That's what we put in our books. The police aren't going to say 'thank you very much' and leave us alone if we turn Abe in. They're going to check our records. And have the IRS on our asses so fast, our heads will spin."

"So what'd you do?"

"Moe, as usual, had all the answers."

I wait as he takes a bite of his sandwich, two thick slabs of seeded rye that barely restrain an inch and a half of fatty pink pastrami. Only in Miami do the food courts serve good deli. And *café con leche*. Tootsie takes a sip of coffee and another bite of pastrami before I realize that he considers the story over.

"So what did you and Uncle Moe do about the stolen refrigerators?" I ask, louder.

"What difference does it make?"

"I want to know why Abe's so angry."

My father sets his sandwich in its clear plastic container and wipes each finger, an elaborate operation that involves the use of one flimsy paper napkin per digit. "I'm not sure," he says once he's through. "It's been a long time. As far as I can remember, Moe doesn't bother to tell Abe the cops stopped by. Instead, he calls Abe's office manager and tells the girl we're through doing business with him. We've got a new supplier and Abe should find himself another schmuck to buy the refrigerators."

The old man's got a pretty accurate memory of events, considering the decades that have passed and his claims to have forgotten.

"Abe phones a couple times after that," he continues. "He wants to know what's going on. We tell our girl—you remember Mary—to inform Abe we're not in. A couple weeks later I see an article in the *Miami News*. Some bums—we figure they're Abe's men—get pulled over with a semi full of stolen ovens and refrigerators. Abe gets off. Must have greased the right palms. But his men get sent away. Next we hear, Abe's selling shoes at Jordan Marsh."

"You haven't seen him since?"

"Not a word."

"And he's still angry?"

"According to you."

"It seems like a long time to hold a grudge," I say, stuffing the remainder of my tuna sandwich in the polystyrene container.

"What do you mean?"

"You didn't turn him in. You could have."

"So what?"

"So why'd he have a fit and throw me out of his apartment after all these years?"

"You're so naïve, Doll. You don't know nothing about human nature."

"What do you mean?"

"I mean you're a lucky girl. Some people forgive and some don't." He stands and picks up his tray. "Not everyone's as warmhearted as your old man."

11

Tootsie

I'm gazing out at the marina, studying the multimillion dollar yachts docked at Bayside Marketplace, when a raspy voice breaks into my musings.

"Been a long time."

My stomach contracts and I rise from my seat at the small outdoor café. Struggle as I might, I can't hide my shock. It's been fifty years since I've seen Abe Kravitz and the man's as emaciated and stooped as a holocaust survivor. I'd never have recognized the well-muscled son of a gun I used to hang out with. His face, hard-boned and swarthy as an Italian's in the old days, is gaunt and sallow.

I called Abe the night before, after Decks dropped me off, to let him know what my daughter told me about her visit. I asked if we could get together. Turned out the old goat had a doctor's appointment in Miami this morning and grudgingly agreed to meet for coffee. I am confident this will *not* be a joyful reunion.

I drop back in my seat and try not to stare as Abe lowers himself into the rattan chair across the table. I'm surprised that Abe—as sickly as he appears—has the strength to wend his way through the waterfront shopping center's parking lot and past the colorful cramped kiosks. Most are stocked with trashy souvenirs for passengers from the cruise ships nearby.

"Long time," Abe repeats. "Heard about Bernice."

I shrug. It's nice of him to say something. "My condolences on Betsy. She was a good woman."

The waiter takes Abe's order for American coffee and leaves the dregs of my *café con leche* on the table. Latin dance music wafts toward us, carrying the salsa beat from a band performing along the wharf a hundred feet north.

As Abe checks the menu, I eye him. The old bastard hasn't aged well. There's nothing left of the tough guy I knew in the late forties, when we had full heads of dark hair, flat guts, and our pick of the dames. Abe had just moved to Florida from Bayonne, New Jersey, same home town as Louie, and Louie helped Abe get a job with Landauer. Abe proved himself smart and aggressive and became one of Landauer's top lieutenants in less than six months. The three of us—Abe, me, and Louie—spent many a Saturday night hitting the nightclubs on Miami Beach, picking up broads. It seems like another lifetime.

"So what am I doing here?" Abe says, tilting his head and studying me. His lips are pursed and his eyes squint in the manner of a scientist examining a rare and repellant insect. It occurs to me I haven't aged so well either. "What do you want?"

"Like I said last night, Becks told me you threw her out. I want to find out what you told her."

"I had to come here for that?" Abe snorts. "I told her more than you did." His eyes narrow. "Does she know anything about your past? What happened with Landauer and Moe?"

"Of course not," I say, waving away the possibility with a flick of my wrist. I'm trying to play it cool but my palms are damp and perspiration drips down my back. "My daughter's nosy and she'll dig around until she finds what she's looking for, or what she thinks she's looking for. She found out about Moe going before the Kefauver committee and came across an article on you." I glance at Abe, then down at the flashy cigarette boats docked at the seawall. "If she finds out—I'm begging you not to say anything. For old time's sake."

Abe laughs, an ugly rasp that draws the attention of the obese pink-skinned couple at the adjacent table. "You want *me* to keep quiet for *you*? Let your daughter think you're a sweetheart? After what you did to me?"

"What are your talking about?"

"You know damn well what I'm talking about. I'm supposed to protect the reputation of a rat? The creep who closed down my business."

"Wait a minute now. I didn't turn you in."

"What do you take me for?"

"I swear it. Some of Moe's friends, cops, showed up at the store and told us you were selling hot merchandise. They asked us to let them know if we came across stolen goods. But we never ratted."

I'm breathing hard and stop talking as a leggy blonde glides by on Rollerblades. Her short, skintight black dress punctuates every curve of her derriere and her thigh and calf muscles ripple with each stride. "Girls today dress like whores," I say, then add, "nothing wrong with that."

"So how'd my men get caught if *you* didn't rat?" Abe persists.

"Damned if I know."

"Come on. Do I look stupid? Who else knew they were heading down U.S. 1 with a shipment of refrigerators?"

I shrug. "I'm telling you, it wasn't us. You never told us where the merchandise came from or when it was coming in. We couldn't have snitched if we'd wanted to."

Abe jumps up, knocking his chair backward, then braces himself on the table with both hands. He leans in until his nose almost touches mine. "Bullshit. I don't know what you and Moe got out of it, but there's no doubt in my mind you ratted." He takes a step back. Perspiration glazes his forehead. "It was stupid of me to come here. I thought you were ready to apologize. To admit you'd turned my men in and wanted forgiveness. But you haven't changed a bit. Still out for yourself."

"Hold on. I took care of Landauer's family. And I did what he—" I start, but Abe interrupts.

"Did you know Betsy left me?"

Stunned by the man's sudden flare up, I shake my head.

"That's right. She was working in lady's undergarments while I sold shoes. She couldn't handle it. Went home to her parents."

"I'm sorry. I didn't know."

Abe waves away the sympathy. "We got back together again. No thanks to you."

"Abe, I swear we didn't—"

"Just leave me the hell alone, will you? And keep your daughter out of my hair. I'm not promising anything."

He releases his grip on the table and stands back. "So if you need anything, like silence about your past, don't call me. As far as I'm concerned, you're a load of horseshit." He turns his back on me and leaves, moving slowly. His shoulders are stooped and his right leg drags.

I rise from my seat and drop a ten on the table, then wait so Abe can reach his car before I head to the parking lot.

Once I get to my car, I reach for the jar of antacids in my glove compartment. Damned heartburn's acting up again. I don't know whether to curse Becks. Or that bastard, Abe. Either way, I need to come up with a plan for stopping my daughter. If she finds out about my past—well, I can't let it happen.

12

Two nights after my father and I visit the mall, the phone rings. I'm scouring a pan of burned noodle pudding but rip off my gloves and grab the receiver. I'm expecting—well, hoping for—a call from Gabe. When we spoke earlier in the day, he sounded nasal, a sure sign he's coming down with a cold. He was in the middle of exams so I offered to drive to Miami to bring him cold medicine, soup and Vitamin C. He told me his health was fine but if I wanted to make him feel better, I could let his dad move back in. That threw me. After a second during which I didn't know how to respond, I tried to explain how devastated I was by his father's affair. Gabe didn't seem to care. I should know better. The Asperger's prevents him from having any idea how I feel.

The caller is Tootsie.

"You remember Ari Plotnik? Uncle Moe's grandson," he says, jumping into conversation without a hello. "I just got an email. Kid says he's a kosher butcher in some *ferschtunkena* Iowa town, I can't remember which. He wants to know if our family has any Kohanim blood. I'll email it to you." Then he clicks off.

I finish the dishes and read the email. Ari's wife has traced her family back to Rabbi Gamaliel or some other Hebraic bigwig and Ari is hot to enhance his own pedigree. You get more face time at the bima, the podium at the front of the sanctuary, if you can prove you're a member of the Kohanim, the priestly tribe.

I email my father that I don't know anything about our tribal history. Then Tootsie copies me the email he sends Ari claiming that the only relation he can find is a Plotnik in Lodz who served as the synagogue's shamus. I suspect Tootsie's lying. Either way, the old man gets a huge kick out of telling the kid that his treasured ancestor was the guy who cleaned toilets for the rabbi.

It turns out to be family reunion week because the next day my cousin Sella—Ari's sister—emails that she'd like to get together. I'm thrilled to hear from her. No one in my family has seen Sella since fifteen years earlier, when her father, Zvi—Uncle Moe's son—demanded we depart his synagogue. We were there for Sella's bat mitzvah, or the nominal recognition that passes for one in an orthodox synagogue where women can't read from the Torah.

Zvi's wife, Leah, hadn't bothered to tell her husband she'd invited us in what turned out to be a botched attempt at family reunification. My father has refused to tell me the cause of his rift with Zvi, but that day my cousin announced we weren't Jewish enough to set foot in his precious orthodox synagogue. As *he* saw it, we were practically gentiles, Reform Jews who'd committed the grievous sin of abandoning the ritual he considered critical to claiming one's rightful place as a descendant of Abraham, Isaac, and Sandy Koufax.

Sella writes that she hasn't seen her father in six years and her mother's moved to New Jersey. Sella still lives in South Florida, though, and wants to meet us. I'm delighted and figure this is an opportunity to reunite with Zvi's family, if not Zvi himself. She accepts my invitation to lunch the next Sunday. Of course, I invite Tootsie.

Sella and her husband, Craig, show up just after noon with a two- and a three-year-old who fall asleep in their stroller minutes after arriving. I try to be subtle about studying Sella, seeking traces of the little girl I last saw in her pale purple bat mitzvah dress, all freckles and curls. She has red hair like Aunt Irene, my father's sister, but missed out on the Plotnik eyes, which tend to be a little close-set. Hers are beautiful, green and almond shaped. I can't remember what her mother looks like but figure the eyes came from that side of Sella's family. My father keeps elbowing me and trying to whisper in my ear. I refuse to listen.

"So what happened between your father and mother?" Tootsie asks once everyone's settled in my family room. "We heard she got smart and left the bastard."

I glare at my father. "What kind of question is that?"

"That's okay," Sella says. "You're right. She couldn't take Dad anymore. When her mother, Grandma Nan, died, mom inherited some money and moved up north."

"Smart girl," my father says.

"Is your father still in the house?"

She shrugs, which I take as a yes.

It's a pleasant enough visit. Sella's bubbly and garrulous, though her husband and kids are quiet. My father tells her about family in the area, distant cousins and the like, which is big of him given that he refuses to talk to any of them.

"You remember your Aunt Irene?" he asks. "Your grandfather's sister? You always looked so much like her. That's why she left you our mother's cameo brooch. You still have that?"

Sella looks confused. "No. But I left home in a hurry. My father threw me out. My mom may have it."

We wait for an explanation. It doesn't come.

Sella tells us she rarely speaks to her brothers and acts surprised when Tootsie says he's in touch with Ari. She seems ill at ease, hesitant talking about family. I'm curious about her estrangement from my cousin, Zvi, but don't want to make her uncomfortable so let it be.

By the time we sit down to lunch, it's apparent Sella and Craig are beset by bad luck. Craig's having a hard time finding work so they've moved into his father's apartment, where they share a room with their children. The jobs Sella's been offered don't pay enough to cover childcare. I offer to look at her resume, to help her find something that pays better. She turns me down.

We have lunch in the dining room—I've set out bagels and bowls of tuna and egg salad—and after Sella and Craig pack their kids and stroller into their van and take off, I walk my father to his car.

"There's something wrong here," he says. "But I'm not sure what. I've got a funny feeling." He hands me a slip of paper with a series of numbers and letters.

I raise my eyebrows.

"Their license plate number."

He waits for me to read his mind but only adds "Just in case."

Two weeks later, I'm in the kitchen loading the dishwasher and the phone rings. It's Sella. Her father-in-law is driving her nuts.

"I wouldn't ask if I weren't desperate. He despises me, hates that Craig married a Jew. I'm afraid we're going to end up on the street." She waits a beat. "I know I have a lot of nerve asking and I'll understand if you turn me down. But all we need is four or five thousand for a deposit and last month's rent on our own apartment. We'd pay you back as soon as we could."

I consider it. She is family. I can afford it. But something holds me back. I feel awful, but the answer is no.

"I understand," she says, "I had to ask."

Two weeks later, I'm in Tootsie's living room working on the *New York Times* crossword puzzle when my father slams his hand on the kitchen counter.

"The little pisher's a liar," he says, drawing my mind away from a four-letter-word for "bites like a horse." I've gotten halfway through the puzzle in the time it's taken Tootsie to decide between Chinese and Italian. I usually place the order but this Sunday he complains that I never get what *he* wants, so, after a brief argument, I give in. He calls for Chinese takeout and, after rooting around in the kitchen for paper plates, plops into the swivel chair across from me. A sneer works its way over his face, his pink rubbery upper lip curling to reveal a neat row of yellowing teeth. He wears a faded green polo that fit twelve years ago when I bought it for him as a birthday present. Now his turkey waddle of a neck looks lost in the voluminous folds of the collar.

I set the newspaper down and lean back, resting my feet on his cocktail table. I can tell from the way he glares at me that he's aching for an argument. I've got nothing better to do until the food comes, so I bite.

Okay," I say, "who's lying?"

"Sella. Your precious cousin."

He gives me this twisted smile, his version of a "gotcha." I wonder what line of logic has led from an argument over my historical failure to send out for what he wants for dinner to this crazy conclusion about Sella. He probably couldn't tell me himself.

"What's Sella lying about?" I ask, hoping to get the argument over with before the food arrives.

"The husband. He's not a Jew. And those aren't her kids."

"How'd you reach that brilliant conclusion?"

"Craig, Greg, whatever he calls himself. He's a *shaygetz*, and so are the boys. You ever see a blond in the Plotnik family?"

"Dad." I draw out the word, putting a couple of bucks worth of annoyance into it. "Sella said Craig converted. He became a Jew long before they met."

"And you believe her? Come on, Becks, you're smarter than that."

I look at my father and shake my head in disbelief. But he has a point. The husband and boys don't look—somehow don't *feel*—Jewish. Even so, what difference does it make? Anyone born to a Jewess gets to wear the Mogen David, the Jewish star. So she's got the boys covered.

The food arrives and my father plunks the cartons of General Tso's chicken and pork fried rice on the table. It's only six o'clock, but the sky is growing dark as thunderclouds roll in from the east. We eat facing the sliding glass doors. There isn't much to look at from the third-story apartment, just a tar-paved walkway that leads between concrete block buildings and small groupings of palm trees and scruffy red hibiscus. What we mostly see is our own reflection, an old man and a middle-aged woman sitting at a tiny kitchen table.

"Have you talked to Sella?" I ask, steering him away from the subject of her sons and husband.

"I called a few days ago. Told her I'd drive up to Broward, take her out for a nice dinner. She says she can't afford a sitter. So I say, let your husband sit." He dumps the remaining General Tso's on his plate. "She was not interested."

"Is that why you think she's lying?"

Tootsie compresses his lips and sits back in his chair. "It's more than that. It's the kids, the husband. I don't know. Maybe there's something to this blood thing. She doesn't even feel like mishpachah." He uses the Yiddish term for family. "I'd call her father but—"

"He's a gonif," I finish for him. A crook. My father paid for Zvi's education, including law school, and is as upset over my cousin's lack of gratitude as he is by Zvi's reputation as an ambulance chaser.

"I haven't heard much from Sella either," I continue. "She sent a card after Rosh Hashanah, apologized for cancelling dinner."

I'd invited Sella's family and my father for Rosh Hashanah along with my friends Aviva and Noah. It was nice but the holiday felt incomplete without Daniel and the boys. I couldn't ask Josh to travel so far and Gabe had a hundred excuses for not coming home.

"Sella emailed me some jokes, but I haven't been all that good about contacting her," I tell my father. "I emailed her about a month ago, suggested we get together now that I'm not so busy. She never replied."

"You going to try again?"

"Why not?"

One hears a good deal about blood being thicker than water. That's how I feel about Sella. I hadn't seen her in years. But she is my cousin, one of the few in Miami, and I want her in my life. She's intelligent and attractive, the kind of daughter I'd have liked for myself. Her life hasn't taken the course I'd want for my children and I feel bad about that, wondering if there's anything I could have done.

These thoughts run through my mind Monday as I dress for a meeting with my editor. After the morning appointment to go over ideas for my article and discuss new assignments, I'm free for the day. I call Sella from the car.

She picks up on the third ring. I hear a man's voice in the background, but can't tell if it's Craig or the television.

"Honey, it's me," I tell her, "Becks Ruchinsky. I'm going to be in your area this afternoon and wonder if you're free."

She's silent.

"Your cousin. Tootsie's daughter. I thought we could get together for lunch."

"Sorry, I didn't recognize your voice. Things are so hectic here. Can you hold a sec?"

I wait. When she comes back on, the noise is gone. "I'd love to see you but we have one car and Craig uses it to look for work."

"That's okay. I'll stop by and pick you and the kids up. Maybe we can run over to the mall since you're so near."

"That's a plan," she says, sounding less than enthusiastic.

The line goes dead. I say her name three times and wait a few seconds. I'm about to hang up when she comes back on the line.

"Becks, you know I'd love to see you. But things aren't going well. I don't think it's a good idea to take off just now."

She sounds worried.

"Is everything okay? You want me to stop by?"

"No." The word comes out in a rush of air. "I want to get together. Honestly. But today's not good. Another time, okay?"

Before I can speak, the receiver clicks.

The phone call leaves me with an uncomfortable, out-of-sorts sensation. She didn't make much of an effort to explain why she can't see me or suggest another date. It seems odd, a bit insulting, after she sought me out. I think back to my father's words: "The little pisher's a liar." I wonder if he sensed something I missed.

After the meeting with my editor, I stop in the newspaper's research department. Maya Dipaolo, with whom I'd become friendly while collaborating on stories, agrees to run a search on Sella and Craig Miles. I feel sneaky. But I *am* an older relative. I have an obligation to look after her.

I sit on a wooden chair at the corner of Myra's desk and read the newspaper as she taps at the keyboard.

"That's weird," she says after a few minutes.

I stand and look over her shoulder. The monitor reads: "Craig Miles, a.k.a. Craig McPherson, a.k.a. Greg Minos."

"What's that mean?"

"I tried a few sites and finally got a hit on the Broward criminal court system." Maya says. "Doesn't look good."

I wait as she scrolls down the page.

"There might be more than one Craig Miles. It's not such an odd name." She tries to reassure me. "I hope it isn't your cousin's husband.

Look at that." She points to a column on the far right of the monitor. The Craig Miles listed on the screen had twice been charged with identity theft, but acquitted. My stomach clenches. Does this mean Sella's a con? Or is she being conned?

"Anything else?" Maya asks. She looks up when I don't answer. "I'm sorry," she says "Maybe it isn't him."

"Yeah, sure." I give Maya a peck on the cheek and turn down her offer of lunch. I have no appetite.

I call my father that night and tell him what I've learned. He insists I let it go — that Sella's a con artist too and I'm better off without her. I decide to drop the subject until after the high holidays, then give her a call.

The following Sunday is the day before Yom Kippur, when it's traditional to visit the cemetery and honor one's ancestors. Normally, I wouldn't remember. But this year Tootsie insists I drive him to Mount Nebo, where Miami's Jews are buried.

Plotniks have been in South Florida for over a half century and, in that time, we've made a nice little investment in Mount Nebo real estate. Problem is, deceased Plotniks are dispersed throughout the cemetery. On a hot day, visiting my dearly departed can turn into a nasty little search-and-*schvitz* operation. Tootsie insists we pay our respects to my mother and every other Plotnik of blessed memory.

It rained that morning and the cemetery's mosquitoes are rejoicing in the condensation of moist, sticky air by flitting around the long grass near the graves, taking an occasional break to suck blood from my ankles. We've visited a horde of uncles, aunts, and grandparents, and are heading in what we hope is the direction of my mother's grave when I notice a pink granite stone set at odd angles to the others. It looks shoved in, as though it might belong to the Zimmermans, who rest in peace between the Plotniks and Goldfarbs. The stone is small, almost Victorian in its ornamentation, and stands more upright than the older stones near it.

It's been a few years since I visited the cemetery and I don't remember seeing that stone before. "Who's buried there?" I ask my father, walking around to the front of the stone to read the inscription. When I see what's written, I step back, almost stumbling across a footstone in the earth behind me. A shiver creeps up my spine. I don't say anything as my father circumnavigates the stones to join me. I watch Tootsie take it in. His face goes from confusion, to shock, to anger. I grab his arm, afraid he'll faint.

"Jesus Christ," he whispers.

The stone is inscribed Sella Plotnik. I read the dates below her name. She's been dead six years.

"I'm so sorry, Dad," I manage to get out, not knowing what else to say. We look at each other. "If this is Sella, then what—"

"I'm not stupid," my father interrupts, turning his back on the grave and heading in the direction of my mother's plot. "The girl's a liar."

I drop my father off at the Schmuel Bernstein and drive home in a daze. I feel sadness and disappointment, then frustration, at missing the chance to know my cousin Sella. By the time I get home, though, I'm in a rage. Not the least of it is my anger at being taken in. My father sensed something was wrong. Why hadn't I?

My father's ability to pick up on Sella's lies reminds me of a book I read about the concept of the "gut reaction." The author described it as a combination of accumulated knowledge and experience, superimposed upon a deep emotional response. I wonder how my gut reaction to Sella and Craig could've been so wrong. And my father's so right. I'd sensed something was off. That's why I asked Maya to do a search on Craig. But I wanted to be mistaken. I dearly wanted this girl to be Sella.

In my eagerness to reconnect with the child I'd known years earlier, I ignored what my gut was telling me. It makes me question my instincts. Could there have been something wrong in my marriage that I didn't see—or refused to acknowledge? Daniel and I didn't have a perfect relationship. But I thought we were fine. We're both busy and I never objected when he came home late because it gave me more time to work. Did he read that as disinterest? And did I sense he was unhappy and refuse to see it?

I bring myself up short. Now I'm making excuses for Daniel. Blaming myself. Just like my mother. She thought she could win Tootsie's love by changing herself—dressing beautifully and preparing elaborate dinners. I'm not playing that game.

"Well, girlie," my father says when I call his apartment that night to discuss our revelation. "Your old man isn't such a fool."

I expect him to give me a hard time about being so gullible. But he doesn't. I hear sadness in his voice, regret as well, and wonder if he too hoped this would be the rare case in which his pessimism was unfounded. We talk a few minutes and make plans for breakfast the next week.

13

Tootsie

I'm hunched over the kitchen table gazing at the darkening sky. It's going to start raining like a son of a bitch soon so I'm stuck in my apartment. I'd planned to call Winchell to line up a game of poker, but I'm in no mood for it now.

I just got off the phone with Becks. It's hard to believe she fell for the scam that pischer was trying to pull off. With the boys away at school and that damned Daniel out of the house, she *wanted* the girl to be her cousin. She needs someone to take care of. The funny thing is I would not have been surprised if the girl was Sella *and* a con artist. Lord knows she'd have come by it honestly. Her grandfather was a swindler and her father isn't much better. I'm sorry Zvi lost his daughter. But I'll be damned if I'm going to call that bastard and offer my condolences.

It's uncanny how people from my past are popping back into my life lately. First Florence confronts me, then Becks digs up Abe. All I need is for Zvi to crawl out from under his rock with *his* old accusations.

I sink deeper into my chair. Five decades as an honest businessman and the past still haunts me. Sure, I did things I regret. But that was another lifetime. There's got to be some way to stop Becks from digging any deeper into my past. If she learns the truth, she'll cut me off. Maybe I deserve it. But it would kill me to lose her now.

I didn't want to bring it up with Becks tonight, but Daniel stopped by an hour before she called. I wasn't expecting anyone and was surprised by his knock on the door. I hadn't seen him in two months. He looked like hell, his hair disheveled and his face a sickly shade of gray.

"Tootsie, please talk to her. Tell her I'm miserable," he said after dropping on to the couch and glancing around the living room.

"I'm not hiding her," I said, trying to make a joke.

"Can't you convince her to take me back?"

"I've tried. But I'm the last person she'll listen to. What does she say when you call?"

"Nothing. She won't pick up the phone when she sees my number. I've tried calling from different lines, but it's no use. She hangs up."

The two of them are a mess. She won't talk to him. He wants her back.

"Keep trying. Send flowers and candy. It worked with Bernice." I try to come up with something encouraging. "She seems lonely too."

A half hour later, Daniel leaves, shuffling off like an old man. I'm afraid he'll start crying in the hallway. There's nothing I can do.

I sip my coffee and gaze outside. The rain's let up though the wind's still blowing. The lousy weather does nothing to ease my sense of doom. The past is closing in like a tiger stalking me in a nightmare. At least Landauer is out of the picture. Last I heard, he escaped from jail and skipped the country to join Lansky's gambling operation in The Bahamas. No one's heard from him in decades. He's supposed to be buried at Mount Nebo. His wife and children abandoned him years ago and he had a lot of enemies so I doubt many people showed up.

It's a miserable end but no worse than what I'll have if the girls learn the truth. It seems an awfully high price to pay for mistakes I made before they were born.

I go into the kitchen and fill the teakettle. There must be some way to convince Becks to leave well enough alone.

When I glance toward the sliding glass doors to see if the rain's stopped, I notice the directory of Schmuel Bernstein residents on my bookshelf. I walk over and pick up the thin blue booklet. Winchell said he'd done time in his twenties for breaking and entering. Maybe he could help me break into Becks' house and toss a few things around. It might convince her to back off.

It's a lousy thing to do. She's got enough problems with Daniel and the extra work she's taken on with that cookbook she's writing. But it might put a stop to her nosing around. It's worth considering. And it wouldn't be the worst thing in the world. She'd feel a hell of a lot worse if she learned the truth about her old man.

The teakettle releases a long, shrill whistle. I turn the heat off and shift the pot to a back burner. Then I return to the living room, open the blue directory, and pick up the phone.

14

I'm up early on a damp Sunday, banging around in the kitchen, when the phone rings. Normally, I'm a late sleeper, but the staccato hammering of rain on the roof awakened me. I finished my book last night and didn't want to begin another this morning so I got up and started the chicken soup I promised my father. He loves when I make it with flanken, the way my mother did.

Less than an hour after I'm up, a rich, intense aroma of simmering onions, chicken, and fatty meat hovers over the kitchen. It's still dark and rain is blowing hard from the east, creating a clatter as heavy wet drops bounce like ping-pong balls off the Chattahoochee floor of the patio before splashing against my French doors.

I'm having a hard time balancing the heavy pot over the sink, so I ignore the phone and continue straining the soup through a colander into a large glass bowl. When the ringing starts again, I pick up. It's my father. I'd planned to wake him with a happy birthday call, but he rises earlier and earlier each year.

"Hi, Dad. Happy birthday."

"I checked the obits this morning," Tootsie launches in. "My name's not there."

"That's great." I try to sound amused. He's made the same joke every birthday I can remember. This is his eighty-sixth.

"Outlived that old bastard, Schatzi Lipschutz. Can you believe it?"

I search my memory. Schatzi Lipschutz? Not a cousin. Maybe one of the old man's business associates? I don't think so. I'd remember that name.

"Haven't got a clue," I concede, which is exactly what he wants. "Who's Schatzi Lipschutz?"

"I'll hold on while you run outside and get the *Herald*."

He buys his paper on Saturday night. It lets him wake me up Sunday with the latest news.

"It's only six. I don't think my paper's come yet. I'm still in my house robe."

"You got a minute," Tootsie says, "I'll tell you about my old friend, Schatzi." The way he pronounces "friend," I'm pretty sure he means *anything but*. Tootsie doesn't concern himself with such niceties as refusing to speak ill of the dead.

Without waiting to hear if I have time, he continues. "The son of a bitch got me mixed up with the Nazis."

My neck's already cricked from holding the phone with my chin while I wash out the pot, so I stop him. I'm curious. But once he starts in with the stories, he doesn't stop. "How about you give me an hour, I'll come get you," I say. "Your chicken soup's ready and I'll bring it over. We'll have breakfast at Rascal House and you can tell the story there."

He agrees readily. The old man never turns down a meal at Rascal House. I transfer the soup into the plastic wonton containers I save from Chinese takeout and load them into a cooler with ice packs.

Tootsie's standing in the portico when I arrive, a section of newspaper neatly folded and clasped in his hand. He scurries over and opens the car door.

"You can't comb your hair for the old man?" he says before easing himself into the passenger seat. He offers his cheek for a kiss, then slams the door and stares at me. It's a purposeful look, deliberate and cynical. I wait for the zinger. It comes. "I don't like being seen with ugly broads," he tells me. "Especially on my birthday. Pull over and put on some lipstick. And do something with that mop."

I haven't bothered with my appearance—jeans and a tee are good enough for breakfast at Rascal House—but I brush my hair and swab on a smear of lipstick to please the birthday boy.

Tootsie's making this weird buzzing at the back of his throat and, after listening a few minutes, I realize he's humming. I can't name the song, but recognize it as one of the Barry Sisters' tunes he'd play on the hi-fi every Sunday morning of my childhood. The sisters sang jazzed up, schmaltzy renditions of Yiddish songs, with plenty of harmony, quite peppy in an Old World East European fashion. My father's in fine form. Why not? It's his birthday. He's having breakfast at Rascal House. And he's outlived this Schatzi fellow.

We land a booth, thanks to my father's status as a fifty-year regular. I slow down on the way to our table to examine the strawberry and pineapple cheesecakes that glisten inside the glass pastry case. After checking out the Formica tables and red leatherette booths for familiar faces, Tootsie stops at the lunch counter to shmooze with an elderly man I don't recognize. I leave him behind and trail the waitress to our table. She hands me a menu the size of a Buick and leaves another behind for Tootsie.

Five minutes later, Tootsie joins me. He tosses the newspaper section he's been clasping on the table and taps his finger on a two-inch obituary. "Schatzi Lipschutz."

I pull the article over and look at a photo of a young man with a 1940s-era pompadour. I read the usual: ninety-year-old retired businessman dies, survived by two sons, donations should be sent and so on.

"Who is he?" I ask.

"Oy, Becks," he says. "The stories I could tell if you weren't my daughter."

I roll my eyes, which should be paralyzed in an upward position from the number of times I've reacted to that line.

"You know Meyer Lansky?" he asks.

"We were never properly introduced, but I remember the name. He got thrown out of Israel in the nineteen seventies. Something about being a crook?"

"A crook, my ass. Lansky was a gangster, a big shot in the underworld. Ran most of Vegas, Miami, and Havana before you were born. By the time he was thrown out of Israel, he was worth millions. He went there to avoid charges of tax evasion." Tootsie snorts. "That's the best the feds could do. Taxes."

He squints at me like I'm supposed to challenge him. Which I don't.

"So what's the story with Schatzi Lipschutz?" I ask again.

"Schatzi." He rolls the name around his tongue, slowly, appreciatively, nodding his head. "He used to live on the Lower East Side of New York, near where your Uncle Moe and I grew up. Lot of tough kids in that neighborhood. We'd fight for the hell of it. The Italian boys would come into the neighborhood and try to make it with Jewish girls. Schatzi and Moe would stop them, wait on corners on Saturday nights and pick fights when the boys came to pick up their dates.

"Your grandmother hated Schatzi, called him a hoodlum, but all the kids in the neighborhood thought he was something else. Here's this big tough Jewish boy, six feet, and he's ready to beat the crap out of any schmuck stupid enough to challenge him. Hoods from outside the neighborhood would try to rob and push around the old guys who ran newsstands, tobacco shops, places like that. You think anyone called the cops? No way. They called Schatzi, or your Uncle Moe if Schatzi wasn't around. The creeps never showed their faces again."

The waitress returns with metal buckets brimming with kosher pickles and coleslaw and we place our order. I wait as Tootsie clasps a pickle between his thumb and forefinger, studies it for a few seconds, and takes a bite. He chews with a lot more noise than is altogether necessary.

I wait until he pauses to make myself heard above his eating. "So what about the Nazis?"

"Hold on. I'm getting there." He swallows. "This all happened in nineteen thirty seven, thirty-eight when things were looking bad. We're still in the Depression and the Nazis are holding rallies around the country. Everyone's worried about anti-Semitism but afraid to do anything about it. Like maybe we're asking for trouble by bringing attention to ourselves.

"Not everyone saw it that way. Including Lansky. From what I heard, some big judge calls him, knows Lansky and his pals don't give a shit what the gentiles think. I don't hear the whole story until years later, but this judge asks Lansky to round up some muscle and break arms at Nazi rallies.

"I'm not going to kid you, Doll. I was no Boy Scout. I wasn't as tough as Schatzi or Moe but I could hold my own with anyone else in the neighborhood. Schatzi's already running numbers for some outfit by this time, and Moe—well, I don't know what Moe was into. But when Schatzi tells Moe he volunteered to take the moxie out of these Nazi bastards, Moe says he'll join up. Moe tells me what's going on and there's no way I'm missing out on this action."

My father takes another pickle, examines it, and takes a bite. He raises one finger, a signal I should wait for him to chew and swallow.

"What did you do?" I ask.

"What do you mean, what'd I do?"

"Did you beat up the Nazis?"

"Sure I did. We went to the big hall where they were meeting. When the bastards came out, we attacked them. Surprise." He raises both hands, fingers outspread.

"Were you hurt?"

He shrugs. "Not much."

I'm getting frustrated. He starts these stories, then cuts them off as they're getting interesting. I try another tack.

"Where were the police?"

My father laughs. "I read in the news that the cops were called in to break up the fight, but it took them a couple of hours to get there."

"Did you ever do anything like that again?"

"Unfortunately, no. A week later, Moe got sent off to basic training. I wanted to join up but I was too young and your grandmother wouldn't sign the papers. Schatzi stuck around awhile and I heard he helped bust up a couple more Nazi rallies in Jersey. Worked with a Jewish fighter who had an in with the cops there. I asked Schatzi if I could join him, but he told me to get lost. Eventually, he enlisted too."

The waitress returns, her arms laden with heavy white china plates of bacon, eggs, and pancakes. Bacon, my father claims, is the only cut of pork that becomes kosher when eaten outside the home.

I break the yolk of my fried egg over my pancakes. As I eat, I imagine my father fighting in the midst of a throng of rioting Jews. It's not hard to envision. I've seen him fight his temper, his left eyelid twitching as he struggles to rein himself in. Sometimes, he'd get so mad at my mom, she'd send us to our rooms where we'd listen to him raging.

"So what happened to the Nazis?" I ask once we're nearly through the meal.

Tootsie looks up from his plate, considers my question. "They kept meeting, but not in such large numbers, and they demanded a police guard. Can you believe that? You've heard of Mayor LaGuardia? Like the airport."

I nod.

"His mother was Jewish and he spoke Yiddish. But he still provided police protection at Nazi rallies. He had to love that."

"And Lansky?"

"What about him?"

"You see him again?"

"Yeah, once, a long time later." He looks over my shoulder and out the window before returning his gaze. "It's funny. No one talked about breaking up Nazi rallies after the war. Hell, after the liberation of the camps, you'd think every German in America loved the Jews."

We eat in silence. At least I do. My father's making enough noise to rouse the dead. Which, in a sense, he has.

Once we're through, I turn around to signal the waitress, who is waiting on a couple in the booth next to us. When I turn back, the man Tootsie stopped to see at the counter is approaching our table. He's tall with elegant silver hair and wears a soft aqua cashmere cardigan over linen pants.

My father introduces me to Winchell Levin as his kaddish, meaning I'm the one who'll say prayers in his memory once he's gone. He tells me Winchell's an old friend from New York.

"You going to Schatzi's funeral?" Winchell asks. "It's at noon today. The old neighborhood will be there, at least those who haven't kicked the bucket."

Tootsie turns to me. "What do you say?"

"Whatever you want." I'm not doing anything. And I'm dying to meet these characters from my father's past. "We can drop the soup at your place and head over."

Tootsie stands and pats Winchell on the back. "We'll see you there."

"Yitgadal v'yitgadat sh'may rabo."

Every one of the old geezers at the graveside service is reciting the mourner's prayer. I'm not. For one thing, I can't remember the words. For the other, Tootsie keeps poking me in the ribs with his elbow and whispering in my ear. It's like a *Who's Who* of *alter cockers* with whacked-out nicknames. Bernie "The Weasel" Shapiro. Mort "Schmutzy" Lieberman. Daniel "Peanuts" Wolinsky. Even the old lady who accused my father of murder is there, in her wheelchair accompanied by a nurse in a white uniform. An old man chats with her, then looks our way.

The whole thing is so incredible, these old guys floating around in their too-large suits, wiping away tears and missing the days when they beat the crap out of each other. My father's riding a seesaw of emotion, crying one minute, chattering rapidly the next. Neither of us mentions Abe Kravitz, who glares at my dad before turning back to the service.

"Peanuts, over there," my father says, pointing to a short bald guy leaning on a walker, "had something to do with the dockworkers strike after the war. And Schmutzy," he says, motioning toward another midget, this one in a wheelchair, "had a fist like a golem."

The high point of the funeral comes about fifteen minutes in, when a gray Ford pulls to the end of the row of cars parked on the right side of the cemetery's main road. Two men in their midforties step out. The driver is tall, an obvious bench presser, his chest muscles straining at the seams of his gray suit. The man who gets out on the passenger side is a trace shorter, with a facial palsy that gives him a permanent, crooked grin. Their identical sunglasses catch the sun's glare and even I recognize them as cops.

If this were an Italian Mafia movie, everyone would be edging back to their car. But these are old Jews who probably haven't pulled off a job in five decades. Everyone, including the widow, a tiny octogenarian with raven black witch hair, looks toward the cops before returning his or her attention to the service. No one gives a damn. The cops keep their distance, hovering ten feet behind the mourners.

My father grabs my arm. "We need to go now," he whispers.

"It's almost over," I say. "Can't you wait?"

"I've got to piss."

He drags me toward my Mercedes, leaning forward to propel himself more rapidly. As we near the car, I recall rumors that floated around the family about my father and Uncle Moe. When I was in my teens, a cousin from New York swore that Uncle Moe and my father had killed a man. I didn't believe it. Now I wonder if the old man's being paranoid or has a good reason to leave. He stares over his shoulder at the cops as we get in the car and drive off. He's scowling and his silence makes me nervous. I wonder if his rapid departure has anything to do with Fat Louie's murder. I don't ask. He's so tense that he's grasping the door handle in his fist. I don't want to upset him more.

It's Tootsie's birthday and, being an obedient daughter, I return him safely to the Schmuel Bernstein. On the way there, he asks if I'll arrange his funeral. He asks me this every time we attend one. I tell him I don't want to discuss it. I'd rather talk about why we had to leave Schatzi's funeral early. He won't answer so I drop the subject. I'll try another time. A half hour after we leave the cemetery, I pull up to his building and watch him shuffle through the double glass doors. He looks more stooped than usual. I'm dying to know why he became so upset at the sight of police officers at Schatzi's funeral. I'll ask him the next time we meet. And hope that he tells me the truth.

15

Tootsie

By the time Becks pulls into the Schmuel Bernstein, my heartburn's killing me. It was a struggle hiding my panic from Becks. When I got inside, I collapsed into a chair in the lobby to catch my breath.

Am I going nuts? It's been five decades since I last saw him, but the man chatting with Florence Karpowsky at the cemetery looked a hell of a lot like Murray Landauer. The bastard's supposed to be six feet under in a grave at Mount Nebo. When I spotted him, it felt as if the devil had risen from hell.

That would explain why the cops showed up. Landauer and Schatzi worked together in New York. Maybe the police heard Landauer was back in Florida and figured he'd be at the service?

To top it all off, Becks pestered me to stay until the service was over. What was I supposed to tell her? That I'd seen a ghost? I shouldn't have brought her to the funeral. I'm becoming too dependent on the girl.

Once inside my apartment, I make a beeline for the kitchen and toss back two antacids. It takes awhile for the pain to subside so I return to the living room to rest on the couch. As my heartburn eases, I consider the funeral. My panic at spotting Landauer. But also the loss of Schatzi. I felt it a lot more than I'd have thought. He'd been a hero to a lot of kids on the Lower East Side, myself included. Truth be told, I never would have become involved with the mob if it weren't for Schatzi. What's odd is that it started idealistically, with this business about the Nazis.

It was a late Sunday afternoon the winter I turned sixteen. I was already six feet tall and as strong as my brother. Moe and I had come downstairs in our apartment building and planned to run out to get a newspaper for Dad. I was surprised to find Schatzi waiting near the bank of mailboxes in the hall.

"I had a visitor last night," Schatzi said. He grabbed Moe's arm and pulled him toward the door. "There's going to be some action."

Schatzi looked at me, then Moe, waiting for my brother to tell me to scram. Moe surprised us both. "Let him come," he said. "Time the kid grew up." I tried to act nonchalant, to hide my excitement at being included.

The three of us stepped outside and turned left, bending our heads against the wind. The snow had stopped falling in the early afternoon, leaving a thick slush of icy water and coal dust on the sidewalk. I winced as I stepped into the raw air. It was only three in the afternoon but already dark and the windows of the tenement buildings emitted a pallid yellow glow that scarcely illuminated the sidewalk. A piercing wind spit slivers of ice down the narrow street and I shivered, as much from the arctic air as the thrill of hanging out with my brother and Schatzi. They were five years older than I was but seemed a generation removed because of their street smarts and reputations as toughs.

"You heard about the Nazis holding their meetings in Yorkville?" Schatzi asked once we were clear of the building and its prying ears.

"Rumors," Moe said. "I heard they were pretty harmless."

"I don't know about that. They're planning a pro-Hitler rally this week. Harmless or not, we're not letting them get away with it."

I hadn't read anything about Nazis in New York, though I'd heard stories about Germans rounding up Jews and taking them away from their homes. A week earlier, Mrs. Gottlieb from next door came over in tears to tell my mother her sister hadn't written in six months. Ma made me leave the apartment.

"Those big shot rabbis can talk all they want about laying low, keeping out of sight of the Christians. But that's crap," Schatzi said. "If someone calls me a dirty Jew, I'll break his jaw. I'm not letting the bastards walk all over us."

Schatzi and Moe took long strides and I had to run to keep up.

"What're you going to do? Beat them up?" Moe said, then laughed. He and Schatzi got in plenty of fights.

"I might. There's this guy, Lansky. Word is out that he's looking for Jews to take on the Nazi bastards."

We stopped at the intersection with Delancey and waited for a truck to pass before we crossed the road. Orchard Street, which was crowded with push carts heaped with vegetables and fruit in the summer, was deserted in the cold. Once across, Schatzi turned his back to the wind to light a smoke. He lit a second cigarette off that and handed it to Moe. When he eyed me, I shook my head. I was afraid I'd get sick and embarrass myself.

"Some judge gave Lansky a call," Schatzi continued after releasing a cloud of smoke. It hung in the cold air. "Wants him to break up the Nazi rallies. Bust some arms and legs too. He called in old favors and is getting young guys, like us, to join. You in?"

"You bet," I said before I realized Schatzi was looking at Moe. My brother and his friend exchanged glances.

"You can come along, but don't get in my way," Moe said. "Anything happens to you, Ma'll kill me.

The subway doors slid open with a squeal and the raw onion stink of unwashed bodies assailed me as I stepped into the car behind Moe and Schatzi. It had been two days since Schatzi appeared in our hallway and we were on our way to the Nazi rally. I'd ridden the subway to visit relatives in Brooklyn, but that had been in the daytime, when the cars were crowded.

Tonight, the nearly deserted subway felt like a ghost train racing into the dark. Two Negroes in tan porter's uniforms nodded off five benches down. Across from them sat a fat man with his arms folded and his bulging eyes half closed. The man kept his hands in his pockets, not bothering to pull them out to brace himself on the sharp turns.

Motioning his head to draw us closer, Schatzi pointed a thumb toward the stranger. "That's Harry Shapiro," he whispered, "one of Lansky's men. Bet he's on his way to beat up Nazis." I glanced at the stranger, who was openly staring at us now. "The big idea tonight is to listen and keep your mouth shut," Schatzi continued. Then to me, "If you can't take the fighting, get out. We don't need to worry about you."

I nodded. The strangeness of riding a subway at night added a tinge of fear to the excitement I'd felt all day. My stomach ached. Ma hated Schatzi and would yell at me if she found out I was hanging around with what she called the "nogoodnik." Schatzi was always getting into trouble and bringing Moe along. As Schatzi got older, his troubles got worse. He'd been picked up by the cops twice in the last year.

The night before, we'd heard Lansky speak. I was nervous then too, but not as bad as tonight. The auditorium was crowded with hard-looking men in their twenties and thirties and a half dozen boys around my age. I tried to look streetwise, slouching against a wall, but I wasn't fooling anyone.

The three of us waited a half hour before a short man with big ears stepped up to the stage, silencing the crowd with his presence. He wore a fancy suit with a pink silk handkerchief in the breast pocket and looked like a businessman or a lawyer. An outfit like that, I expected the man to have a classy voice. But what came out of his mouth was straight from the old neighborhood. Turned out the guy was Meyer Lansky. And he'd grown up on the Lower East Side, just like us. He told the crowd where to meet the next night and that it was okay to break bones—arms, legs and ribs were fine. But no killing.

The man was a rousing speaker and the throng cheered him on. I'd never heard anything like it. Lansky made it sound like it was our patriotic duty to take out the Nazi bastards, that we were fighting for America and for the suffering Jews in Europe. When he asked for volunteers, every hand in the hall shot up.

But that night, hanging on to the subway's metal overhead bar on the way to the Nazi rally, my stomach contracted. I'd been in plenty of fights and could hold my own with the kids who wandered into our neighborhood looking for trouble. But in a few hours I'd be taking on grown men. Moe and Schatzi had done a fair amount of street fighting and would be okay. I didn't want to embarrass myself by getting beat up. And I sure as hell didn't want to end up in jail or the hospital. That would kill Ma.

I pictured her standing over me in a hospital bed, crying like she always did when Moe and I got in fights. I turned my back on Moe and Schatzi and stared at my reflection in the window. The ache in my stomach had worked its way up and lodged like a melon in my chest.

"You want to move it, buddy?" A deep voice broke into my reverie.

It was the man with the bulldog eyes. We'd reached our stop. I stumbled out of the subway car and ran to catch up with Moe and Schatzi, on the platform and heading for the stairs. When we reached street level, we buttoned our coats against the cold and turned south. No one spoke as the faintly-lit street filled with a dozen or so men, most young and broad-shouldered with a stony set to their jaws. Moe, Schatzi, and I joined the small army as it advanced down the block past closed storefronts and restaurants. Eventually, we stepped into the shadows of the buildings across the road from a brick auditorium.

We waited an hour, then two, shivering in the frigid air and whispering to one another as we listened to cheering from the auditorium. No one told us what the signal to act would be, but I figured we'd know when it came. My feet were almost numb with cold when I heard the crash of shattering glass and saw two bodies fly through a window to the right of the auditorium's entrance. In seconds, three thugs I recognized from the night before had scampered up the fire escape on the side of the building.

I raced after Moe and Schatzi toward the auditorium and ran to the top of the broad staircase. Men in khaki outfits and business suits dashed like angry ants from the entrance, trying to escape the Jews who greeted them, punching and kicking as they tried to descend. In seconds, Moe was swinging the nightstick he'd stuffed down his pants and Schatzi and I were using our fists on everything that came within arm's length. The cheers we'd heard from the building moments earlier were replaced by the grunt of fist meeting gut and the heavy breathing of men in combat. Blood trickled down my cheek and my knuckles burned, but I kept swinging and connecting.

Stopping for a brief moment to catch my breath, I saw Schatzi slam his fist into a heavily-muscled man in a brown shirt guarding a short, plump character with a Hitler-style moustache. Maybe it was the mustachioed man's look of contempt for the fighters as he approached the stairs, or the fact that two hoodlums in brown shirts lunged at Schatzi as he neared the plump man, but it was obvious the fellow at the center of the goons was big in the Nazi organization.

I was stunned by the rage on Schatzi's face as he attacked the bodyguards, splitting the lip of one with his right fist, then using his left to send the other plummeting down the stairs. When he reached the fat man, Schatzi went berserk, slamming his fist into the man's nose and sending blood splattering over both of their shirts. Then he landed his fist in the man's gut, sending him sprawling to the ground before kicking him in the ribs. When I heard the crack of bone breaking and the man's screams, I ran to stop Schatzi. Moe was behind me as I tore him off the blood-soaked man.

Seconds later, the grunts and curses that had pierced the night stopped. The only people left in front of the auditorium were me, Schatzi, Moe and a few disheveled men in brown shirts who looked too broken to do any damage. The scream of a siren grew louder as I raced behind Moe and Schatzi down the cold deserted street.

I rise from my couch and walk to the sliding glass doors. It's almost dark. The purple-edged storm clouds that hover over Miami remind me of the cold, dank winters I hated in New York. I turned eighty-six today and I feel old. For fifty years, I played it straight. So did most of the guys I knew then. But Landauer's back and that doesn't bode well. Schatzi's funeral and Landauer's appearance are frightening reminders of my own mortality. I need to prepare myself and my girls for the worst. I pick up the phone and dial Becks. She answers on the third ring.

16

Monday morning, I wake up in a miserable mood. Tootsie called last night and wouldn't hang up until I agreed to handle arrangements for his funeral. Everything's got to be just so. He's selected the caterer (me) and location (my house) for his *shiva* reception and insists on mailing me the list of people to invite. Schatzi Lipchitz's death, no doubt, brought on all this planning. But it's hard enough to deal with end of my marriage. I don't need to think about losing my father.

"I'm not asking that much," he says. "Someone's got to do it. Your sister won't talk to me and the grandchildren don't know from funerals. What am I supposed to do? Leave instructions with your *ferschtunkena* cat?"

"How about Daniel?" I offer, joking.

"What about him?"

"You think he's such a great guy. Ask him to do it."

He's silent a moment. "Maybe I will."

I grit my teeth. I don't know if he's kidding. He and Daniel are close. In fact, Daniel felt I was being too hard on my father when I refused to talk to him after my mother died. Back then, when Daniel brought the boys to see their grandfather. Tootsie'd ask him to talk to me about repairing our rift. Daniel tried—unsuccessfully. Now the tables are turned. Two weeks ago, Daniel asked Tootsie to have a word with me. I told my father I could handle my own marriage.

After I agree to my father's instructions, we chat about Schatzi's funeral. My father won't explain why we had to leave so suddenly. He still insists he was tired and needed a bathroom.

Then he gets down to what he's really calling about.

"I forgot to tell you. I need a ride to the lawyer tomorrow. I'm changing my will."

This comes as no surprise. Tootsie changes his will every three months depending on who's ticked him off or pleased him. On our last visit to Solly Horowitz, Tootsie put my son Joshua back in his will after he broke up with the non-Jewish girl he'd been dating.

"What are you changing this time?" I ask.

"What's it to you?"

"I *am* driving you down there. Don't I have a right to know?"

"No, Miss Smarty-Pants. It's none of your business."

I beg to differ. But I'm a good daughter and agree to pick him up at ten for his ten thirty appointment. Naturally, he hangs up without a goodbye.

When I was a child and accompanied my father to his attorney's office, we'd meet Solly's father in the first-floor luncheonette of the downtown Miami skyscraper where he worked. It wasn't much, just a few metal tables and a counter that seated four. My father never spelled it out, but I assume he was uncomfortable in the lawyer's lavish office. The plush navy carpeting and gold-trimmed, Napoleonic desk may have intimidated him or, more likely, reminded him how much he was spending on legal advice. The men got their business done over a cup of coffee and a pastrami sandwich. I'd sit at the counter with an iced tea.

Solly takes a less formal approach with my dad. Always impeccable in his Brooks Brothers suits, he trots out to the waiting area and welcomes Tootsie with a hug. Then he introduces him to the receptionist as his late father's friend. After instructing her to bring coffee and Danish, we return to the same office his father used. A sleek, beveled-glass desk with polished steel legs has replaced his father's antique gilded desk. Teak bookcases full of heavy legal texts line three walls of the large office. The most impressive part of the office, though, is the wall of floor-to-ceiling glass that frames a panoramic view of the royal palms that line Biscayne Boulevard.

It's obvious why my father insists on these visits, which could be handled by phone. When he retired, Tootsie surrendered his status as a successful businessman. That couldn't have been easy for a man with my father's ego. When he visits Solly, the two of them rehash events from when Tootsie still owned the business. His visits with Solly bring him back, for a brief period, from the invisible world of the aged.

When Solly invites us back this morning, Tootsie gives me a dismissive nod, which I ignore. I follow the men down the hall and join my father in one of two green paisley wingback chairs that flank the lawyer's desk. Once the ceremonial cheese Danish is consumed and small talk exhausted, Solly settles back in his chair.

"So, Mr. Plotnik, you want to change your will?" His glance in my direction is an unspoken "again."

Tootsie flattens his palms on the desk and leans in toward Solly as though offering a valuable stock tip. "I've been doing some thinking. About the past. I've been a lucky guy. A successful business. A wonderful wife and children. It's time to give something back."

"That's very commendable," Solly says.

"Yeah, well." Tootsie shrugs. "I've thought it out and decided to leave twenty-five thousand to the Karpowsky Center. That's the part of the Schmuel Bernstein that works with Alzheimer's patients."

Alzheimer's patients? I think. *Tootsie never gave a damn about Alzheimer's patients.*

"Any special reason?" Solly asks. Then he frowns. "You haven't been diagnosed with —"

"Don't talk crazy. I'm sharp as a tack. It just seems like a worthwhile cause." He looks at me and then Solly, his face darkening. "Is there something wrong with giving them dough?"

"Not at all. It's a wonderful organization." The lawyer raises his hand in assurance, then scribbles on a yellow pad. "Anything else?"

"That's it."

"I'll make the changes and mail it to you. Stop by when you're ready to sign." He rises and we follow him back to the waiting area.

"Good to see you, Mr. Plotnik." he says, shaking my father's hand. Then to me, "Take good care of your father. You're lucky you still have this character around."

I smile and drape my arm across Tootsie's shoulders. "Don't I know it."

The elevator's crowded so I wait until we return to the car, pull out of the parking garage, and stop at a light to pop the obvious question.

"So what's the deal with the Karpowsky Wing?"

"What do you mean?"

"Since when do you care about Alzheimer's disease?"

"I've always cared about Alzheimer's."

"Really?"

"Yes, really. A lot of old guys at the Schmuel Bernstein have it."

"Anyone you know?"

"Not offhand."

"So what's with the donation? And why now?"

The light changes and I take a left. Tootsie doesn't speak for a block or two.

Then, defensively, "Everybody's got to go some time. Why not spend my hard-earned money where it'll do some good. There's plenty to go around. You girls don't need it all."

It's not the first time he's accused us of hovering like hungry vultures over his so-called fortune. I refuse to take the bait.

"It's so sudden. You ran into Mrs. Karpowsky two months ago, and now you're making a donation to her family foundation. This wouldn't have anything to do with Fat Louie, would it?"

My father glares. "Such as?"

"Such as trying to make amends to his widow?"

"Could be. Or not. Either way, it's none of your business." He stares ahead, jaw clenched.

I drop him off at the Schmuel Bernstein and return home. I'd love to know what this is about.

I swear as I pull around the semicircular paved driveway in front of my house. The lawn man's late again and the grass is up to my ankles. When Daniel was home I wouldn't have minded. It was his job to complain to the yard service or do the mowing himself. I slam the car door and stomp up the stairs to the front porch. The Mercedes' air conditioner barely wheezes out cool air and I'm anxious to escape the heat. Tootsie's refusal to explain his largesse to the Karpowsky Center irks me and I haven't eaten in hours. I want to go inside and make lunch.

I put my key to the doorknob but, before I can insert it, the door swings open. I hesitate, more perturbed than worried. I've been careful about locking doors, especially since Daniel left. Then I remember. I left the house through the garage that morning but must have forgotten to pull the front door fully closed when I got the newspaper earlier in the day. Still, I'm a bit uneasy. I live in a safe neighborhood, but who knows? Plenty of strangers drive down my street on their way to cleaning and lawn maintenance jobs.

I go into the kitchen and wolf down a tuna on rye. When I finish, I head to the dining room, which I turned into an office after Daniel left. The sandwich has carbed me into a state of relaxed bliss and I'm ready to get to work. But as I turn the corner from the hall into the dining room, I slam to a halt. A chill edges up my spine. Someone's pulled the drawers of my file cabinet off their treads and dumped the contents! Paper is strewn across every surface—the floor, the dining room table, my grandmother's walnut buffet.

I stand frozen a full minute, holding my breath and taking in the scene. Then the adrenalin kicks in and my shock turns to anger. Who would do a thing like this? My first thought is Daniel? Was he looking for something he could use against me in a divorce? But that's unlikely. He knows where I file my papers. And a man who calls daily, pleading with his wife to take him back, doesn't break into his estranged wife's house. Then again, I never thought he'd cheat on me.

But the alternative is worse. Robbers looking for jewelry or drugs? I'm so furious that I race around the room, grabbing papers off the chairs and table, not even considering that I should call the police.

I'm on my knees scooping up old correspondence and muttering to myself when it hits me. Whoever did this could be in the house! I freeze and listen but all I hear is the thumping of my heart. I try to convince myself they're gone. They'd have heard me enter the house and escaped out the back door.

Even so, I have to force myself upstairs, taking one dreaded step at a time and straining to hear intruders. My chest hurts and my breathing is uneven as I imagine Josh or Gabriel finding my body crumpled at the bottom of the stairs. I brace myself against the wall to remain steady as I ascend the steps, then tiptoe past the boys' rooms. They're untouched, which is a relief. But a few steps on, at the entrance to my bedroom, my heart sinks. It's a nightmare. The contents of my bureau have been dumped on the ground and my clothes are strewn across the bed, carpet, and chairs. The sight of my bras and underwear on the rug leaves me feeling naked and vulnerable.

I run into the closet, where my dresses and nightgowns are heaped on the floor. My jewelry box is splayed open across a black beaded evening gown, and bracelets and necklaces form a tangle of silver and gold on the fabric. But the good pieces, including my mother's diamond necklace and opal ring, are still inside the box. Nothing is missing. Why would anyone break in and leave behind valuable jewelry?

When I return to my bedroom, a splotch of red catches my eye. I gasp. The intruder has scrawled ASK YOUR FATHER in red lipstick on the mirror above my bureau. The writing is thick and deliberate as though written with controlled rage. A tube of my lipstick, the end smashed, lies on the bureau. Beneath the words, affixed to the mirror with duct tape, is a brown envelope. I race around my bed, panting, to tear the package down.

Inside are two yellowed newspaper articles held together with a rusted paperclip. A photograph falls out when I release the clip. As violated as this break-in makes me feel, the lipsticked scrawl and clippings are even more alarming. This isn't a random burglary. The intruder who tore my home apart and left the envelope is someone who knows me. And my father. They're sending us a message. Goose bumps rise along my arms. This has got to be related to my father's story about Fat Louie and the Jewish syndicate. But who knows I'm looking into it? My father. And Abe.

My mind races through my options—should I call my dad, contact Daniel? How about the police? I grab the phone next to my bed and dial 911 but replace the receiver. My father must have done something horrible to provoke such a violent invasion.

What'll happen to Tootsie if the police get involved? Could he land in jail? My breathing returns to normal as my fear subsides. No one's in the house. I'm safe. I need to talk to my father before I call the police. And I need to find out what the clippings are about.

Pushing aside a tangle of bathing suits and the cat, who's followed me upstairs and settled among the mess, I sit on my bed and read. The first clipping is similar to the article I found at the historical museum about Uncle Moe's testimony before the Kefauver Commission. No surprises there. The second is a two-paragraph item, dated 1949, reporting that my father and uncle's business was awarded a lucrative contract to supply restaurant equipment to several Miami-area hotels. Scrawled in pencil at the top of the clipping is the notation "S&G?" The handwriting is identical to the scrawl on my mirror.

The photograph unsettles me. It's an old police shot, taken in what looks like a morgue. A man's bloated body, pallid in the harsh tones of the black-and-white photograph, lies on a metal table. The face, or what was once the face, is a pulpy mass of lips, nose, and mouth that have been partially chewed away by . . . I don't want to think about it. I turn the photo over and find a caption. It's dated May 17, 1948, and reports that a gangster known as Louis Giovanni washed ashore on Miami Beach the day before. According to the clipping, the body was wrapped in linen as though prepared for a traditional Jewish burial. Miami Beach police, the article says, have no leads.

I become nauseated, then dizzy, and lean my forehead against the bedpost to stop the room from spinning. My house has been ripped apart by someone who wants to frighten, maybe hurt, me. My father has altered his will to support the wife of a dead gangster's charity. And a stranger has left me newspaper clippings—and a grisly photo—that date back fifty years.

If I had any doubts before, I'm sure now that the break-in has something to do with my dad's past. I recall his reaction to the arrival of the officers at Schatzi's funeral. The old man *is* hiding something. But what could be so awful he won't tell me? I sit on my bed, torn.

Only one person can tell me what this is about. But I'm afraid he'll hand me more lies. I haven't called the police because I want to protect my father. If I tell him that, could he be selfish enough to lie to me? I can't rule it out so make a deal with myself. If I sense he's making up more stories, I'll go to the police. It's the only way I'll feel safe again.

I call the locksmith and wait while he changes my locks.

Then I dial my father.

It's time we had a talk.

17

My father didn't say anything about going out tonight and I'm surprised by what sounds like a rumble of thunder and loud cheers in the background when he answers his cell.

"Don't you have anything better to do with your life than pester your old man?" he says when the noise dies down. "This is a lousy time to talk."

"Where are you?" I have no patience for his games.

"Where do you think? I bowl Monday nights."

"I forgot."

"You would. What's so important you have to interrupt my game?"

"I can't discuss it over the phone."

"Hold on a sec." I hear the low grumble of men's voices before he comes back on the line. "I'm going to be here a few hours. If it's so important, come here."

"To the alley?"

"That's where I bowl."

I debate a moment. I'm tense and angry. And frightened of leaving the house, then returning alone later. The intruders could come back. My stomach clenches at the prospect. But I'm not going to be able to sleep until I talk to my father. Might as well drive back to Miami and confront him. If anything seems out of order when I return, I'll call the police before entering.

"Do you still bowl at Lopez Lanes?"

"Where else?"

"I'll be there in an hour."

I make it to Miami in record time and park my car next to a tall metal lighting fixture. It throws sharp-edged pools of light on the patches of broken tar and gravel that are all that remain of Lopez Lane's parking lot. The bowling alley was a dump when I went there as a kid forty years ago and the neighborhood has continued to deteriorate. A ten-foot metal fence protects the parking lot from the vandals and thieves who drove the adjacent businesses away. Two scratched and faded red bowling pins twice the size of a grown man tower over the entrance.

Walking into the bowling alley is like descending into a Las Vegas version of hell. The crash of heavy balls hitting solid floors and the crack of high-velocity plastic colliding with wooden pins creates an unrelenting racket, broken occasionally by the cheers of men's voices. Covering the floor is a jarring interweave of purple, red, and black triangles interspersed with yellow images of bowling balls and pins. Small groups of men gather at orange and red plastic tables with molded seats, at the front of which rests a computer monitor. No one seems to be eyeing the large overhead screens that post team scores.

It's not hard to find my father. He's with the group of older men sporting wrist, knee and elbow braces. Tootsie, not to be outdone, wears a wide black belt that supports his back.

I'm so torn between anger at my father and desperation for his reassurance that I break into a trot when I spot him. My throat tightens and my jaw aches, forcing me to swallow a few times to control the sobs that threaten to swell up from my chest.

"Dad." My voice breaks with the word.

Three heads turn in my direction and a deeply-tanned, silver-haired man in a coral shirt frowns. It's the man I met at Wolfie's, Winchell Levin. He taps my father on the shoulder.

Tootsie turns around with a smile that fades when he sees me. He puts the paper cup he's holding on the plastic table and strides to where I'm standing.

"What's wrong?" He tries to put his arm across my shoulders but I step away.

"Someone broke into my house."

"My God. Are you all right? "

"I'm fine."

A cheer goes up from my father's teammates and he glances at the overhead screen.

Then, turning back to me, he says, "You look awful."

"I'll survive."

He shrugs. "What did they get?"

"That's what's so weird. They didn't take anything."

"Did you catch them in the act?"

"I was home a half hour before I noticed anyone had been there." I tell him about the mess in my dining room and bedroom.

"I'm so sorry, Doll. It's odd they didn't take anything."

I cross my arms and hug myself. "I think they wanted to scare me and get a message to you." I look him in the eye. "And I think you know who broke in."

My father looks at me a second too long. He opens his mouth to speak but a voice breaks in.

"Plotnik, get over here." It's a man with a black wrist brace. "You're holding up the game."

My father raises a finger, motioning his friend to wait. "This is my last frame. Give me a minute. Then we'll talk."

I drop onto a bench a few feet from the alley and watch my father approach the ball return and pick up the black speckled ball he kept in the front hall closet at our home in Coral Gables. Before we were old enough to bowl, he would bring Esther and me to Lopez Lanes to watch him practice. I loved the way he'd send pins ricocheting off the walls with his powerful swing. Esther was his favorite, which is doubly sad now that they're not talking, and it was a special treat to be included when he took her on their regular Saturday afternoon outing to the alley. Esther told me he was the best bowler in Miami and I believed her. She worshipped our father.

He's got the same great form tonight but, when he releases the ball, it veers to the left and clips three pins. He raises both palms in a gesture of resignation as he approaches the ball return. Then he takes a few seconds to study the pins, cocking his head right then left before letting the ball fly. For a few seconds, he's the old Tootsie, raising a fist in the air as the ball edges to the right and sends the remaining pins clattering to the ground. And I'm a little girl again, proud of my dad and confident he'll make everything right.

But the feeling doesn't last. And that upsets me. After what happened tonight, I don't know who he is or if I can trust him. It's frightening how the most important men in my life have let me down. First Daniel. Then Tootsie. I thought they had my best interests at heart. But I have to face the fact that they're not the people I thought they were. Those men were fantasies I created out of my own need for strength and constancy. My world is shifting and I don't know if I'll ever regain my ability to trust. But old ways of thinking are hard to change. I want to believe Tootsie's the powerful father who'll protect me from the monster in the closet. Maybe that's why I keep returning to him after all I've learned.

After shaking hands with his teammates, my father packs his ball into its case and returns to where I'm sitting. He nods toward a heavy oak door behind me. A brass sign mounted on the wall above it reads "Gutter Lounge."

"We can talk in there."

The thunder and cheers of the alley fade as the large door shuts behind us. I follow my father to a cracked leather booth that forms a semicircle around a thick wooden table embedded with navigational maps. The small room is surprisingly cozy, with two walls of booths and a handful of tables. It's deserted except for a young woman who looks up and smiles at us, then returns to polishing the bottles of colorful liquors that line the glass shelves of the mirrored bar. The room smells vaguely of mold and ammonia, but the heavily varnished table looks freshly polished. As my father slides into the booth, he asks the bartender to bring two beers.

While we're waiting, I pull the envelope from my purse and slip out the yellowed clippings and morgue photo. I place them on the table, facedown. Tootsie eyes the clippings, but continues to chat about his game, recalling the old days when he never scored under two fifty.

After the bartender delivers the beer, I take my hand off the clippings.

"The guy who broke into my house today left these." I push the articles and morgue photo before him. "He took a tube of my lipstick and scrawled 'ask your father' across the mirror."

Tootsie looks shocked but says nothing as he peruses the article about the Kefauver commission and tosses it aside. It takes him less than a minute to read the business announcement about his and Uncle Moe's restaurant contracts. When he sees the morgue photo, he brings a hand to his mouth. Panic flashes across his face so rapidly I'm not sure I've seen it. Then he flips the photo over and reads the caption.

When he's through, he slaps the table with an open palm. "Son of a bitch." His pupils are tiny and black and his jaw muscles are taut.

"Do these articles mean anything to you?" he says, tapping the pile of clippings.

"I'm the one who should be asking that question."

He scowls and nods. "You're right." He takes a sip of beer and positions the mug dead center on its coaster. "These clippings were probably stolen from me, but I don't know anything about the photo."

"What're you talking about?"

"Years ago, someone mailed me every article that mentioned my business. At first, I thought it was a friend. That was until whoever sent them started adding nasty notes. I should've thrown them out long ago."

"Where are they?"

"Who knows? I stuffed them away so many years ago that I forgot about them when I sold the business. As far as I know, they're still in the warehouse."

Before retiring, my father owned a building that housed his showroom, office, and a ten-thousand-square-foot warehouse. The warehouse was a dusty, foul-smelling storeroom with a leaking ceiling and dozens of floor-to-ceiling metal shelves where he kept the pots, pans, ovens, and refrigeration he exported to hotels and restaurants in the Caribbean. When he sold his business, he also sold the warehouse and inventory.

It's a good thing my father got paid up front because the new owner bought his business with drug money. After he was busted, the showroom and warehouse—which were in a rapidly deteriorating neighborhood in downtown Miami—remained deserted.

"So you want to tell me what these articles are all about?" I say.

My father shrugs. "Why not? You heard of S and G?"

"That's the group Uncle Moe testified about?" I don't remind him he was cagey when I asked about it earlier.

"You got it. A bookie operation out of South Florida. It was run by Meyer Lansky, his brother, Jake, and some other tough guys. Back then, everyone and their uncle had a piece of Miami. It was what they called a free city—no single gang owned it. Each group had its own operation and its own set of hotels and restaurants."

"What's this got to do with you?"

"Not a hell of a lot. Except that if you wanted to do business in Miami, you did it with gangsters. They had the money and owned the hotels and restaurants. What were Moe and I supposed to do when they came in asking us to outfit their restaurants and bars? Say no thanks, we just deal with legit operations? We weren't crazy. The cops knew which gangsters owned which restaurants and never bothered to shut them down. Who were we to judge?"

"So why did whoever left me the articles make such a big deal of your doing business with them?"

"I have no idea. If King Kong had walked into my store looking for a refrigerator, I'd have sold it to him. That's called doing business. I wasn't running a charity. Maybe it's an old competitor. Someone still jealous we did so good in the old days. Who the hell knows?"

I look at him. We both know it can't be that.

The oak door swings open and his friends, who've changed out of their bowling shoes and peeled off their elbow and knee braces, enter. One of the men—he can't be much older than I am—nods at my father and points to a large table at the far end of the bar.

Tootsie waves. "I'll be with you in a couple."

I slide the morgue shot toward my dad's beer glass. A corner of the photo curls from the damp. "And this?"

He flips the photo over. "What about it?"

"This have anything to do with you?"

He grabs my elbow. "Don't talk crazy. Yeah, it's Louie. I already told you. Landauer ordered the hit." He lets go of my arm, then takes a swig of beer and slams his glass down. Foam sloshes onto the table.

My father has all the answers, but they mean nothing. I have no idea why an intruder broke into my house and left the clippings. I tell my father as much.

"I'm calling the police. There's no way I'm going to feel safe until I find out what this is all about."

"Don't." The word comes out in a rapid eruption. He looks around. "Did you change your locks?"

"Of course."

"Give me time. I got a few enemies. Who in the business world doesn't? And some of those characters you met at Schatzi's funeral? They were upset when I left the game. Including your friend Abe. But I can't think of anyone who'd want to hurt you or me. Maybe one of the old guys is senile, thinks he's back in the forties and wants to piss me off." He rests his chin on the intersection of his twined fingers. "You want me to stay with you, keep an eye on things? I will."

I reassure him that won't be necessary.

"Then go home. It had to be Abe. The bastard had his fun. It's nothing to worry about."

"That's easy for you to say. You're safe eight stories up at the Schmuel Bernstein. I'm the one who's going to be sweating each time I walk into my house."

"I'll talk to him."

"To Abe?"

"Abe and whoever else is involved. I'll find out what they're after and take care of everything."

"How?"

"I don't know yet. Pay him off. Whatever it takes. You need to be careful in the meantime."

I'm not convinced. But I rise and stuff the envelope back in my purse. I glance at him a moment and contemplate telling *him* to be careful. But he knows better than I do what we're up against.

"Don't stay out too late," I say before I lean over to give him a kiss.

"Not to worry."

As I open the door that leads to the bowling alley, I turn to wave. My father remains where I left him, staring at the table. His hand trembles as he brings the glass to his lips.

When I get home, I'm nervous about entering but force myself to go inside. I'm too keyed up to sleep. I hate to call so late, but I need to talk to someone—to Esther. She knows our dad and might have some ideas. She mentioned earlier in the week that Monday was a teachers' workday and she'd be going in late. I hope she's not sleeping.

"You're up late," she says after her husband, Bruce, hands her the phone. He's used to my late night calls and asks how I'm doing before passing the receiver on. Bruce is an attorney and very logical so he's a great help when it comes to talking things out. I'm not ready, yet, to talk to him about a formal separation from Daniel. That would mean acknowledging, at least to myself, that I'm ready to end my marriage.

"Dad really did it this time," I say when Esther comes on the line. Then I fill her in on the break-in and Tootsie's reaction.

"My God. Did you call the police?"

"Not yet. Dad said he's pretty sure he knows who did it and will confront them. He might have to pay someone off."

"Did he say who? Or why?"

Esther and I talk at least once a week but I've held off on telling her about Mrs. Karpowsky's accusation or my meeting with Abe. I didn't want to stoke her anger against our father. I'm beyond worrying about that now. I fill her in and tell her that Tootsie suspects Abe's behind the break-in.

"The old man's a real piece of work," she says. "Stay away from him."

"I can't do that. Not after we got back together."

"But look at what's happening to you."

"I'm the one who's digging up the past."

We don't speak for a moment.

Esther's rebuffed me on several occasions when I've asked why she's not talking to Tootsie. I try again.

"I am sorry, Becks, but it's like the message that intruder left. You need to ask Dad. If you push hard enough, he'll explain. But I don't feel right telling you myself. You have a good relationship with him and I'd hate to be the one to ruin it."

There's no need to mention my relationship with Tootsie is already less than ideal. I'm so angry I'm tempted to cut him off again. But I can't do it. He's as vulnerable now as I am and I'd feel terrible if anything happened to him. But it's time to stop pussyfooting around. Esther and that damn intruder have it right. I've got to find some way to force my father to tell me what this is all about before one of us gets hurt.

18

Tootsie

After Becks leaves, I remain in the booth and stare at my beer coaster. A buxom blonde in an Oktoberfest costume smiles back, offering up a ceramic stein and an invitation into her uncomplicated Teutonic world.

If only life were so simple.

I set my glass down and drop my face in my palms. My hands tremble so badly I have to steady them with the weight of my cheeks. The break-in at Becks' shook me. My knees feel weak and my breath comes in short, shallow gasps. I glance toward the corner of the restaurant where my friends joke and laugh. I hope no one noticed Becks' anger or my despair.

For a brief moment, I wonder if the intruder was Winchell. But no. he turned me down when I suggested it. Said it was a sick idea. So the intruder *had* to be Abe. That son of a bitch. What kind of psycho goes out and scares an innocent woman? It's hard to believe Abe would pull off a break-in. But how well do I know the guy? We were friends two, maybe three years before everything went down the toilet. I assumed Abe mailed the clippings years ago, though I never figured out why. But how did he get his hands on Louie's morgue photo? My mouth feels dry and my palms grow damp as one possibility occurs to me. The same way he covered up Moe's murder.

"Tootsie." It's Winchell, standing at the edge of my table. I didn't hear him approach. "You coming? We saved a seat."

I glance toward the others. No one looks my way. "Not yet."

"Something wrong with Becks?"

I hesitate. Winchell knows Becks is poking into my past, but doesn't know why. "It'll be okay. I'll join you and the boys in a minute."

Winchell shrugs and rejoins the bowlers.

I consider the clippings. Abe had a lot of nerve bringing them to Becks' house. As if *he* never broke the law. And what kind of bullshit is that—ask your father? Now I have to tell Becks something. If I tell her the truth, I'll be cut off from her and the boys. I can't handle that. After what happened today, Becks will be even less forgiving than her hard-nosed sister.

I'm so fed up with this damned secrecy. It'd be a relief to tell Becks about my past, to get it out in the open before someone else blows it—like that bastard, Abe. But I can't risk it. Becks is all I have now. I've got to convince Abe to get off her back.

I get up from the table and join my friends. Five minutes later, we head back to the Schmuel Bernstein. No one notices my anxiety as I say good night and head upstairs. The minute I hit my apartment I dial Abe.

"What the hell were you thinking, breaking into Becks' house and leaving those clippings?" I say the instant he picks up.

"I don't know what you're talking about."

"Don't hand me that bullshit. She came to see me tonight. Told me everything. So what are you after?"

"Nothing. I don't want nothing."

"It's been, what, fifty years? What do you have to gain by frightening my daughter?"

"You don't give up. I'm telling you, I don't know what you're talking about. If someone broke into your daughter's house, it's not my problem. It had to be somebody else you screwed."

I hesitate. Abe sounds convincing. But he's the only one who knows Becks is poking around. He could've broken in. Lord knows breaking and entering was one of the skills he developed back in Bayonne. But he'd have needed help, a younger guy, to do that much damage. That wouldn't be a problem. No, it had to be Abe.

"You have a beef with me, see me," I say. "But you bother my daughter again and I'll break your legs." I slam the phone into the receiver.

I thought I'd feel better after the call. But I don't. Images of Becks alone—watching television, working at her desk, asleep in bed—haunt me. She has a big house with lots of doors and windows. I think about calling her, telling her to make sure everything is locked and secured. But I can't do it, not this late. I'd scare her more than she already is.

I turn on the television and watch fifteen minutes of a late night talk show before abandoning the effort and picking up a book. It's hard to concentrate on the words but I keep trying. Every time I look up from the page, my chest constricts and I go back to reading to drive away the fear. It's three in the morning before I rise from the couch and enter the bedroom. Even then, the image of Becks' frightened, angry face returns, keeping me awake. I catch a glimpse of sunlight filtering through my bedroom blinds before I finally drift off.

19

I arrive at the synagogue at nine thirty the Saturday morning after my meeting with Tootsie and slide into the last row, stepping around three sets of knees before dropping into the plush velvet seat next to Mindy. The flowery scent of expensive perfume fills the air, creating a heady counterpoint to the musty odor of the prayer books that lie open on congregants' laps. From back here, the room is an ocean of black shoulders draped in undulating waves of blue-and-white *tallits*, the fringed shawls worn by Jews during prayer. Here and there, the pastel of a woman's dress breaks the dark pattern of men's backs.

Many of the worshippers, myself included, are here for the bar mitzvah of Zach Birnbaum. He sits on the raised dais at the front of the congregation, a small figure in an oversized wingback chair between the larger forms of his parents, Aviva and Noah. The rabbi's just led the congregation in the prayer honoring Judaism's founding fathers and mothers, and it's growing close to the moment when Zach goes to the lectern to read from the Torah. I smile when he brings a hand to his face and Aviva pushes it away. I've seen those gestures hundreds of time. The poor kid's nervous and needs to bite his nails. Aviva won't let him. Today he becomes a man—at least, according to Jewish law.

I hate arriving late for the service but I overslept. I've had trouble falling asleep all week. My father's assurance he'd contact Abe did little to convince me I'd be left alone and I startle awake at every little creak in the house. I wonder if I'd feel so skittish if Daniel were living at home. He was a good sport about running downstairs to check the doors and windows when I imagined noises at night. In the two months he's been gone, I haven't felt his absence as strongly as I have since the break-in. It's not just his physical presence either. I felt a certain confidence around him, a knowledge that whatever happened, he'd get me through it. It seems a lifetime ago.

I've picked up my prayer book and am trying to locate the page we're on when Mindy elbows me across our shared armrest. I look at her and raise an eyebrow.

"Daniel," she whispers.

"What about him?" I keep my voice low.

"Over there."

I follow her gaze to the front of the synagogue and gasp. Mindy grabs my hand.

Blood flows into my cheeks and my stomach lurches. I struggle to focus on the service but can't draw my eyes from Daniel's back. He's almost six feet four inches and sits a head taller than anyone else in his row. His shoulder twitches and he glances over it, no doubt sensing my stare. A woman I don't recognize is seated next to him. I clench Mindy's hand when Daniel leans in to whisper to her. At least it's not Dawn. Having Daniel show up with a woman his sons' age would be too humiliating.

Damn Aviva. She's one of my oldest friends. What was she thinking, inviting Daniel to Zach's bar mitzvah? And the nerve of him—bringing a date. Then I remember. The invitation arrived months ago—before our separation. In all the excitement after the break-in, I forgot. Besides which Daniel plays basketball with Noah on Sunday morning and has as much right to be here as I do. Not that this makes me feel better. I wish I'd steeled myself for this moment.

I spend most of the service trying to figure out who the woman is. A new girlfriend? The bastard. I hope he'll have the decency to leave as soon as the service is over and skip the reception.

I struggle to relax and focus on Zach's voice as he chants his Torah portion. He does a wonderful job, his voice cracking only once. The rabbi concludes the service and, while we're standing and singing the closing song, I catch Daniel's gaze. He smiles and waves. I turn toward Mindy and pretend I don't notice.

Who am I kidding? He's not leaving after services. He wouldn't want to hurt Aviva and Noah's feelings. With a sinking sensation, I realize there's no escaping an encounter with Daniel and his date.

Mindy and I join the crowd that rushes to the front of the synagogue to hug and congratulate Aviva, Noah, and Zach. That done, the two of us leave the sanctuary and head down a broad, marble-tiled corridor to the hall where the cocktail reception is being held. Mindy, whose husband is visiting his mother in Indianapolis, pastes herself to my side, a stocky, middle-aged bulldog prepared to run interference with Daniel.

We stop at the entrance to admire the decorations—gold lamé table runners over black linen tablecloths and an endless array of hors d'oeuvres on silver platters. Mindy and I help ourselves to the flutes of champagne and delicate lamb chops offered by white-gloved waiters before making a beeline to the table with seating cards. Mindy and I are at table six. I sneak a peek at Daniel's and relax. He's across the room at table eleven.

I'm about to break the good news to Mindy when a hand presses the small of my back.

"Becks." My heart skips a beat. It's Daniel.

I do my best to compose my face before turning around.

Daniel smiles hesitantly as he takes the elbow of the woman who sat next to him in the synagogue and propels her toward me. They make a handsome couple, him in his best black suit and her in a red dress that shows off a tiny waist. I hold my breath, expecting the worst.

"Have you met Sarah, Noah's sister?" Then, to her. "This is Becks. My wife."

I breathe again. Of course. Sarah. I met her years earlier, before her husband died. She was blond then. Noah must have asked Daniel to sit with her.

We shake hands and ask about each other's children.

Then Daniel asks Mindy and Sarah to excuse us, explaining we have a few things to discuss. He does it with such finesse that it doesn't occur to me to refuse when he steers me to a two-person table near the bar. He pulls my chair out before seating himself, then leans in toward me and gets down to business.

"Why don't you answer the phone when I call?" He sounds angry and hurt.

"What's there to say?"

"Plenty. I made an appointment with a marriage counselor last Wednesday and was embarrassed when you didn't show."

I heard his telephone message about the appointment and ignored it. I didn't think he'd go without me.

"There didn't seem any point in my coming. You've already decided I should forgive you and let bygones be bygones."

"Aren't you being a little simplistic?"

"No, you're the one who's being simplistic." I start to rise, but he grabs my arm and pulls me back into my seat. The man and woman at the table to our right stare, then avert their eyes.

"Becks, I made a mistake. A big one." He drops his voice. "I never cheated on you before and regret what I did more than you can imagine. But that's past. I've taken care of all your expenses, called every day. Why are you being so stubborn?"

All I can think about is getting away from him. "Do you really think it's that easy to forget that you slept with another woman?"

"I'm not saying it's easy. But you could answer the phone and talk to me. Your silence isn't getting us anywhere."

"I don't know that talking will help." I take a deep breath to control the sob that's welling up. "What you did . . ."

He stares down at the table. When he looks up, his eyes are damp. I avoid meeting them with my own.

"I'll do whatever it takes to get you back."

"I don't know." My voice is flat and expressionless with the effort of controlling my emotions.

"What do you mean?"

A half dozen couples I recognize mingle, smiling and laughing, near the bar. Daniel and I went to dinner and sat through Little League games with them years ago. A few were at our sons' bar mitzvahs. With a pang of sorrow, I recall how proud Daniel and I were as we watched our boys read from the Torah, of how united we felt in our love for each other and our sons. Why are those couples together when we aren't? Do the men still find their wives desirable? I feel like such a failure, such a fool. Mindy stands by the bar, watching us, a bodyguard in a frilly pink dress. She gives me a little wave and I nod back.

"I don't know if I *can* forgive you," I tell Daniel. "I told my father what happened and he said get over it. But I can't. It's not as simple as you and he think."

Daniel grabs a napkin off the table and crushes it. "I knew it would come to this." He sounds resigned.

"What are you talking about?"

"Your parents. Your father was a lousy husband and your mother put up with it."

"What's that got to do with us?"

He half rises in his seat and leans in toward me. "I'm not your father." He speaks slowly and deliberately. "I won't treat you the way he treated your mother." There's pain and bitterness in his voice.

"Well, you've come damn close."

Our eyes meet. And we're both glaring.

He drops back in his seat and scrutinizes me. "If what your father did was so awful, why do you forgive him but not me?"

Daniel's hit a raw nerve, raising a question I've been asking myself. I resented my father most of my life for cheating on my mother and swore I'd never put up with that kind of behavior. But here I am, spending time with a man whose indiscretions were far worse than Daniel's.

"I haven't *forgiven* him," I say, struggling to work it out. "But he's the only father I have and he's getting old. I can't change who he is. But I don't have to put up with the same behavior from you."

Somehow I feel stronger, verbalizing the reason I won't take Daniel back. Perhaps I *am* doing what I wish my mother had done when my father cheated on her. I don't know if that's bad or good. All I know is Daniel cheated on me. And being around him is painful.

I sip the last of my champagne and stand. "Have a great time at Zach's party."

He rises but doesn't follow me.

I leave the reception without a word to Aviva or Noah and pray they're having too much fun to notice my absence. I helped Aviva plan the menu and the decorations and have been looking forward to this day. I feel terrible about leaving. But I can't bear another minute in the same room as Daniel.

When I pull up to my home, I hesitate before I get out, then let myself in through the front door. The house feels larger and emptier than when I left that morning. My cat, Mulligan, races downstairs and takes a running slide across the hallway to greet me. I reach down and scratch behind his ears. At least I'm not alone. Although it's not even noon and I'm joining my father at seven to see a play, I go into the kitchen and pour myself a glass of Chablis.

"*L'chaim*," I say, raising the glass to Mulligan, who watches me from the kitchen table. "To life. And to the end of my lousy marriage."

20

Tootsie and I are standing outside the Stage Door Theater in Fort Lauderdale, recovering from the schmaltzy Yiddisher vaudeville show that's sent half the elderly audience into laughter and the rest into tears. We've just emerged from the darkened theater and everyone's blinking in the glare of daylight and digging around in their pockets and purses for car keys. A gaggle of "mature" women in stiletto heels and velvet tracksuits file onto the bus for Harbour Villas. Two gray-haired gentlemen wait politely beside the door as they board.

Suddenly, my father grabs my arm.

"You see that?" He squeezes my elbow and propels me toward a poster advertising the show.

I look where he points, at the photograph that dominates the poster. The show's cast is hamming it up, the women showing their ankles beneath sparkly evening gowns and the men posing like overstuffed kishke in black tuxedos. In the middle of the photo is an obese woman in a strapless, black, sequined dress that does nothing to flatter her ham hocks of upper arms.

Cynic though I am, I have to admit they put on a rousing show, belting out Yiddish songs and delivering a rapid-fire barrage of Jewish jokes. The audience laughed and sang along to the music. The theater grew quiet, though, when the heavy woman in the black sequins stepped into the spotlight and rendered an excruciatingly sentimental a cappella version of "My Yiddishe Mama." The song's a real tear jerker about the sacrifices a Jewish mother makes for her children. I was embarrassed to find myself damp-eyed.

Tootsie coughs, a short bark that brings me back to the photo.

"Yankel Fleishman," he says, tapping a corner of the glass in which the poster is framed. He points to an image of the old man who came on stage before the performance to discuss the Jewish theater. He looked about ninety and spoke in such a heavy Yiddish accent that I had a hard time understanding him. "A big star when I was a kid. Like an angel, he sang," my father says. "His voice brought tears to your eyes. I told you about Meyer Lansky?"

I nod.

"Even Lansky cried when he heard Fleishman's 'Yiddishe Mama.' "

"Is that what they wrote in *Variety*? Fleishman makes Lansky cry?"

"Don't be an idiot."

"Then how do you know?" I say. "You went to a nightclub to hear 'Yiddishe Mama' with a sobbing gangster?"

"As a matter of fact, Miss Smarty-Pants, I did."

I purse my lips, fold my arms.

"You don't believe me?" He looks around to see if anyone's listening. "Get in the car. I'll tell you over dinner."

A busty Latina in a thigh-hugging skirt seats us at a booth across from the revolving dessert display. I can't keep my eyes off the chocolate layer cake. My father's eyes are on the waitress's rear. After much debate, we agree on corned beef sandwiches, which is living dangerously in a Cuban diner that serves pork chops five ways.

"So you liked the show?" Tootsie asks after the waitress takes our order.

"It was okay. A little schmaltzy."

"What do you know? When I was growing up on the Lower East Side, that's what we listened to. The old guy I showed you.

Fleishman. He was huge. We'd go to the Yiddish vaudeville to see him every year for my parents' anniversary. When I was in New York after Esther was born, I heard him again."

"With Meyer Lansky?"

He shrugs. "In the same room."

"What were you doing in New York? Shouldn't you have been in Miami with Mom?"

"What I was or was not doing at home with your mother, may she rest in peace, is none of your damn business." He looks over his shoulder. "I was in New York. On a job."

My father's told me so many stories I can't keep them straight, but I remember something about his working as a nightclub bouncer while my mother was pregnant with Esther. I mention it.

"That didn't pan out. I got fired when this big shot claimed I made advances on his Doll. Truth is, the broad came on to me when he went to the can. I turned her down so she told her boyfriend I was fresh. The manager had to let me go." He shakes his head. "Esther was born a week later."

"That must have been tough."

"You don't know from tough. I didn't tell your mother until after Esther was born. I needed a job, and fast. I told your Uncle Moe and he asked around. Found out some of his friends needed help in New York. Someone strong who could work on the docks and keep his mouth shut."

"That would be you."

He grimaces and nods. "I'd have taken anything. A week after your sister was born, I was on the Orange Blossom Special heading to New York. I felt like a heel leaving your mother but what was I going to do? I had a wife and a kid to feed. Moe said a guy named Sammy would meet me at the station. I should look for a redhead."

He stops talking when the waitress returns to tell us they don't have rye bread. Her accent is so thick I can barely understand her. My father has no problem and tells her to bring whatever she's got.

"Sure enough," he continues, "the train pulls into Penn Station and this skinny red-headed guy is waiting for me. Short fellow. Old enough to be my father."

"What's this got to do with Lansky?" I ask.

"Keep your mouth shut and I'll tell you." He glares at me. "I introduced myself as Moe's brother and he gave me this tough guy handshake, like he's got something to prove. I figured he's the boss and don't squeeze back. He hailed a cab—my first time in a New York taxi—and took me to a classy hotel. Sammy told me to come upstairs once I'd dropped my suitcase in my room. And to shake a leg.

"I had a quick shower and shave and headed up to the room he told me to visit. When I got there, I heard men talking, but the sound died out after I knocked. I'm not going to lie to you. I was nervous. When I tried to make conversation with Sammy in the cab, he ignored me. And I knew your Uncle Moe had some questionable friends. Sammy finally let me in."

The waitress drops off our diet sodas. They come in huge, plastic, blue-pebbled glasses.

"It was a big room, a fancy hotel suite," my father says after taking a sip. "A man with movie star looks, a little older than Sammy, leaned against the desk at the front of the room, talking to a couple of guys my age. Dark hair, dark eyes. I figured him for an Italian, maybe Mafia. Sammy introduced him as Yehuda, though, and I realized he was a Jew. He didn't crack a smile the whole time I was there. And I could tell he was in charge from the way no one interrupted when he spoke. He talked to the two guys in Hebrew. But different from what I'd heard in shul.

"Yehuda asked me a couple of questions about my work. Being polite, I thought. Then he got down to business. Asked if I'd I heard of the *Haganah*, the Israeli underground. I told him no. Remember this is 1947, nobody knew from the Israeli army back then. He explained it was a secret defense force set up by the Jews to fight the British and Arabs. My job, he said, was crucial to the future of Israel. I had to work on the docks and keep my eyes open. When I asked what I was looking for, he wouldn't say. Just told me to make sure the Italians and Irish dockworkers did what they were told. And to report to Sammy if they didn't."

"I still don't see what this has to do with Lansky," I break in when he stops to blow his nose.

"You want to let me tell the story or not."

I nod.

"I spent a miserable winter loading cargo from piers along the Hudson River, mostly from the Jersey side. None of the dockworkers talked to me, probably thought I was a spy, which I was. They had to be stupid not to figure something's up. Here's this Jew, new to the union, working with the Italians and Irish.

"I kept my eyes open but nothing suspicious happened. I worked like a dog, loading whatever the bosses told me to load and freezing my ass off in the process. Everyone did their jobs, kept their mouths shut and I had no idea why Sammy and Yehuda decided to plant me there."

He scoots back in his seat and leans in toward me.

"Then one particularly lousy morning, about a month after I started at the docks, all hell broke loose. A blizzard a couple of days earlier had turned New York into a frozen hellhole and it took two hours to get to work. I was in a lousy mood. We were working on the pier, loading wooden crates—heavy sons of bitches labeled fertilizer—and had a hard time wrapping the cables to lift them.

"We finally finished and stepped away to let the crane operator load the crate onto the ship. Everything went fine at first. But as the crate crossed the ship's rail, a slat fell off and crashed to the dock. Another slat fell and then another. I was getting nervous, thinking maybe we hadn't secured the cables tight enough and I'd be in trouble, when a box slipped out from between the broken slats and tumbled to the pier. It broke open and a half dozen machine guns rattled to the ground."

"I thought you said the crates held fertilizer?"

"That's how they were *labeled*. The foreman took a look at the cargo and yelled for everyone to clear out of the area. Next thing I knew, Sammy raced up, grabbed my arm, and forced me to run at top speed from the shipyard. I didn't know where he came from, but he was the boss so I obeyed.

"His car was parked outside the terminal and we jumped in and took off. I was full of questions but Sammy, Mr. Silent, had nothing to say until we were clear of Jersey City. When he opened his mouth and told me, I was ready to slug him. I'd been loading weapons all morning. An illegal shipment headed for Israel."

"You had no idea?" I ask.

He shakes his head. "None."

"Didn't you wonder why they needed a spy on the docks?"

"Sure. I asked but no one would tell me. And I couldn't afford to make waves. Most crates were labeled heavy machinery or fertilizer. Turns out I'd spent the month loading weapons headed for Palestine. This Yehuda had arranged for me and Sammy to keep an eye out to make sure none of the longshoremen learned about it."

My father stops speaking while the waitress serves our sandwiches. I take a bite and spit it out. The meat's stringy and the bread's stale.

"Is that what Sammy told you?" I ask once my father peels his eyes from the waitress's retreating derriere.

"I learned most of it later. I don't think many people knew then but the U.S. sold a lot of its surplus World War II equipment to the Arabs. The Jews, who were fighting for statehood, got bubkes. At first they had no money. By the time they got some, the U.S wouldn't ship military hardware to the Mideast. Makes you wonder where *their* sympathy lay. We heard rumors the British were banking on the Arabs if war broke out after they left. Which, in fact, it did."

He stops talking and shakes his head. "You didn't learn this in religious school?"

"I don't remember it."

He takes a bite out of his sandwich and chews slowly.

"Maybe I wasn't paying attention," I add.

He laughs. "Maybe. The way I heard it, Ben-Gurion—before he became prime minister—convinced a group of rich American Jews to help the Israelis purchase surplus ammunition and weapons-making equipment. It shouldn't have been a big deal. But the only way Israel could get the stuff was to smuggle it in."

"And that's where Lansky came in?"

"Smart girl." He reaches across the table and taps my forehead. "At the time this was going on, the Mafia controlled the shipyards in New York and New Jersey. And Lansky had friends in the Mafia. So Ben-Gurion's wealthy friends introduced Yehuda—a gunrunner from way back—to Lansky. And Lansky convinced the Italians to tell Yehuda when weapons were headed to Arab countries. Maybe stop them from reaching their destination."

"So Lansky helped Israel?"

"Sure he helped. He was a Jew. He lined things up with his Italian buddies, who told the longshoremen what to do. The thing is, a lot of these dockworkers were Italian. They could've been fans of Mussolini. Who knows what they'd have done if they knew the cargo was headed to Israel."

"You didn't know this while you were working the docks?"

"I knew something fishy was going on. But it wasn't my place to ask."

"What happened after the weapons were found?"

"As far as I was concerned, nothing. I hung around New York a few more days. Sammy thought I might be needed. It was all over the papers. Something like thirty crates of machine guns were intercepted on their way to Palestine. I'm not saying I'm glad I worked at the docks that winter. I was miserable. But you got to admit those gangsters were one hundred percent behind Israel."

I'm not going to debate him on that subject. "So where did your meeting with Lansky fit into all this?"

"Keep your pants on. I'm getting there. The night before I left town, Sammy told me Mr. Lansky would like to meet me. He was going to the theater that night to hear Fleishman and wanted I should come. I took a cab with Sammy and sat at a table with a dozen tough-looking guys. Some, I guess, were Mr. Lansky's friends but some looked like protection. Sammy introduced me and Mr. Lansky was very nice, asked if I had a wife, kids. I told him yes and he thanked me for my help. Can you believe that? Meyer Lansky thanking me?"

That doesn't need an answer so I don't offer one.

"When Fleishman came on stage, everyone was silent, especially the guys at Mr. Lansky's table. Everyone knew he was a huge fan of the singer. Sure enough, Fleishman wrapped up his act with 'Yiddishe Mama.' I was trying to be a tough guy, but I was near tears. And I couldn't help myself, I looked around. Lansky sat there with a white hankie, dabbing his eyes. That big, tough gangster was crying." My father shakes his head. "Just goes to show. Once a Jew, always a Jew."

I don't know that crying over "Yiddishe Mama" qualifies anyone as a Jew. But I keep my mouth shut and push my plate away. I gave up on my corned beef sandwich after the first bite.

"The next day, Sammy and I took the Havana Special back to Miami. I got to tell you it was great getting back to your mother and Esther. Your sister was a little doll."

A shadow crosses his face and I realize how much he misses Esther.

"I learn later that Sammy was trying to get in good with the Miami Jews. That's what brought him up to New York to help Lansky." Tootsie laughs. "Turned out he lived in Miami Beach and had a daughter of marriageable age. Problem was the Jewish mothers wouldn't let their sons date a gangster's daughter. But working for Israel, that's another story. His plan must have paid off. His daughter married a Jewish accountant, a fellow named Irving Tannenbaum. Years later, Irv told me Sammy wouldn't let him into the business. Sammy said that working as a wise guy was fine for Sammy's generation. But not for an American-born Jew."

"Sounds like you went straight too."

"You bet. After the trip to New York, I was ready for a legitimate job. Uncle Moe had connections in the restaurant business so we decided to open a restaurant supply company. You know the man I talked to in the theater, the old guy sitting in front of us?"

"What about him?"

"He ran one of South Florida's largest bookie operations before opening a cafeteria. One of our best customers."

I picture the wizened old man in the plaid golf hat. "You're kidding."

My father shakes his head and goes back to his sandwich.

I wonder how many of the old guys at the Stage Door Theater have similarly illicit pedigrees. I'm not entirely comfortable with my father's story about Meyer Lansky. It's as if he's trying to convince me that being a member of the mob was a good thing, something you did out of loyalty to other Jews. I'm not buying it. Not after what his buddies did to my house. Jewish or not, Lansky and his kind were mobsters and murderers. Which, I have to admit, made Tootsie a thug. What upsets me the most is that he's proud of it.

I'm not letting my father off the hook for the break-in. He says I'm a nag when I ask if he's contacted his so-called friends. His condescending attitude and refusal to recognize how badly this frightens me drive me crazy.

My father chews deliberately, his chin resting on his upturned palm as his jaws labor at the corned beef sandwich. I'm about to tell him what I think of Lansky and his gangster pals when Tootsie stops chewing. His eyebrows form a vee of concentration. I expect an insight from him, maybe an admission these hoodlums weren't the wonderful characters he paints them to be.

But no. It doesn't happen. Instead, he spits a hunk of fatty meat into his paper napkin.

21

Tootsie

Becks is unusually quiet on the drive home tonight and, when we turn off the I-95 ramp for downtown Miami, I ask if I've said something to upset her.

She shakes her head. "I'm down. I saw Daniel this morning at Zach Birnbaum's bar mitzvah."

"And?"

"And we had a fight."

"About what?"

"Everything. Nothing. Moving back in together."

She looks at me from the corner of her eye, daring me to comment. I'd like to press her, to find out if there's anything I can do to help. But I keep my mouth shut. I don't need her telling me again that it's none of my business.

When I get upstairs to my apartment, I go to the sliding glass doors and stare into the Schmuel Bernstein's garden. It's dark and the palm trees are scarcely visible. Across the lawn, lights flicker on in one of the upstairs windows of the nursing home. The grounds are deserted except for a raccoon trying to upend a garbage can.

I'm down tonight too, sad and disappointed. The actors put on a terrific show and it brought back great memories. Afterward, at dinner, I enjoyed sharing them with Becks. But as I spoke, I realized I was trying to convince her that the gangsters I knew weren't the monsters she paints them to be. Lansky and his cronies did a lot of good, helping the Israeli underground fighters acquire weapons. Becks seemed unimpressed.

She didn't say anything tonight, but she's made no secret of her contempt for these men. I can understand it. They were criminals. I suppose I was too and regret some of the things I did. But whether she likes it or not, a lot of those men are friends I grew up with, people I admired as a kid. It seemed natural to follow in their footsteps. Although I knew what they did wasn't kosher, it was the best option for a kid from our neighborhood who wanted to make it in the world. It didn't occur to me until I was married with a child that I had another choice.

And now Schatzi is dead. Moe too. They had good lives. Truth be told, most of us did pretty well for ourselves. Even if our jobs weren't entirely straight, we married and had kids who went on to legitimate careers. Some of my friends even went to college. I thought about going before the war. But that was craziness. My father didn't have the money to send me. And by the time the GI bill came along, I'd lost interest.

Back then, the neighborhood men Ma called nogoodniks were the ones who made real money. Drove big cars like Schatzi's, went out with good-looking dames, and dressed sharp. The guys who left the Lower East Side for Brooklyn and points north helped those left behind when they could. If Schatzi hadn't put Moe in touch with Landauer, neither of us would've come out of the army with a job.

You had to be tough to survive back then. I needed it on the streets of New York, where I had to fight Irish and Italian kids almost every day. And I needed it to get through the stinking war. When I left the army and moved to Miami, the only assets I had were my size and my fists. Moe had the same skills and made a nice living working for Landauer. There was no reason I shouldn't do so the same. And I never hurt anyone. If people wanted to spend their dough betting on numbers, who was I to judge? It was business. How could I know things would turn out so miserably?

I go to the kitchen and open the refrigerator. Nothing worth eating so I shut it again. When I turn around, I spot Bernice and the girls' photos. Their eyes, dark and accusing, follow me as I return to the living room. I don't know how much more of this secrecy I can bear. Hiding my past has become torture. My world would be so much less complicated if everything was out in the open. But then I'd be alone, shunned by my daughters and grandchildren. And life wouldn't be worth living.

22

I'm dozing on the family room couch with the television on after dropping off Tootsie when the phone rings. It takes a few seconds to identify the sound and I'm half awake when I pick up the receiver and mumble "Hello."

"Becks?" It's my sister, Esther. She sounds surprised. As though she expects me to be out on a date. Or, more likely, asleep.

I glance at the clock on the cable box. It's almost midnight. "What's going on?" We're both problem sleepers so I figure she's called to chat.

"Listen, I . . . " She hesitates. "I'm sorry to call so late, but Bruce is out of town and . . . I need to talk to you. I got some scary news yesterday."

I'm completely awake now and flip off the television. "What happened? Are the girls okay?" Her two daughters are away at college.

"They're fine. But I went for my mammogram yesterday. Then afterward the radiologist suggested I get an ultrasound. He didn't want me to wait. He did it right away. And something's wrong. My doctor wants me to have a biopsy."

"My God." My heart skips a beat. "Did he say what it is?" I don't want to use the word cancer, but what else could it be?

"Not yet. Just that he saw something, maybe just calcifications, and needs to probe further."

"What's that mean?"

"He says the biopsy will tell us more. I have it scheduled for Tuesday after school."

"I'll come up. I can get a flight tomorrow. Or drive." My sister lives in Greensboro, North Carolina so it's a short flight away. She teaches third grade and I want to be there when she gets out of class so I can accompany her to her appointment.

"Are you sure? You already have enough going on. I told Bruce and he's flying home now. He's supposed to start a trial in Atlanta on Tuesday."

She doesn't need to spell it out: there's nothing like having a sister near when you're in trouble.

"I'll leave in the morning," I say.

"Would you? I'm so scared." Her voice quavers. "How am I going to tell the girls? They're coming home from college for Thanksgiving."

Esther's daughter Michelle is a senior at the University of North Carolina, Chapel Hill, and Ariel is a junior there. We joke that Ariel still needs to let go of the umbilical cord, she's so attached to Esther. She'll be panic-stricken if her mother has cancer. I don't know that my own boys would be any less upset if I became ill.

"I don't think I can handle this."

The fear in her voice frightens me and I search my mind for comforting phrases. "You'll be fine. You'll get through it." Then, without thinking, I say, "Daniel will help."

I'm surprised at my words. I've done everything possible to avoid my husband.

Esther knows this. In fact, she's the only one who supported me in my decision to spend time away from Daniel. Aviva and Noah think we should go for marriage counseling and Mindy, like my father, thinks I should forgive Daniel and take him back. But Esther and I suffered together through our parents' arguments and she's as familiar as I am with the toll infidelity takes.

"Could you call Daniel, let him know what's going on?" she asks before I can sort through my thoughts. "I know it's not easy for you. But I trust his judgment. I'd feel so much better if he got involved. If you want me to call . . ."

"No, I'll do it." I try to sound reassuring. She's got enough to think about. "Why don't you come here and see him? Let him take over your care. Whatever it is, you'll move to Boca Raton and stay with me."

"Really? I was half hoping you'd offer. I can fly down early this week." She hesitates a moment. "And don't say anything to Dad."

Before I can protest, she hangs up.

It's no mean trick getting to sleep that night. I picture my sister in a hospital bed, hooked up to all manner of tubes and wires. All I can think about is how I'll handle it if Esther has cancer—or worse, dies. I'm battered and emotionally drained by events of the last few months. First Daniel betrays me. Then my father reveals his ugly past. But Esther having cancer? Everything pales before that.

Lying in bed with my eyes open, I search for the bright spots in my life. Josh calls every Friday night to see how I'm doing. I love that he feels so protective toward me. He has a tendency to take care of others, though, and I'm afraid he'll make Daniel's and my problems his own. Gabriel sends funny emails—the closest he comes to expressing affection. But it's not like having a sister to confide in. Esther and I have shared a lifetime and know we can count on each other to get through the rough patches.

When Esther's youngest was diagnosed with Hodgkin's lymphoma at eight, I flew to Greensboro for a week at a time so she and Bruce could put all their energy into Ariel's medical care. My friend Aviva lived next door at the time, thank goodness, so she kept Josh and Gabriel until Daniel got home from the office. It seems so unfair that this is happening to Esther after what she's been through. Daniel loves her almost as much as I do so I know he'll do everything he can to help her.

Daniel's an early riser so the next morning at seven, I dial his apartment. As anxious as I am to set things up for Esther, I'm uncomfortable making the call. I chew my nails as I wait for him to answer. For a fleeting second, I wonder if he's alone.

He picks up on the third ring. "Becks? Is everything okay?" My heart leaps at the familiar voice. He sounds concerned and surprised, but very much awake.

"I'm fine. So are the boys. It's Esther." I struggle to keep my voice from shaking.

"What happened?"

"She called last night." I repeat what Esther told me.

"Did *you* suggest she see me?"

"She suggested it," I lie. "Are you free this week?"

"For Esther, of course."

A wave of relief drapes my shoulders and I settle back in my chair. Daniel will take over.

"Do you know which scans she's had?"

"She mentioned a mammogram and ultrasound. She's supposed to go in for a biopsy Tuesday."

"I'll call her before I leave for the office and set things up. Tell her to hold off on the biopsy. I'd rather she do it here. I'm pretty sure I have time Wednesday morning. Can you bring her in then?"

"Sure." I experience a flutter of panic as I realize that Esther will expect me to go with her to his office.

He hesitates. "And, Becks, it's been long enough already. Don't you think we could . . ."

"I've got to run." Up until now, our conversation has been civil, even warm. But I'm not ready to go any further. Hearing his voice leaves me emotionally raw and tender. "I have a lot to do before Esther arrives."

My hand trembles as I hang up the phone.

By six that night, when I've promised to pick up my father for dinner, I'm exhausted. Part of it is the strain of talking to Daniel. It was a relief to hear his reassurance he'd take care of Esther. But our conversation left me feeling lonely and lost. I can't believe it's been a little more than two months since we separated.

I've survived by talking to my sister and focusing on my writing. The time away from Daniel has given me a chance to think about what I want in life. Right now, it's the opportunity to work on the cookbook I promised myself I'd write. I'm just a few pages in, but I feel like I've got something solid, something other cooks will find useful. And writing it makes me feel closer to my mother, helps re-create the wonderful times we spent in the kitchen.

Tonight, though, I've worked myself into a state over Esther. I'm afraid of the worst—that Daniel won't be able to help her. If the news is bad, I don't know what I'll do. Who I'll confide in. I let my mind wander to Bruce and Esther's girls and how devastated they'll be if anything happens to Esther. I'm making myself sick with worry. And I have to honor her request not to tell my father. He and Esther haven't talked in over a year.

"Daniel stopped by this morning," my father says as he slides into my car at the entrance to his building. "He asked me to talk to you." Tootsie watches me, gauging my reaction.

My face grows hot but I keep my mouth shut. I had no idea the two were in contact. I shouldn't be surprised. Tootsie called Daniel now and then to ask medical questions and they'd remain on the phone talking about sports. They have some sort of bond I don't understand considering how different they are. Or how different I thought they were. I don't like the idea of Tootsie and Daniel discussing our breakup and feel betrayed by my dad's willingness to talk to him.

It's November and, despite the early hour, the city is entering the shadowy netherworld of twilight. The few souls walking along the sidewalk appear as black-and-white ghosts floating between pools of light thrown off by streetlamps. The sky grows darker as we head down Biscayne Boulevard and the lights spanning the condominium towers across the bay form a wall of twinkling stars.

"So what did Daniel want?" I ask, already knowing the answer.

"He wanted me to talk to you about getting back together. He regrets what he did and misses you."

"And you believe him?"

"Of course I do. He's a good man. He cheated on you once. That's not something you end a marriage over."

I glance at Tootsie and he looks away. He must know by now how little I respect his advice on marriage. His affairs destroyed his relationship with my mother and turned her into a bitter person. I won't let that happen to me. I never told Tootsie how witnessing his treatment of my mother prevented me from trusting Daniel or any other man for a long time. I debate bringing it up, but don't. I doubt my father would understand.

"I know what I'm doing," I say, struggling to keep the anger out of my voice. "You and Mom worked things out your way. I can take care of my own marriage."

He shrugs. Then he looks out the window and back at me. His eyes are sad and I realize how upset he is by our breakup. I appreciate his concern. But it's something I need to deal with alone.

When we arrive at Wasserstein's Deli, it's crowded so we sit at the counter at the front of the restaurant. The backless stools are small and hard and Tootsie keeps squirming. It's noisy here, near the crowd waiting for tables, so we eat and head back to the car.

"Did Daniel say why he came to see you *today*?" I ask once we're on the causeway crossing the bay to his apartment. I'm afraid Daniel said something about Esther.

"I don't know why he stopped by *today*, but he looked miserable. He talked about how much he misses being part of a family. He's got a point, you know. Thirty years is too long to throw away. I asked what happened with his chippie. Did she dump him? He said no. The affair was a mistake."

I cringe. That's it? A mistake with a "chippie." Is that how my father sees Daniel's affair?

"He loves you, Doll."

I can't have this conversation. It's painful and can only end in another argument over how he mistreated my mother. The last time that happened we didn't speak for years. I'd hate a repeat of that. I need him too much now. It's been a nightmare of a weekend and I want to go home.

I drop Tootsie off, refusing his invitation to come upstairs. My father adores Daniel, and I know he'll launch into his spiel about what a great guy he is. I don't need that. And I'm afraid I'll let word of Esther's condition slip.

Two days later, Esther arrives with an envelope of films. She talked to her doctor but says we can discuss his findings after she meets with Daniel and has a better idea of what they mean. We stay up late talking and baking my mother's chocolate chip mandel bread, which is gone by the morning. It's wonderful to have her around, though it makes me realize how lonely I've been banging around this big, deserted house. She brings two books on breast cancer but we ignore them. I've looked forward to her arrival with trepidation, afraid that the fear of cancer has changed her, maybe stripped her of her sense of humor. But she's still got me on the floor laughing with stories of her students.

My sister is shorter and smaller-boned than I am but much better at sports. In the last few years, she has taken to wearing her athleticism like a badge of honor. When she's not working, she tends to hang out in pricey sneakers and brief running shorts that show off her well-defined quadriceps. As a teenager, she always followed the latest fad so I'm not surprised that she packed an impressive collection of lightweight nylon shirts and tees emblazoned with the names of marathon sponsors. She brought me a tee shirt with the names of several Greensboro eateries. It was, she joked, the tee shirt I'd appreciate the most.

Our little honeymoon of eating, sleeping and laughing ends the minute we get in the car Wednesday morning. Daniel's agreed to see Esther at nine thirty. I'm so nervous on the ride to his office that I run a red light.

"Hey, I'm here to be cured, not killed," Esther says. "Calm down. It's just Daniel." She pats my shoulder and a surge of warmth engulfs me. She appreciates how hard it is for me to face him.

It's been two months since I visited Daniel's office and the place looks shabby. The hedges in front of the compact brick building need a trim. The lawn service is overdue and dollar weed competes with small patches of brown grass for control of the lawn. Though it's officially his office manager's job to oversee the building's upkeep, in reality it fell to me. I get a certain sense of satisfaction knowing something at his office has paid a price for my absence.

When Esther and I enter the office, two elderly women glance up from the champagne leather armchairs I chose for the waiting area ten years ago. They're still in good shape, though not in the precise arrangement I left them. I motion Esther to sit and step up to the receptionist's window.

"Esther Potok is here to see Dr. Ruchinsky."

The receptionist, Mary, looks up with a welcoming smile that quickly changes to shock. "Mrs. Ruchinsky. I didn't know you were coming with Mrs. Potok." She glances down at her schedule book, then over my shoulder at Esther. "I'll let Dr. Ruchinsky know his patient is here."

I steal a glance into the office through the tiny window behind which Mary sits. A woman walks behind her and I catch my breath. Mary whispers, "Dawn left."

I manage a weak smile. Of course. Everyone knows. Mary blushes, then closes the opaque sliding glass window as I return to Esther.

Having helped out in Daniel's office when members of his staff were sick, I know it's customary for a nurse or assistant to escort the patient to an examining room. But ten minutes after we sit down, Daniel opens the waiting room door.

"Esther," he says, though he's looking at me, "it's good to see you."

I open my mouth to say hello, then close it. My tongue feels like sandpaper and my limbs are weak. I'm shocked at this unexpected reaction. A sense of loss rushes over me, but I can't tell if it's from the sight of Daniel or from a sudden recognition that this is real—that I could lose Esther. I fight an irrational longing to run into his arms and beg him to reassure me she'll be fine. Daniel glances at me, eyebrows furrowed, and I sense he's reading my mind.

Daniel's become gaunt since I last saw him and the high cheekbones that gave his face a compelling Slavic intensity look like bony parentheses. His hair is beginning to curl behind his ears, which means he hasn't had it cut in weeks. When his eyes search mine, I look down. My stomach contracts.

"Why don't the two of you come back now?" he says.

Esther rises.

"I'll wait here," I manage to whisper. I don't know if I'm capable of standing. "When the exam's over, call me in."

They leave the waiting area, Daniel's hand across the small of Esther's back.

I'm hiding behind the *Southern Living* magazine I left in the office months earlier, trying to conceal my reddened face, when the older of the two elderly women in the waiting room reaches for her companion's hand. The two appear well-heeled, with short, blunt-cut, silver-gray hair and beautifully tailored pantsuits. They look so much alike that I wonder if they're sisters.

"You're going to like Dr. Ruchinsky. He's the finest oncologist in Palm Beach County," the older one whispers to her companion. "And he's so kind. I don't know how I could've gotten through this without him."

I keep my eyes glued to the page, but turn my head slightly to better hear what they're saying.

"When I found out about Joseph's cancer, I was devastated. Dr. Ruchinsky spent as much time comforting and explaining things to me as he spent on Joseph's medical care. He did everything he could." She touches a manicured pinkie to her cheek and wipes a tear.

I catch her eye and look away. She leans toward her friend and takes the woman's other hand. "I promise. You're going to get the best care. Everything will be fine."

The women continue speaking but drop their voices to a range I can't hear. Their conversation reminds me of how I felt when Daniel broke away from his old partners to start his practice. When I'd run into doctors at the gym or grocery store, they'd reassure me he'd do fine, that he was a terrific doctor and they'd send their patients to him. I felt proud of being married to such a well-regarded man. Now I wonder how such a kind and gentle person could have treated *me* so poorly. What happened to the Daniel I knew? I loved being "Dr. Ruchinsky's wife"—not just because he was a successful and well-respected physician, but because he sincerely cared about his patients and wasn't afraid to show it.

"Dr. Ruchinsky asked if you'd come back to his office."

I look up from my magazine and check my watch. Has it really been twenty minutes? Mary stands at the open door, smiling. I follow her down the narrow hall and past the examining rooms to Daniel's office. When I step inside, he's sitting behind the antique walnut desk we shipped home during a vacation in Vermont. The glassed-fronted barrister's bookcase we picked up a year earlier is crammed with books and journals. Colorful framed photos of the boys at the beach, horseback riding at camp, and standing with Daniel and me in their high school graduation robes line the top of the bookcase. Everything's familiar—and strange. Esther sits across from Daniel, her hands folded in her lap. Her face reveals nothing.

"I'm afraid there's something there," Daniel says once I've pulled the door shut and settled into the chair next to Esther. "I've gone over Esther's scan and want to schedule a biopsy for tomorrow."

I take my sister's hand and give it a squeeze. It's cold and damp. She doesn't squeeze back.

"So the question is where do we go from there?" He nods toward Esther. "It's your decision, of course, but I've been through this with many patients. Barry Simon can do the biopsy. He's a good surgeon and I can set it up for you tomorrow if you want. Once we hear back, you can decide what to do.

"In any event, if you need radiation, chemo, surgery, whatever, we can arrange to do it in Boca. I'd also be glad to call your doctor in Greensboro if you'd rather go home. Either way, I'm here for you."

He talks a bit longer, explaining Esther's medical options and answering her questions. I'm surprised by how coherent she is. I'm numb and, after a few minutes, realize how deeply disappointed I feel. I was sure Daniel would announce Esther's doctor misread the mammogram. That she was fine. I counted on him to, somehow, pull a rabbit out of his hat and make her cancer disappear. But even Daniel can't do that.

When he stands, Esther and I rise. Daniel reaches to open the door for us and hesitates as his hand touches the knob. He looks at me, then diverts his gaze.

At the reception desk, he gives Esther a hug. I stiffen as he approaches and he steps back.

The first five minutes of the drive home, we don't speak. Daniel's office is fifteen minutes from the house and we return along Jog Road, passing gated communities with elaborately landscaped entrances. When we turn into my neighborhood, Esther looks at me. "I'm glad I came. It's a relief to be with you."

I tell her she's welcome to stay as long as she wants, that I plan to be with her for every appointment and procedure.

"I'm sure the doctors in Greensboro are fine," she continues, "but they're not Daniel. He's so reassuring. And he took the time to explain what I'll be going through. My doctor at home usually can't be bothered."

I take in what she said and recall the conversation between the elderly women in Daniel's office. Esther's right. Despite everything, I never lost respect for Daniel's medical skill. He's devoted to his patients. Sometimes too much so. Any real difficulties in our marriage before the affair stemmed from the time he spent with patients and away from the family. He was, as Esther once put it, a package deal. The same qualities that I loved in him, his sensitivity and ability to tune in to people, made him a great, if overworked, doctor.

Esther seems to read my mind. "You know he still loves you."

I give a quick nod.

She reaches across the console and puts a hand on my arm. "I can't believe the Daniel I know, the guy I just saw, cheated on you. I still love him, but hate him for what he did to you. We talked a little before you came in. He regrets his affair and hates himself for hurting you." She reaches into her purse and pulls out a mirror and lipstick. Since we're heading home and won't be running into anyone, I realize she's putting on makeup as a delaying tactic. She gives a little pout to smooth her lipstick, then turns back to me. "And thirty years is a long time."

She sounds like my father. I didn't have an answer for him. And I don't have one for her.

I pull into my driveway but we both remain seated. I'm worried sick about my sister's cancer. But I must admit there is a certain irony to Esther's illness. As awful as death and sickness are, they bring families together. When my mother was dying, Daniel kept Esther and me sane. He spoke with her doctors almost every day during the last few weeks of her life, and helped us make the agonizing decision to let her go. Although my mother and Tootsie were divorced at the time, I resented him for being in Las Vegas with his bowling buddies when she died. Esther's husband was in the middle of a trial. Only Daniel stood by.

Now that Esther may be gravely ill, may even be dying, I'm turning to Daniel again. I wish I could talk to my father about Esther's illness. I don't know how much help he'd be but at least he could share the emotional burden. But I have to honor my sister's request. That leaves Daniel once more. At the end of the day, Esther's illness is forcing me to reevaluate my feelings toward Daniel.

At his office today, it struck me; I'm still in love with him. Our marriage may be worth saving. But first, I have to convince myself he can be trusted, that he's the old Daniel in whom I could confide, who'd be there for me no matter what. And I need to forgive him, to step away from the hurt and resentment I've been harboring and open myself to the generous and loving man I married. I hope I can do that.

23

The next Friday, Esther's flight to Greensboro is running late so I park in the garage and keep her company at a coffee shop in Fort Lauderdale International Airport. Her biopsy revealed she has invasive ductal carcinoma and she's returning to Greensboro to tell the girls, who are coming home from college for the weekend. She's returning to Florida for the lumpectomy so Daniel can oversee her care.

When she called to tell the girls about her diagnosis, Ariel and Heather took the news better than expected. Both wanted to fly to Boca Raton to be with her immediately, which she refused. Bruce is handling things well, calling Esther every night. When she returns to Florida on Monday, she'll have the surgery then decide whether to go with chemo and radiation therapy. She spent hours talking to Daniel and me and searching the internet and seems comfortable with her decision.

I'm a little calmer about her prognosis knowing that Daniel's set up a thorough plan of action. He seems optimistic she'll come out of this fine and I trust his judgment. The second time I went with Esther to Daniel's office, it was easier to be around him. But I still refuse to join her in the examining room. I prefer the three of us meet more formally in Daniel's office.

I'd risen too early to shower that morning so, when I get home, I do so. While washing my hair, I consider the article I'm working on for the mid-December food section. I'd like to find a tropical spin on Hanukkah recipes and thought I'd take a look at early issues of Miami newspapers in the Miami Library's archives. By the time Esther boarded her plane, though, it was too late for the long drive. I'm disappointed because I'd hoped to see Gabriel while I was down there. We haven't spoken in a few weeks and I'm eager to make up after my refusal to let Daniel move back home. I talk to Josh almost every Sunday, but I miss Gabriel and feel left out of his life. He's close geographically, yet emotionally so distant. I decide to spend the rest of the day searching the internet for historical information about the holiday and its culinary traditions. I'll call Gabriel tonight.

It's been almost a month since my house was ransacked and I'm no closer to knowing who broke in. My father and I have been back and forth on the subject a half dozen times. He seems convinced I'm not in danger. But I'm not comfortable taking his word. Maybe he's telling me things are fine so I won't go to the police with what I know about his background.

I have thought about visiting Abe, telling him what my father said when I asked about their disagreement—which is what I presume he meant by "ask your father." But I'm afraid to initiate contact. The vehemence of his anger when I visited and the savagery with which he vandalized my home terrify me. Plus it's not the type of thing you do—show up at someone's house and announce, "I asked my father and he said he never ratted on you." For all I know, Tootsie turned Abe in.

The shower wakes me up and, after throwing on a sweat suit, I head downstairs to start work. As I near the first floor, I hear noise in the kitchen, as though the television's on. I stop for a moment, then smile, picturing my cat on the counter, lying across the remote control. Mulligan's developed this habit of landing on it when he jumps on the kitchen counter, turning on the television. Then he sits there until I shove him aside. I was frightened by the noise the first time he did it and it took me fifteen minutes to find the remote beneath his belly. As though reading my mind, Mulligan trots out of the kitchen and rubs up against my legs.

"Let me guess," I say, reaching down to scratch between his ears, "you wanted to watch the funniest cat videos?"

After the last break-in, you'd think I'd know better.

When I walk in to the kitchen to flip off the television, I come to such an abrupt halt that the towel wrapped around my hair drops to the floor. I open my mouth in a silent scream, then close it. The man I'd noticed talking to Mrs. Karpowsky at Schatzi's funeral sits at my kitchen table with a half-filled cup of coffee. He's roughly the same age as my father, but is shorter and has a stockier build. Skin droops beneath his eyes and jowls, giving him the melancholy, hangdog appearance of a bloodhound. He wears a formal, heavily-starched, white guayabera with sleeves that extend below his wrists to reveal short, pudgy fingers encased in gold rings. He smiles at me gently and inquisitively like an old friend delighted to have surprised me with his visit.

Standing behind him is a squat, bulked-up Latin with a bowling ball head. A black spit of a goatee and mirrored sunglasses add little to his appeal.

He's pointing a gun at my chest.

And he is *not* smiling.

I step back, too stunned to scream.

"You must be Tootsie's girl," the old man says, rising from his chair. He pronounces it 'goyl' and the conciliatory tone of his voice is more frightening than anger. "Becks, isn't it?"

I nod. It's a struggle to hear his words over the thumping of my heart. I want to know how he got in and what he's doing here, but I'm too scared to speak.

"Sorry for the surprise visit, but old habits die hard. This is my friend, Pinky." He motions toward the bruiser, then frowns. "You want to lose that gun."

Pinky sets the ugly metal object on the kitchen counter but keeps a hand on it.

The old man drops back into his chair and motions to the seat opposite. "Sit. Please. We have a lot to talk about."

I move mechanically, one leg then the other, until I'm seated across from him. I can't believe this is happening. In my own kitchen. The newspaper I left on the table that morning lies open to the crossword puzzle, which is filled with unfamiliar handwriting. "Who are you?" I ask. I'm not feeling altogether confident but decide to take the man's greeting as a sign he's not here to kill me.

"I'm a friend of your father going way back. Maybe he told you about me. Murray Landauer." The hair on the back of my neck rises. He reaches a hand across the table and I take it, hoping a firm grip will hide its trembling. "He and a buddy, fellow named Louie, worked for me years ago. Sound familiar?"

I'm so frightened that my "yes" emerges as a croak. I picture my body splayed across the wooden table in a pool of blood and imagine the boys coming home and finding me dead. Idiotically, I wonder how Daniel would handle this. Would he try to be a hero and attack these men? Probably not. Daniel's too realistic. The old man seems sane but Pinky looks like he could shoot a man—or woman—without a twinge. I want to kick myself for not calling the police after the first break-in.

"My sympathy on the loss of your Uncle Moe. I heard he died young."

I thank him, not knowing how else to respond. Why bring that up? It's like every gangster in town wants to console me for my uncle's death.

"I heard the Plotnik brothers went legit and did okay for themselves. That's wonderful," he says. "Tootsie raised two lovely daughters, one of whom, so I hear, has been poking around in the past."

I'm starting to catch on.

He smiles again, a benign, gentle smile, and points a gnarled finger at me. "That would be you. Would you care to share what you've learned?"

I try to focus, to figure out what the man's after. It's got to be the story about Fat Louie. I can't think of anything else. So I tell him what I know, starting with Tootsie's sighting of Florence Karpowsky at the Schmuel Bernstein. "He felt terrible about turning Louie in," I conclude. "He had no idea things would turn out so badly for his friend."

As I speak, Mr. Landauer makes occasional eye contact with Pinky, who remains standing next to the counter with his lids half closed.

"And your visit to Abe Kravitz?" Landauer asks when I'm through. "How'd that go?"

"Is that who told you I was asking around?"

The old man jerks forward in his seat and any resemblance to a bloodhound disappears in a cold scowl. "*I'm* asking the questions."

I can sense the menacing power of the mobster my father feared and struggle to hide the terror in my voice. "I was doing research for work and came across an article about Abe's conviction. He was a friend of my dad's. I don't care about Abe's record. I thought he might tell me more about my father and Uncle Moe."

"What'd he tell you?"

"Nothing. He threw me out."

Mr. Landauer smiles, barely moving the corners of his mouth. "And how about the little visit with your father after the break-in?"

I jump from the chair. "That was you?" The man's familiarity with my recent movements and family frightens and infuriates me.

He leans across the table and enunciates his words. "None of your fucking business. Sit down. I told you. *I* ask the questions."

My throat constricts and I swallow a few times before continuing. "My father told me Abe robbed trucks and sold him and my uncle the stolen goods. They quit buying from Abe after police came by looking for stolen refrigerators." Then, speaking rapidly, "My father and Uncle Moe did *not* turn Abe in." I don't know if I believe that anymore. Or if it matters. I can't believe this goon broke into my home because of refrigeration stolen fifty years earlier. There's got to be more to this *and* my father's past than I know.

"Of course they didn't turn Abe in." His voice is thick with sarcasm. "They were *much* too loyal for that."

Landauer hands his mug to Pinky, who pours another cup of coffee from the carafe on my counter and brings it to the table. The old man leans back in his seat and scrutinizes me. "You seem like a nice girl, so I'm going to play it straight with you." He takes a slow sip of the steaming brew. "Your father's full of shit."

"I can't believe . . ."

He slams his hand on the table so hard that I jump. "Shut up and listen. My friends had a reason for leaving that crap in your bedroom. It's too bad you didn't have the smarts to figure it out. If you did, you wouldn't be talking to your old man and I wouldn't be here today. Your father killed Fat Louie as sure as I'm sitting here. Then he let *me* take the rap. And that's just half the story. So here's what you do. Go back to your father. Tell him that you met me. And let him know I haven't talked to my wife and kids in sixty years. You can also let him know that if he doesn't tell you the truth, his life isn't worth a red cent. Neither is yours. You got that?"

I nod, too frightened to speak.

He stands. My heart skips a beat as Pinky reaches for his gun, then tucks it into the waistband of his pants.

"I'll return," Landauer says. "And if you're father doesn't confess." He glances at Pinky, then me. "You got two boys, right. Well, he knows what I'll do."

He walks around to my side of the table and pats my head. "Don't get up. We'll show ourselves out."

Pinky picks up Landauer's cup and places it in the sink. I'm terrified. Landauer knows about Josh and Gabriel! They could be in danger. My stomach heaves. I'm afraid my knees will buckle if I try to stand so follow the two men with my gaze as they leave the kitchen. I'm too weak to do anything but stare after them for several minutes after the back door slams.

When I hear their car pull away, I pick up the phone and dial the Boca Raton police. I love my father. But this has gone far enough.

The two officers who show up fifteen minutes later are polite but exchange skeptical glances when I tell them about the intruders waiting for me at my kitchen table. As I describe the visit, I understand their skepticism; except for the threats, Landauer's visit sounds too civilized. After I've shown the men where we sat and point out the coffeepot and mug Pinky and Landauer touched, the policemen suggest we go to the family room to talk. Officer Lopez, a baby-faced cop in his early twenties with a shadow of a mustache, stays with me while his partner, Officer Amodio, checks the house. We make small talk about the neighborhood and Boca's growing crime rate.

"All clear," Amodio says when he rejoins us. He's a foot taller than his partner and carries an extra ten pounds, most of it shelved neatly above a thick black belt. "Your rear sliders are easy to break into so you might want to replace them. But from the scratches on the front doorknob, I'd say your visitors picked the lock and entered there."

"Wouldn't they worry about being spotted?"

Amodio shrugs. "I guess they scoped out the area before entering. I called the station and a detective will be here soon."

He inclines his head toward the kitchen. "That business you mentioned earlier, about seeing one of the men before. Did you catch his name or any of the other people at the funeral?"

"My father identified a few people, but not Mr. Landauer." I'm uncomfortable lying, but decide not to mention that I recognized Landauer's name from my father's account of Fat Louie. I don't want to go there—at least not yet. My goal at this point is to feel safe. If that means telling them about Tootsie's past later, I will. But I want to talk to the old man first. He must have had a good reason for failing to point out Landauer at the funeral.

The doorbell rings and Lopez—announcing "that'll be Detective Cole"—answers it. I'm surprised when an attractive silver-haired man in a navy sports jacket strides into the hall. He's broad-shouldered but slim and the angle of his eyes suggests Asian blood. Where the other police officers look official in their heavy black uniforms and shiny badges and guns, this man could be a doctor or lawyer or insurance salesman. I follow the officers to the kitchen to show the detective where Landauer sat, but Cole raises his hand directing me to stop at the entrance.

"Have you touched anything since the intruders left?" he says, walking briskly to the counter and glancing into the sink. Amodio must have told him about Landauer helping himself to coffee.

"Just the phone and my chair," I say. "And the front door when I opened it for the officers."

He nods and sends a silent signal to the policemen, who wish me luck and leave through the garage door.

After Cole checks the kitchen, we return to the family room, where he spends fifteen minutes going over the same territory I covered with the uniformed officers. I can't seem to get comfortable on the couch and cross and uncross my legs as we speak. He stands before me, blocking my view of the television, arms crossed. What time did I arrive home? Did I notice anything odd before going upstairs? Were the men wearing gloves? The answer is no.

Detective Cole asks if I recognized the intruders and I repeat my story about seeing Mr. Landauer at the funeral. He cracks the barest of smiles when I describe Landauer as a bloodhound and asks me to come down to the station to meet with a sketch artist. I agree, though I don't know how much good it'll do. Landauer's been out of the country for years, according to my father, and Pinky looks like every other punk with a shaved head.

When the detective questions me about my conversation with Mr. Landauer, my palms grow damp.

"What do you mean by threatened you?" he asks. "Did he say he was coming back to harm you?"

"He didn't spell it out. He said he'd be back if my father didn't tell me the truth. He mentioned my sons."

"Do you know what he meant?"

"Just that they'd be in danger."

I'm a lousy liar—thanks, I suppose, to an open face and penchant for blushing. The detective picks up on it. He keeps at me for what feels like hours, posing questions from multiple angles. Why were we at the funeral? Does my father know the older man? It's not easy to avoid bringing up my dad's criminal past and I grow increasingly resentful about the position Tootsie's put me in.

"Why don't you call my father?" I say, sick of this exercise in deceit.

The detective assures me he will.

Just then, the doorbell rings and Detective Cole opens it to one of the tallest women I've ever met. She's more than six feet and walks into the hall slowly, gazing around. The creases around her eyes suggest she's nearer fifty than forty, though the curves revealed by her well-tailored black suit hint at the body of a weight lifter. She carries a red tackle box and follows the detective into the kitchen. He tells me to wait at the door.

Cole speaks to her in a voice too low to hear, then turns to me. "Why don't you show Pam every surface the intruders touched?"

I show her the cup and coffeepot, and indicate where Pinky left his gun and Landauer sat. Then I return to the doorway to watch her. She sets several vials and brushes on the table before selecting a small feathery brush and dipping it in black powder. It looks like she's painting as she swirls the brush in the sink and on my countertop, then on the cup and carafe. I can't tell if she's found fingerprints but suspect she has when she covers the carafe handle with what looks like packing tape, then lifts it off and attaches it to a card. Next she wipes the edge of the cup with a cotton swab.

It strikes me—stupidly after all I've been through—as unfair that I'm the one who'll have to clean up the kitchen once the technician leaves. It's not bad enough my house has been ransacked and I've been threatened by strangers. Now I'm being grilled by the police and will have to spend half the afternoon removing fingerprint dust from counters.

This is all Tootsie's fault. And I'm ready to kill him.

24

"What's the big God damn secret?" my father says the minute he opens the door to my Mercedes. He slides into the passenger seat and slams his door. "You couldn't tell me what you wanted to talk about over the phone?"

I'm parked at the entrance to the Schmuel Bernstein, picking up Tootsie for what I know is going to be a rough night. Two nurses having a smoke on the front porch glance up as the door clangs shut. Terrific. The old man's on the warpath. I can't wait until he hears about Landauer. And the police.

It's been five hours since the aging gangster paid me a visit. Two since the detective left my house. I realize I'm being optimistic but hope the police will find the intruders from the prints. I ran to the car the minute they left, leaving the cleanup for later.

On the drive over, I made myself crazy debating how to ask Tootsie the questions Landauer raised. I've never been this angry at my father and breathe deeply to calm myself. Attacking him will get me nowhere and if I don't wrestle the truth out of my dad soon, my life and my sons' lives may be in danger. The police reassured me they'd look into Landauer's whereabouts and talk to Tootsie. But that won't happen until tomorrow. I need answers now.

When I called my father an hour earlier, he refused to see me, claiming he couldn't "sacrifice" his Friday night poker game. I told him I couldn't see him Sunday and he relented. Even so, it's hard to believe his door slamming is because of a couple of missed poker hands.

"I ran into Sadie Goldfarb at breakfast this morning," my father announces once he settles into the car. "She said her daughter, Mavis, saw Esther at the grocery store Wednesday. You want to tell me what's going on?"

Great. Like I don't have enough problems.

"She needed to get away," I lie, "to take it easy, go to the beach. It gets cold in Greensboro."

There's no way I'm getting into his relationship with Esther tonight. Normally, I'd hedge my answer but am too angry to worry about sparing his feelings. I thought I'd start yelling at him the minute he got in my car. But I decided to hold off and attempt a rational discussion when we reached the restaurant. That's enough compassion for one night.

"Esther told me not to let you know she was in town. She wouldn't tell me why."

Tootsie shrugs. The movement releases the dead animal stench of wool that's been stored without washing. It's dark so I turn on the car's interior light. I'm surprised to see my father in the cheap leather jacket Daniel bought on our honeymoon in San Francisco. I had no idea he'd given it to Tootsie. It reeks like a dump.

I open my window and pull onto the road.

"You going to tell me what's going on with you and Esther," I say, "because I'd like to know? Being forced into the middle of your argument stinks."

Tootsie looks away from me, and remains staring out the window as we take the causeway to Miami Beach. It's dusk and streetlights are beginning to flicker to life. The sky is hazy blue and the narrow stratum of clouds that hover above Biscayne Bay reflect the faded pinks and oranges of the setting sun.

When we exit the causeway on Forty-First Street, Tootsie starts in with his complaints. It's Esther's fault they're not getting along. She didn't call him the last time she was in town. She forgot his birthday last year. She never acknowledged his Hanukkah gift. None of this explains their rift. When he accuses me of monopolizing her time, I lash out.

"You know I've got my own problems. This is taking a toll on me too."

"What is?"

I catch myself. "You know, having a houseguest."

"So why doesn't she stay with me? Sleep on my sofa."

I laugh and he glares at me. My father has a one-bedroom apartment and never invites anyone to stay with him. If relatives ask, he offers my house.

"Why would she do that?" I say.

"Because, for Christ sake, I'm her father."

"How long has it been since you talked to her?"

He stares out the window.

I pass the stately homes along Alton Road, figuring I'll cut across the island farther north to reach Pino's, the restaurant my father chose. Most of the homes along this thoroughfare date from the 1930s and have a dignified charm and understated elegance absent from Boca Raton's stucco mini-mansions. The soil down here is richer too so the landscaping is lusher.

I'm speculating how to bring up Landauer's accusations when it hits me. Esther knows something I don't. That's why she isn't talking to Dad.

I hit the brake and come to a stop on Alton.

"Hey watch out," Tootsie yells as the driver behind us honks his horn.

I gun the motor, breathing heavily. That's got to be it. Esther knows what's going on. Whatever she learned has to be pretty dreadful if she hasn't told me. It's not going to be easy, but I have what I need to confront my father about Landauer's accusations.

"Does Esther know about you and Fat Louie?" I ask when we stop at a red light.

He chews his lip before answering. "I told her. But she didn't take it too well."

"How'd she react?"

"Your sister's always judging me, just like your mother." His glances toward me, his eyes slit. "She thinks I was responsible for Fat Louie's death."

"Why?" Then I hazard, "You didn't know your boss would kill him, did you?"

"Don't talk crazy." He looks away. "Of course not."

Pino's Pizza is buzzing tonight. It's six twenty and the pizza, minestrone soup, and soft drink special is good for another ten minutes. An elderly couple get up as we enter, and Tootsie grabs my elbow and steers me into their booth. He motions a waitress over to bus the table, then studies the menu.

The place is packed. Families with small children crowd into high-backed red leather booths while couples of all ages share the small wooden tables that fill the center of the room. The waitress takes our order. We decide to go with the early bird special.

"Something happened this morning," I ease into the subject. "It has to do with Fat Louie."

He gives me a quick glance. "What? Did Esther say something?"

"She didn't say a word. But I think there's more to the story than you're telling me."

He grimaces.

"Come on, Dad. How bad could it be? I'm not Esther. I'd never cut you off."

It's dim in the booth, but enough light flickers off the candle to reflect the fear in my father's eyes. And I realize that's exactly what he's afraid of. Why he's withholding the truth. He thinks I'll abandon him. The thought saddens and empowers me and I realize that if I don't force him to tell the truth now, he never will. I need to know. Ever since my house was ransacked, I've been afraid to enter my home. Landauer's break-in has terrified me. I can't live like this. Josh and Gabriel are due home for Thanksgiving. I'm thinking of telling them to remain at school.

Pino's bustles with the clatter of china and cutlery and the slap of pizza pans on metal stands. A child in the booth behind us whines and a man two tables away laughs. But our heavily-padded booth creates a cozy, cushioned space. It's safe and private in here and, though we can hear each other, our conversation is absorbed in the clatter and hum of restaurant noise.

"Mr. Landauer broke into my house today," I say. My father's head shoots up from the menu. "I found him and his bodyguard in my kitchen."

Tootsie jumps up, but his thighs hit the table and he drops back into his seat.

"When?" The word comes out in a whisper. He pulls a handkerchief out of his back pocket and mops his brow.

"This morning. When I returned from taking Esther to the airport."

He stares at me a second, eyes wide. "Jeeze. I thought I recognized him at Schatzi's funeral. But I wasn't sure. I heard he was dead. What did he want?"

I tell him about my encounter with Landauer. He cringes when I mention Pinky's gun. "He said to tell you he hasn't seen his family in sixty years. And that, if you don't tell me the truth, he'll come back and . . . he didn't say. Just that you'd know." A chill like iced water ascends my spine. My father, who's chewing the edge of his thumbnail, turns pale.

He's about to speak when the soup and pizza arrive. I want to push for his response, but I can see from the way he dives into the minestrone that he's grateful for the break. I pick at my food in silence, interrupted only when the waitress appears with soft drink refills. When she leaves with the metal pizza plate, my father sets his glass down.

"I'm sorry, Doll." He shakes his head from side to side, deliberately, like a buffalo warding off flies. "It must have been horrible coming home to that. I've spent my life trying to forget that bastard and what he forced me and Moe to do. But if we hadn't cooperated, it might have meant our lives."

"What are you talking about?"

The couple at the table to my left look over. I've raised my voice.

"I told you I discovered Louie double-crossed me and Mr. Landauer." Tootsie whispers.

"Yes."

"And that Mr. Landauer found someone to kill Louie."

I nod.

He leans outside the booth and looks left, then right, before turning back to me. "That someone was Moe." He hesitates. "And me."

A knot forms in my gut. I already sensed my father had more to do with Louie's death than he admitted. And I'm not surprised my uncle was involved. From what Tootsie's said over the years, Moe had some tough friends. But my dad a murderer? I swallow and fight a building nausea. The threats to my life and Tootsie's start to make sense.

"When Landauer figured out what Louie did, he yelled at Moe and me. He said we're the ones who brought in the bad apple, we got to get rid of it. He didn't come out and say so, but it was clear he expected us to take Louie out."

"You're kidding."

"I wish. Well, I didn't like it. Neither did Moe. But what choice did we have? Landauer was connected with some characters who'd be glad to do the job. Kill me and Moe too. We figured better Louie than us." There's pleading in his voice.

"Moe ran into Louie a few days after Landauer's outburst and learned Louie's wife, Florence, was in New Jersey visiting her folks. That's when he came up with his plan. I'd invite Louie over for Shabbat dinner at your grandmother's, then get her out of the house. Moe would shoot Louie and dispose of his body before Ma returned. It sounded nuts to me, but it's all we had. Moe insisted he knew what he was doing."

My father speaks rapidly. He seems relieved to be talking.

"The next Friday afternoon, I gave Louie a call. Remember, he had no idea I was on to him. I told him my mother was making noodle pudding, his favorite, why didn't he come to dinner. My father was out of town and Louie could take my old man's place at the table.

"I guess Louie saw this as an attempt to rekindle our friendship because he agreed. Your Grandma Yentl set the table with her nice white linen and fine china. We hadn't told her what happened with Louie and my job, but she knew there were problems between us. She was glad we were making up.

"Moe and I sent our wives out to dinner, saying we had to work that night, and went to Grandma Yentl's with Louie. She'd prepared a regular Shabbat meal. Chicken soup with matzo balls. Brisket she'd simmered all day. The noodle pudding. Once we finished dessert, Moe gave Grandma a couple of bucks and told her to take Mrs. Horowitz from upstairs to see a movie. We'd do the dishes. Mrs. Horowitz agreed and the ladies took off.

"Moe, Louie and I stayed at the table, talking about old times. I found myself chattering, nervous about what lay ahead. Moe knew this so he played older brother, telling me to get my ass in the kitchen and start the dishes. I was in there, with the water running and the dishes clattering, when I heard a pop. It wasn't loud—Moe used a silencer. But I knew what it meant. I felt sick but returned to the dining room."

"Uncle Moe shot the man?"

"You'd better believe it. Louie lay on the floor, blood down the front of his shirt. I didn't know how Moe did it—I didn't even want to know how he learned to do it—but the only place blood splattered was on Grandma Yentl's tablecloth."

"Was he dead?"

"Don't be an idiot. Of course he was dead. I had to hand it to Moe, though. He planned everything. Pulled out a bag of rags he'd stashed under Ma's couch and used them to wipe up the blood. Sent me to drive his car to the alley behind Ma's apartment building. I was sobbing like a baby as we rolled Louie into the tablecloth and dragged him down the back stairs to Moe's trunk. Your uncle was a cool character. I don't think he felt a thing."

I've heard enough, but my father keeps talking. I don't think he'd stop if I asked.

"Moe arranged everything. He drove to the Miami River and pulled behind a shack where two goons waited in a filthy skiff. They watched with dead eyes—you know, like they'd seen it all—as we dragged Louie's body across the old dock. I had to stop twice to puke in the river. We got Louie in the boat and took off, driving to Ma's apartment in record time and changing into clean shirts in the car. When Ma turned up a half hour later, we were doing the dishes. Moe told her he spilled Manichewitz on the tablecloth and would take it to be cleaned. We joined her for a glass of tea and a piece of honey cake and made it home by eleven."

My father's face is flushed and the armpits of his blue polo are soaked. He leans back and looks at me, eyebrows raised, as though daring me to respond. I'm not fooled. The pleading I'd seen in his eyes remains.

I'm sickened by what Tootsie told me and don't know what to do with his confession. I'm shocked and angry—but my anger is tinged with pity. He's had to live with the knowledge he murdered a friend. It could not have been easy.

I want to believe my father when he says he had no choice. But he's lied before. It's been hard enough coming to terms with the notion that he associated with gangsters. But a cold-blooded killer? That may be more than I can handle.

I wonder if my mother knew. And if so, what choices she had. She loved my dad. And turning him in would've sent him to prison, leaving her alone with a small child. I can see why Esther won't talk to Tootsie. I'm tempted to leave the table and let him catch a taxi home. I glance around the restaurant—anything to avoid his gaze. My fingers are numb from grasping the edge of my chair.

My father studies me, reading every muscle on my face. I try to smile, but my lips feel stiff and it probably comes across as a grimace. He slides the check around the table without looking at it; my eyes follow his hand. I'm torn between disbelief and horror as I try to adapt to this reality. This *alter cocker*, with his soft gut, his waddle of a neck, a killer? It seems so far-fetched, so part of the distant past. As though he's talking about someone else. But he isn't.

He drops a twenty on the table and rises. I slide out of the booth and lead him through the parking lot to my car.

"Jeeze, Dad," I say once we're buckled in. He turns to me as though awaiting a verdict. "I can't believe you've lived with this secret so long." It's the best I can do.

The Miami skyline draws near as we cross the causeway. The view has changed a lot since I was a kid. The office towers are taller and more densely packed. Steel and glass fill the horizon. People on the street come in every shade of red and brown and white and are as likely to speak Creole or Spanish as English. It's entirely different from the Miami Tootsie knew as a young man. The only remnants of that era, of the years when Miami was a Mecca for glamorous movie stars and underworld figures, are old men's memories and crooked gravestones in Mount Nebo Cemetery.

When we reach the campus of the Schmuel Bernstein, my father tells me to pull into a parking spot. There's more. We sit for a few minutes, listening to the frogs chirruping and my air conditioner wheezing.

"Your uncle and I almost got away with it," he says without looking at me. "Your uncle was sharp and did a good job of covering our tracks. No one could trace Louie's death back to either of us. But word had reached the street that Louie was double-crossing Landauer. A cop saw the two goons who took Louie's body out to sea returning in the skiff the night Louie died and knew they worked for Landauer."

He stares straight ahead. "The police were having a hard time tying Landauer into some other hits and, when they found blood in the boat, they were sure they could nail him. When they offered me and Uncle Moe immunity, we took it. What choice did we have? Landauer pleaded to first-degree murder and was lucky not to end up in the chair. Last I heard, he escaped while being transported to a hospital in the 1960s and made his way to the Bahamas. I couldn't believe it when he showed up at Schatzi's funeral. That's why I left so suddenly. I couldn't be sure it was him, though. It's been fifty years."

"Weren't you afraid he'd come after you and Uncle Moe?" The idea of my father living with this guilt and fear of being hunted down for so long disturbs me.

"When he first escaped from prison, yes. But then nothing happened and I figured he'd made himself a life. I'd have helped him if he wanted it."

Honor among thieves, I think, but don't say as much to my father.

"So how are you supposed to let Landauer know I've told you the truth?" Tootsie asks.

"I don't know. That's what makes me so nervous. I'm afraid he'll show up again."

"God forbid." He flips the AC vent on and off a few times, then turns to me. "Tell you what, Doll. Go home. Or better yet, you and Esther stay with a friend or have Daniel move in. I'll make a couple of calls and try to close the books on this."

"What'll you do?"

"That depends on Landauer."

"Don't do anything crazy. We can always explain to the police."

"No." The word comes out in a quick breath. "What'll you tell them? That your father killed a man fifty years ago?"

"If that's what it takes to be safe."

"Please. I'm begging you. Hold off. Just a few more weeks. I promise I'll take care of things." He opens the passenger side door. "Sweetheart. Becks, I'm sorry to put you through this. It happened so long ago. Try to forgive me."

"You're still my dad," I say as he gets out. "I'm glad you told me the truth."

He cracks a faint smile, but says nothing. I watch through my rearview mirror as he passes through the automatic glass doors of his apartment building.

As I back out of my parking spot and pull onto the road, I wonder if I meant what I said or came up with words *he* wants to hear. The whole thing's so crazy, so horrible. And I'm concerned about reassuring *him*. My father murdered a man, for God's sake. I try to convince myself he had no choice. But I don't know if I believe his story.

As I drive home, I ask myself if I'll come back. If I can face my father, knowing he took a life. I'm tempted to tell the police what I've learned. But the statute of limitations on murder never runs out and, as horrified as I am by what he told me, I don't want my dad to spend his last years in jail. I've never been in such a dangerous and untenable position. I hate it. And it's all because of my father's lies.

25

Tootsie

"Well, look at what the cat dragged in," Winchell says as I let myself into the Schmuel Bernstein's card room after leaving Becks. He motions me to the table where he and his poker buddies are clearing a hand. "You want to fill in? I'm not doing so good."

Ira, a retired cardiologist, purses his lips into a smug grin and squares off the pile of bills in front of him. The other men—Friday night regulars Bill and Jack—eye me like a piece of steak they're ready to tear into. Each has a lousy little pile of bills on the table.

"Why not?" I say. A few hands of poker may take my mind off Becks. I drop into Winchell's chair and throw a ten on the table. But it's no good. Three hands in, I'm down fifty bucks. I can't concentrate. Becks' forced smile at the restaurant and halfhearted attempt at reassurance keep returning. I make my apologies and go upstairs.

I'm not a big drinker but tonight I need one. After letting myself into the apartment, I go straight for the fifth of Dewar's under the kitchen sink. I take a swig from the bottle, then pour two fingers into a glass and bring it into the living room.

Damn that Becks. Sticking her nose where it doesn't belong.

When she dropped me off tonight, she seemed anxious to assure me she loves me, but her words rang false. My heart was beating so hard when she told me about Landauer's break-in I thought I'd pass out. It's bad enough he threatened me. But to threaten my daughter? Bastard. Of course she's scared. The man's a monster. And no one wants to believe their father is a murderer. I'm sick about burdening her with this.

There must be some way to earn back Becks' respect, to persuade her I'm not a callous murderer. Maybe if she knew what my life was like back then, why my involvement in the syndicate, even Louie's death, were inevitable. Who the hell knows if she'll understand—or walk away? I sure as hell didn't expect Esther to write me off.

I take another sip. The heat from the Dewar's travels down my gullet and sends a comforting glow through my body, but it doesn't calm me. Losing Becks may be the least of my problems. More important is getting Landauer to back off. It was shocking enough spotting the bastard at Schatzi's funeral. What the hell does he want from me or Becks? I paid him off years ago. If he wants more money, I'll give it to him.

My hands tremble. Time has done nothing to ease my fear of the mobster. The bastard would smash a man's face in at the slightest provocation. A joke about his thinning hair. A comment about his wife. I don't want to come up against that animal. But this is my daughter. My Becks. I need to get in touch with Landauer and find out what he wants.

I take the last sip of Dewar's and set my glass on the cocktail table. Then I reach under the sofa for my white pages. It's a long shot. A delaying tactic. I leaf through the *L*s. Of course Murray Landauer isn't listed. The old bastard's still wanted by the police.

There's just one way to reach the man: Abe Kravitz. He was Landauer's lieutenant when the mobster was sent up and everyone knew he masterminded the old man's escape. Abe's got to know where he is.

My palms are damp when I dial Abe's number.

"Abe, it's Tootsie," I say when he answers.

"So what."

"I hear Landauer's back in town. He paid a visit to my daughter."

"No kidding."

"You knew?"

Abe is silent.

"Can you put me in touch with him? Maybe you got a phone number where I can reach him?"

"I'll tell you, Tootsie, I don't know if I can help you."

"What do you mean you don't know?"

"Why should I? You screwed me. I got no reason to put you in touch with anyone."

"Abe, I'm begging you. This is my daughter. Do you know how to reach him?"

Abe hesitates. "I might."

A sigh of relief escapes my lips. "Then tell him this. I'm not a rich man but I've got a little stashed away. It's his. Just leave Becks alone."

Abe, again, says nothing.

"You got that?"

"Yeah, sure."

"Listen Abe . . ."

I hear a click at the other end of the line.

All I have now is hope. And prayer. And a desperate need to make Becks understand how my life took such an ugly turn before she learns the worst of it.

26

The next Monday night, I arrive home late, having wasted an evening at the opening of a new Mexican restaurant in Ft. Lauderdale. I would love to tell my editor that there's no point in running a review of the greasy spoon. But he left a six-inch slot in Wednesday's newspaper for the article and I have to give him something, even a negative review. That's one reason I prefer writing about food, rather than critiquing restaurants. I feel guilty about panning a business—worse when it's starting out. But I owe it to readers to be honest.

I let myself in the front door and cringe when I notice a light in the kitchen —then remember Esther's back in town. She was supposed to rent a car from the airport and go to the hospital for blood work and a chest x-ray before letting herself into my house. Tomorrow morning's her lumpectomy.

I haven't told Esther about Landauer's break-in. Why worry her? It can wait until after her surgery.

I went to the Boca Raton police station the Saturday after the break-in despite my dread of getting the second degree from Detective Cole. I was relieved he wasn't around when I met with the sketch artist, who created remarkably accurate drawings of Pinky and Landauer. Shortly after I returned home, my dad called to tell me he got a phone call from the detective. Tootsie sounded angry but wouldn't tell me what they discussed.

Esther stands at the sink and looks over her shoulder when she hears my footsteps.

A head of romaine lettuce, a tomato, and a cucumber sit on the black granite in front of her.

"So how'd it go with Tootsie?" she says, pulling out a drawer and riffling its contents. "I meant to call about your dinner Sunday." She denies any interest in our dad but asks about our get-togethers.

I reach under the counter and hand her a knife and cutting board.

"Actually, we had dinner Friday instead of Sunday. And it could have been better."

"What happened?"

"He knows you're in town and he's pissed off you didn't call."

"So."

"So I told him you don't want to see him."

"He okay with that?"

"What do you think?"

She shrugs. "Where'd you end up eating?"

"At his favorite pizza joint, a place off Collins." I hesitate, then decide to dive in. "I asked him what he told you about Fat Louie. He came clean."

She stops in the middle of slicing the cucumber and stares at me. "He didn't."

"I almost wish he hadn't. I can see why you're angry with him. I'm still reeling. He told me how his boss forced him and Uncle Moe to . . . to do away with Fat Louie. You know the details?"

"Enough that I don't want to hear them again."

She makes precise, even cuts in the cucumber and I wonder if she's taking her time to consider what I've said or if it's her habitual slowness. I could put an entire salad on the table in the time it takes her to slice a cucumber.

"Did he tell you about Landauer going to prison?" I say.

"The gangster who ordered the killing?"

"Right. He ended up taking the rap while Dad and Uncle Moe got off."

She stops slicing to look at me. "He never mentioned that."

"He told me just before I dropped him off. He's been looking over his shoulder ever since."

She shakes her head and returns to the salad. "I'm not worried. He always lands on his feet."

She's rather cavalier about our father's safety.

I can't abide her puttering around with the vegetables and offer to make the salad. She agrees and drops into a chair at the kitchen table.

"You know I've been trying to get closer to Dad since Daniel and I separated," I say.

"Why?"

"I thought it'd make me feel better if I had a relationship with him."

"You've got to be kidding."

I turn and give her a dirty look. "He isn't much help. But with the kids gone and this business with Daniel . . . well, he *is* family. And he has told me about his past, stories about growing up in New York. I did some research about Jewish gangsters, trying to find out about the people Dad named. You've got to admit, that's pretty interesting about his hanging out on the sidelines of the mob. At least it was until I found out . . ."

"That Dad's a murderer?"

I put her salad in a glass bowl and slide it in front of her without answering. There's no point in bringing salad dressing. She watches every calorie. Where I'm tall and substantial with curly hair I've abandoned to Florida's humidity, she's tiny and thin and would be delicate if not for the sinewy arm and leg muscles she developed training for marathons. My love of cooking extends to a love of eating, so I'm always fighting my weight. She has little interest in food.

"What is it with you? Why are you digging into Dad's past?" she says after picking at her salad.

I hesitate. I've been asking myself the same question. "I'm not sure. It's like one day Dad's this fairly normal person, a man I know and understand. Then he turns out to be a gangster. Remember when we were growing up and Dad would return from a trip with these great presents, all excited about watching us open them? I thought he was the best father in the world. We didn't know until later he was cheating on Mom."

She nods.

"Now I find out he's not the great dad who brought us gifts and he's not the horrible man who cheated on Mom. At least, he isn't just those people. He's an aging gangster, a criminal. I don't know when he's telling the truth anymore. I think he was straight with me Friday night. But who the hell knows?"

"You don't give up, do you?"

I laugh.

"Anything else I should know?"

I bite my lip, wondering how much to tell her. She handled the news about Abe's break-in pretty well. I owe her the truth if she's going to stay with me. "I told you Dad suspected his old friend, Abe, of breaking into my house?"

"Yeah."

"I started digging around and learned he did time for dealing in stolen goods."

"No way."

"And Dad and Uncle Moe did business with Jewish gangsters who owned hotels and restaurants."

"That doesn't surprise me."

I root around in the refrigerator to give myself a moment, then grab a diet soda and sit in the chair opposite her. "I need to tell you something else. You may decide not to stay with me after you hear it."

She looks up from the salad, fork poised in the air. "You're a gangster too?"

I laugh. "Not that." Then more soberly. "I should have told you. But I didn't want to worry you. It was selfish, but I . . ."

"Just tell me."

"Word reached Dad's old mob boss, Murray Landauer, that I've been poking around in the past. I think Abe told him. Landauer showed up here a week ago. Broke in with his bodyguard while I was in the shower. When I came downstairs and found him, I freaked. He threatened to come back, to kill me and Dad if Tootsie didn't tell me the truth. He also knew about the boys. That's why Dad finally told me the whole story."

"My God. Did you call the police?"

"Yes. But I didn't mention the gangster business or Fat Louie's murder. All we need is Dad in prison."

"I have no problem with it." Esther stabs a tomato. "That's where he belongs."

At first I think she's joking. But she's not smiling. She's known about Louie's murder for a while. It can't have been easy hiding it from me.

"Why didn't *you* call the police when you learned about Dad's past?" I say. "Or tell me."

"I felt Dad should tell you himself. He said he would." She pushes her bowl away. "I don't know. When you come right down to it, there didn't seem to be any point in telling anyone. It's history and it's not like Dad went on to murder other people."

"But a man is dead because of him and Uncle Moe."

"I'm not saying he shouldn't be punished. He should. I think. I don't know anymore." She brushes a lock of hair off her forehead. "It's not our job to turn our father in. Wives have the right not to testify against their husbands. So why should we testify against our father?"

I can't argue with that. I'm sure she's discussed this with Bruce. I pick up Esther's bowl and fork and place them in the sink. Then we retire to the family room and stretch out on the couches.

"So you still want to stay with me? In spite of Landauer's break-in?"

She shrugs. "You're still here. If you feel safe, so do I. And it's cheaper than a hotel." She pulls my patchwork quilt up to her neck. "But if you don't get answers from Tootsie soon, you ought to tell the police about Louie."

I assure her I will.

"It's a relief to learn you finally know about Dad," she says. "You can see why I'm not talking to him."

"Oh, I understand. What's strange is I'm not sure how *I* feel about the whole thing. It was so long ago. I'm horrified by his role in killing Fat Louie and angry that his lies led to the break-ins at my house. But I shouldn't be surprised. His whole life's a lie. The funny thing is, up until now, it hasn't affected us."

"Don't be so sure."

I wait for her to continue, but she's quiet, staring through the French doors to the patio. I follow her gaze. The white mesh chairs that go around the patio table are stacked one on top of the other. Daniel pressure cleaned them a week before I threw him out. It seems such a long time ago. After a few minutes, I lean across the couch to see if Esther's sleeping. Her eyes are open.

"What are you thinking?"

"I've got my own little confession." She sits up and crosses her legs. "I'm not sure why I didn't tell you or anyone else. At first, I couldn't talk about it without crying and, then later, I was embarrassed. It seems unimportant now, but it bothered me for a while. You remember my boyfriend, Darrell?"

"The creep who stood you up for senior prom?"

"Yeah. It was because of Dad."

"What'd Dad do?"

"He didn't *do* anything. When Darrell's parents learned who Tootsie was, they forbid him to date me. He ignored them. Then, two days before the prom, Darrell said his parents threatened to take away his car if he brought me as his date. I was devastated. I ended up staying home while all my friends partied. And I couldn't tell anyone why."

Her eyes are damp.

"How'd Darrell's parents hear about Dad's past?"

"Everyone in Miami knew. Except us."

"Is that true?" I mull that over. Did my friends' parents forbid them from coming to my house because of my father?

"I don't know. I asked Dad about what Darrell said. He claimed it was a lie. That Darrell made it up to get out of taking me to the prom."

I'm stunned. What kind of father would let his daughter suffer that much pain and rejection to hide his past? Esther didn't deserve that. With a jolt, I wonder if he's lying to me too—about contacting Abe and Landauer. Does he think I'll forget about Landauer's visit? Can he be naïve enough to think they'll leave us alone?

Esther gazes at me, then down at her lap. She has to be thinking the same thing.

"So how'd you learn the truth?" I ask.

"Dad told me."

"But I thought you said . . ."

"It was last year, when he was visiting for Rosh Hashanah. You remember. Bruce had just been accused of stealing from a client's trust account. Of course it turned out to be the bank's mistake. I guess Dad wanted to comfort me. He got this crazy idea that I'd feel better about Bruce being a crook, which he *wasn't*, if I knew my father had been involved in a murder."

"That makes no sense."

"Not to you and me. But this is Tootsie we're talking about. And who knows what goes on in his mind?"

That night, lying in bed, I can't let go of what Esther told me. Our father's confession about his past opened up old wounds for her too. I've had to deal with my father's absence most of my life, with the fact that he was away on "business trips" during my piano recitals and school awards ceremonies. He never praised anything I did no matter how hard I worked. I can forgive that. And I've been trying to let go of my resentment for the way he treated my mother.

But I don't know how to deal with the ugly truth of the murder. I need time away from my father. I can't forgive Tootsie. At least not while I'm living in fear of Landauer's return.

That night, I sleep in short spurts, waking frequently to the sound of creaking doors and footsteps that turn out to be Mulligan prowling my room. I'm worried about Esther's surgery tomorrow. As is so often the case with my late night ruminations, I imagine the worst—that she'll have more advanced cancer than the doctors anticipate or the cancer will spread. I've lost my husband and it feels like I'm losing my father. I don't know how I'll live without Esther in my life.

27

"Get up. It's six o'clock."

I groan and drag my arm from across my eyes. I couldn't have slept more than an hour or two. Esther perches at the edge of my bed holding out a cup of coffee. I shimmy up against my pillows and accept it. She's already dressed in a soft pink skirt made of tee shirt fabric and a matching top. She smiles but her face is pale. Today's the big day, I realize with a pang of anxiety. We need to be at the hospital by seven.

Last night before bed, Esther told me the surgeon assured her the lumpectomy would be a brief, outpatient procedure, but that she might be at the hospital all day waiting to come out of anesthesia. Dr. Simon would take lymph nodes from under her arm during the surgery to make sure the cancer hadn't spread. She'll have to take it easy for a few weeks to heal from surgery before going on to chemo or radiation therapy. We'll know more about her options after the pathology reports come back.

I sit up and swing my legs over the side of the bed and my sister returns downstairs. I've showered and am in the closet reaching for jeans when it strikes me that I should dress a little nicer. Despite my insistence I'll be fine, Daniel is adamant about staying with me while Esther's in the operating room.

I throw on a comfortable paisley knit dress and dab on foundation and lipstick. I tell myself it's not for Daniel, that I always make an effort to look good when I visit the hospital. But there's more to it. I know it's terribly superficial but half the people on staff at the hospital doubtless know about Daniel's affair. I don't want to be pitied as the aggrieved wife of Dr. Ruchinsky. And that means looking attractive and confident.

When Esther and I arrive at the surgical waiting room, a nurse ushers us back to the pre-op holding area. Despite the nurse's warmth and reassurances, the place unnerves me. It's a large open space with black linoleum flooring, a speckled, acoustical-tiled ceiling and six curtained bays behind which patients chat with family members. Daniel is at a desk reading charts when we get there. He says he went in early this morning to round on patients and doesn't have office hours until two. I feel awkward, yet relieved. The constant beeping of heart monitors unnerves me and the oxygen tank and blood pressure machine in Esther's bay remind me that all surgery is risky. I stand by Daniel's desk in uncomfortable silence while Esther goes behind the curtain to put on her hospital gown. We're both a little too eager to join her when she announces she's changed.

In a few minutes, Dr. Simon stops by to chat with Esther. He's followed by an anesthesiologist. Esther will be unconscious for the entire procedure and may have some soreness in her arm for a few days after. With each doctor's visit, the cramping in my stomach worsens. What if the cancer has spread? Will they remove her entire breast? I keep my questions to myself. When the orderly comes for her, I grab Daniel's arm. His muscles tense beneath my hand, then relax. Once the double doors to the surgical suite swing shut behind her, I let go.

There's a lot to be said for being married to a doctor. The hours are lousy and you're always playing second fiddle to your spouse's patients. But when your husband or wife is a doctor, you can count on him or her to help you and friends and family navigate the daunting universe of medical care. It's at times like this—when I face a frightening medical situation—that I most appreciate Daniel.

My husband may have cheated on me and caused more pain than I imagined possible. But he's a good doctor and has never lied to me about a family member's prognosis. So when he tells me Esther will be fine, I believe him.

Daniel suggests we wait for Esther in the hospital coffee shop. Dr. Simon has promised to call once surgery's over. Neither of us are hungry so, after the waitress brings coffee, Daniel returns to his paperwork and I read the novel I've brought along.

It's hard to concentrate as I imagine Esther on an operating table, vulnerable and alone. Every now and then, Daniel risks a glance my way which I'm careful to avoid. After a half hour, he taps my hand.

"Becks, shouldn't we . . ."

I stop him with a shake of my head. "Not now."

The wait seems endless. I jump each time a pager beeps or a phone rings. It always belongs to another doctor. An hour after we enter the shop, Daniel's phone rings. I don't understand most of the medical terms he uses and the call is brief. When he smiles and hangs up, I release my breath.

"It looks good," he says, rising. "We can see her in ten minutes."

28

The earthy orange scent of turmeric greets me as I step off the elevator to my father's floor at the Schmuel Bernstein. I haven't seen Tootsie in over a month and wonder if a new resident, maybe an Arabic Jew, has moved in and is toiling over exotic stews in her kitchen. I picture a tiny woman with raven black hair and wrinkled hands pinching and rolling out dough and sautéing eggplant for mouthwatering bourekas. The cilia in my nose quiver as I pass the door before the old man's. I slow down and take a deep breath, savoring the musky aroma and willing it to calm my nerves.

I'm still appalled by my father's story and haven't come to terms with the claim he and Uncle Moe had no choice but to murder Fat Louie. And although Esther's lumpectomy went well and the doctors said her lymph nodes were clear, her health has been uppermost on my mind. She is back in Greensboro, where she's started chemotherapy. We talk every day.

Esther's visit, and her determination to beat breast cancer, inspired me to get back to work on my cookbook. I've spent a few hours every day for the past month testing my mother's recipes. I've also developed a few of my own, putting a spin on traditional dishes and adapting Middle Eastern Jewish recipes for the American palate.

I've been waiting for my father to call, to tell me he's contacted Landauer or Abe and that everything's okay. But Tootsie's kept his silence and I didn't want to see him until he could assure me I'm safe. Finally, this morning, I get a call. He sounds hesitant, afraid I'll hang up. He reminds me it's the first night of Hanukkah and invites me over for latkes. Daniel, the boys, and I have celebrated

Hanukkah with my father's potato pancakes since the kids were born. When my father asks if the boys are coming, I tell him Josh is at school and Gabriel is studying for an exam.

The truth is, a month ago, when I told Josh about Landauer's threat, he was shocked. He's an easygoing kid and I was surprised by the vehemence of his anger at his grandfather. I don't think he'd have visited his grandfather if he *was* in town.

Gabe was another story. I didn't know if a phone call would be sufficient. It can be hard to get through to him. I hoped that, by visiting, he'd pick up on enough of my emotional cues to realize how upset I was over Landauer's threat. We needed a face-to-face meeting.

I called him the Monday after the break-in to set up a date and he gave me every excuse for not getting together—a paper he had to write, an upcoming exam. I announced I'd be on campus the following Friday for lunch and hung up.

That Friday, when I finally found a parking spot near Gabe's dorm and called him, he said he'd already eaten. I was irritated but agreed to meet him at a lake on campus where we could sit on the grass and talk. Gabe hadn't been home in a month and I was curious to see if he'd changed. His hair was still close-cropped, but he'd grown a pale blond goatee that softened the square, hard lines of his face. I wasn't thrilled with his pierced ears but kept that to myself. He always had a hard time fitting in and, if that's what it took to make him comfortable, so be it.

Gabe listened passively as I told him about finding Landauer in my kitchen. When I was through, he shook his head. I was hoping for a bit of shock and dismay but the danger didn't seem to register. I hoped he might offer to come home for a weekend or two—feel protective toward his mother. His reaction stunned me.

"Mom, don't you think it'd be safer if Dad moved back?"

"What do you mean?"

"I don't think the man would've broken in if Dad lived there."

So much for my effort to raise liberated men.

I struggled to keep my voice from growing shrill as I explained that Landauer's visit came in the middle of the day, when Daniel was working. And that his father's presence would hardly impede a man with a gun. I'd planned to ease into Landauer's implied threat to Gabriel and Josh, but lost my temper.

"Maybe *you'd* like to have Dad move in with *you*," I said. "Landauer said he knew I had two sons and suggested you might be in danger too."

"You're making that up."

"It's why I came here today. To put you on alert. I don't know what that monster is capable of."

"There's no way he'd come down here."

I was about to straighten him out when a duck with a fleshy red wattle limped toward us. He stopped and glared at me like an ugly, petulant child.

"He wants food," Gabriel said. "Ignore him."

When the duck gave up and waddled toward a young couple picnicking closer to the lake, I rose from the grass.

"I know you mean well, but I can handle this myself," I said. "Meanwhile, please be careful. Landauer's old but he's dangerous. He's not the kind of person to make idle threats."

Gabriel stood and brushed the grass off his rear. "Whatever you say."

I didn't know if he meant it or not. But at least he was aware of the danger. And I took some comfort in the fact he works out and can take care of himself.

Tonight is the first time I've come to Tootsie's latke party without Daniel and the boys. I grow tearful on the drive over, contemplating the changes our family's endured in the last year.

First, Gabriel takes off for college, turning Daniel and me into empty nesters. Then Daniel has an affair, leaving me alone in the house. I didn't see either of the kids over Rosh Hashanah or Yom Kippur since both were tied up with mid-terms. And now it's Hanukkah. I'm in no mood for a celebration. The main reason I'm here is that I hope Tootsie's Hanukkah gift will be an announcement that Landauer's out of my life.

"Let yourself in," my father yells when I knock on the door, "and leave my gifts on the hall table."

He's been hard at work in the kitchen and the deliciously greasy aroma of shredded potatoes crisping in hot peanut oil greets me in his hallway. I find him leaning over a pan on the oven, a grease-stained apron stretched across his belly. Truth be told, Tootsie's latkes are a lot tastier than the frozen hockey pucks my mother bought at the grocery when we were kids. Latkes are the only recipe he got from his mother and I appreciate the effort he puts into making them. I kiss his cheek and reach for one of the crispy potato pancakes he's set out to drain on a paper towel next to the frying pan. He's in the middle of a batch and the potatoes look like tiny bird nests bubbling in oil.

"Take a look at your Hanukkah present," he says, motioning toward the kitchen table with a spatula. Not a word about why I haven't called or whether he's contacted his "friends."

A small box, wrapped in blue-and-white paper with dancing dreidels, sits dead center on the table. I pick it up and feel its heft in the palm of my hand. It's solid and heavy for such a tiny package. When I tilt the box, nothing shifts.

Tootsie comes around the kitchen counter and stands across the table from me. He hugs his chest, hands tucked into his armpits, and rocks back and forth in an agony of anticipation. "You going to open it?"

"What's the big hurry?"

"Just open the damned thing."

I tear the colorful paper away to find a brown cardboard box sealed with masking tape. Once that's off, I disentangle the gift from crumpled sheets of aged, yellowing newspaper. I'm anticipating a paperweight for my collection.

Instead, I find a gun.

I'm so surprised I almost drop the weapon. I've never touched a gun before and the cold, hard steel feels foreign and dangerous in my hand. It's an ugly little snub-nosed revolver, shiny stainless steel at the barrel with a dark walnut grip

"What is this?" I ask, placing the weapon on the table. "Is it loaded?"

Tootsie picks up the gun, spins the cylinder, and delivers the verdict: "Empty." He sets it back on the table. A smile edges his lips. Something's up.

"All right," I say. "You want to tell me what this is about? You know I hate guns."

"You don't recognize it?" He snorts. "It's the gun your Uncle Moe gave me when we opened the showroom near Overtown in sixty-two. I showed it to your mother and she wasn't too pleased either. But it was a rough neighborhood. Lots of whores and pimps hanging out on the corners. Moe and I kept guns in our office."

"Why'd you move into such a lousy area?"

"That's where all the showrooms were. Everyone went there for their restaurant supplies."

"Did you ever use it?" I motion toward the gun with my chin.

He looks at it, then back at me. His smile is gone. "I almost blew off a *schvartze's* head with that gun."

I cringe at the derogatory Yiddish term for black person. He misinterprets my reaction as disbelief.

"You heard me right. Your mother knew about it. You were probably too young to be told." He pulls out a chair and sits. I join him across the table and make myself comfortable. This is going to be a long one.

"What happened?"

"It was a Saturday, around two in the morning if memory serves, when the cops called. The store's burglar alarm went off. When I got to the store, your Uncle Moe was there along with two cops. A colored kid, maybe twenty, tried to break in through our roof but fell into the skylight. He was lying on the floor surrounded by glass shards and with his arm twisted at a weird angle. Poor kid was sobbing."

"That's awful."

"You haven't heard the worst of it. Moe was holding a gun to his head." Tootsie curls his lip. "You know what my brother, that son of a bitch, did? He handed me the gun and said, 'I got a rap sheet, you don't.' I stood there like a schmuck until it hit me. Moe wanted *me* to the shoot the kid."

"Uncle Moe really asked you. . ." I'm horrified. My uncle was no angel, if my father's account of Louie's death is to be believed. But to kill a defenseless kid!

"You heard me," my father says. His face is red. "I was as shocked as you are. So I looked toward one of the cops, a fat-faced Mick not much older than the kid on the floor. I figured he was going to tell Moe to lay off. Instead, he shrugged and said I had a right to protect my property. I couldn't believe it. This bastard broke into the business I spent my life building, ready to take what I worked hard to get. But to murder him?"

"Did you let him go?"

My father looks at me, his eyebrows raised. "Of course I did. What the hell kind of person you think I am?"

I'm not about to answer that.

"I got mad all right. But not at the kid. At Moe. He's five years older than me and, like an idiot, I always listened to him.

But this was sick. I grabbed the gun out of his hand, walked into my office, and locked it in my drawer. Then I came back and told the cops to get the kid out of there before I killed *them*. They called an ambulance and the boy got hauled out on a stretcher. After they left, I gave Moe a piece of my mind. He acted like the whole thing was a big joke, said he'd used the threat of my arrival to frighten the intruder. Idiot."

My father rises and returns to the kitchen, where he removes the latkes from the pan and places them on a paper towel-covered plate. They turned a little too brown while we were talking. Tootsie brings the plate to the table, then returns to the kitchen for bowls of apple sauce and sour cream. I'm silent, eating the crispy potato pancakes and digesting what he told me.

"You think Uncle Moe would've killed the kid?" I say when I've had my fill.

"You didn't know your uncle if you need to ask."

He's got a point. My uncle was kind to me and, as far as I knew, a good husband and father. But I was a child when he died and most of my memories of him revolve around holiday dinners, magic tricks, and the Barbie outfits he and Aunt Gert bought me. I recall his temper though, yelling at my father and Aunt Gert. My mother whisked Esther and me from the room when he started up. And then this business about Louie's murder. Maybe he *would* have killed the intruder.

My gaze wanders back to the gun. "Why give it to me?" I ask, picking it up and putting it back in the box. "What am I supposed to do with a gun?"

"Kill Daniel?" He laughs. "I don't know what I was thinking. I found it last night while cleaning out the closet in my bedroom. I wanted to see how you'd react."

That's quite an admission. Pissing me off, then watching me sputter, is one of his favorite pastimes.

"I should've dumped it years ago. Your Uncle Moe's gone. The cops we met that night are six feet under. I guess you could call it a memento of Miami history. A lesson in business one-oh-one."

"What's that supposed to mean?"

He stands and takes our plates to the sink.

"You think you're doing some good, hiring people, helping the community. But after a while you realize no one gives a damn. We knew we were taking a chance, buying property near Overtown. The cops warned us to be careful. I figured we'd be fine. Treat our neighbors fairly. Be treated fairly in return. It didn't happen that way. Most people in the neighborhood were fine. But a couple of animals ruined it for everyone. A week after we opened, we hid a prostitute in the store when her pimp came looking for her with a club. She was on the street the next morning. Then this kid falls through the roof." He shrugs.

I clear away the glasses, then drop the box with the gun in my purse.

"You going to keep that thing?" my father says.

"You gave it to me."

"Don't be ridiculous. I'll get rid of it." He reaches for my purse, but I pull it away.

"You call Landauer or Abe yet?"

He shrugs. "You don't need to worry."

"Did they promise to lay off?"

I wait for more but he sets his jaw.

I pat the side of my purse, where the gun is lodged, and walk to the door. "It's mine now."

My purse feels heavy when I sling it on to the Mercedes' passenger seat. I head out of my father's neighborhood and turn north on Biscayne Boulevard to mount the ramp on to I-95. As I drive, I consider taking the gun to a shooting range and learning to use it. After all, who knows when or if Landauer will show up again? The idea of carrying a gun—"packing heat"—is appealing and gives me a little shiver of power.

Could I shoot someone? Even if my life was in danger? I might. I consider what I would do with a gun if I found Landauer and Pinky in my kitchen. Or if they came near Josh or Gabe. Then I catch a glimpse of myself in the rearview mirror. I'm smiling. It's a twisted grin and I don't like it—or the emotions the gun evokes.

I make a U-turn on Biscayne Boulevard, then cross the Miami River and pass under the towering marble-and-glass behemoths that line the Brickell Avenue financial district. After a few miles, the skyscrapers give way to elegantly landscaped estates and I pull off at a roadside park that faces onto the bay. It's dusk and I don't spot a soul as I cross a grassy field to the water's edge.

More than twenty years have passed since that kid broke into my father's store. Fifty since the Kefauver hearings on organized crime. Law-abiding citizens have wrested control of Miami from the gangsters of the forties and the cocaine cowboys who put Miami on the map in the eighties. We're more civilized now. At least that's what I'd like to believe.

Across the bay, Key Biscayne is a faint grid of lights flickering low on the horizon. The gentle splash of waves against the rocky shore and the distant hum of a skiff motoring to safe harbor create a music of their own. I pull the gun out of my purse and reach back to build leverage in my right arm. Then I release the solid metal projectile into the air. The stainless steel glints in the moonlight as it arcs up, then drops toward Biscayne Bay. It makes a faint splash as it hits the water.

29

Tootsie

I slide the frying pan in the sink and return to the living room. I've left the balcony doors open and a cool breeze fills the apartment. It's been miserably hot lately and I hope this signals the end of our heat spell. I go outside and ease myself into the white wicker chair. It creaks under my weight. Across the open lawn, lights flicker off in the nursing home.

I'm surprised Becks agreed to come over tonight. The last time I called, a few days after telling her about Fat Louie, she was too busy to talk but said she'd get back to me. She never did. I considered phoning a week later but put it off to give her time to cool down. I've been a nervous wreck waiting to see what she'd do and it took all my willpower not to call until today. Thank God she's forgiven me. The girl has a lot of sense. Unlike her father. What the hell was I thinking, wrapping that gun and presenting it to her as a Hanukkah gift?

I didn't expect her to be so shocked. It's a lousy chunk of metal, for crying out loud. I forgot she'd never seen it. I didn't keep a gun at the house when she was growing up. Didn't need one there. But my business was another story. I spent my working hours in Miami's worst slum surrounded by whores and pimps, then went home to a beautiful house in Coral Gables. Sometimes I didn't know which of my worlds was real—the big house in the suburbs or the gritty downtown business. What I *did* know was that I had to protect Bernice and the girls from the world I'd escaped.

And I succeeded. At least until now.

That Landauer is one nasty bastard and Abe isn't much better. I've called Abe twice, asking if he's set up a meeting with Landauer, but he refuses to talk. It's typical. Landauer's got a cruel streak and probably delights in the knowledge I'm sweating over his next step.

I didn't tell Becks or Esther, but my problems with Landauer didn't end when he went to jail. If fact, they just got worse. And Moe, that schmuck, was no help.

It was a Monday morning and I was at my desk, rushing to finish a bid I'd stayed up writing the night before. Profits had been down for a few months because our biggest customer, a resort called Paradise Palms, decided to take its business elsewhere. If I didn't find more business soon, we'd go under.

I always got to the office by eight but Moe rarely sauntered in before nine. That day he showed his face at ten. "Toots, you got to come outside and see what I got."

I glanced up to find him standing in the door to our office grinning like a hyena. "Later," I said and went back to work.

"You can afford five minutes. I'm telling you, you've never seen anything like this." He grabbed my arm and dragged me to the front of the store.

"What the hell do you . . ." My jaw dropped as he opened the door.

Parked in front of the building was the most beautiful car I'd ever seen. Every angle of the powder-blue Mercedes was as perfectly proportioned as a Broadway actress. Its front fenders had the rounded slopes of a woman's breasts and the sun sparkled like a diamond necklace across its chrome bumpers. The rear of the Mercedes was a smooth, creamy blue that invited you to run your hand along its curvaceous lines.

I couldn't believe it. Jews didn't buy Mercedes. Everyone knew they'd been made by Nazis who exploited concentration camp prisoners. And the expense? I could barely make the payments on my Oldsmobile.

When I asked Moe what he paid, he gave evasive answers that implied the car was hot. I went inside, disgusted.

It was a busy day and I didn't have time to think about the Mercedes until later, after everyone had left the store. How had my brother paid for it? Moe and I earned the same salaries and lived in similarly-priced homes so I knew he hadn't saved enough money for the car. Even stolen, the Mercedes was out of his range. Something felt off. And knowing my brother, it wasn't legit.

There was only one way Moe could have raised enough money to buy the car. As I put down my pen, I realized the idea had been eating at me all day. Moe handled the Paradise Palms account but hadn't been all that upset when we lost it. I'd written that off as typical of his lazy ass approach to doing business. He told me a competitor was selling equipment to the resort at cost and we couldn't compete without losing money. Like a moron, I believed him.

But what if Moe had taken the account for himself? I felt sick as I sat in my brother's chair and searched his desk. It took a while but I found what I was looking for—ten Paradise Palms purchase orders, all marked paid. I was speechless. That son of a bitch sold thousands of dollars' worth of ovens, grills, and walk-in refrigerators to the resort—and cut me out of the deal.

I had trouble sleeping that night and got into work before sunrise. Hours later, when I heard Moe in the front office flirting with the girls, I stepped outside our office.

"Get your ass in here."

Moe looked up and smiled, taking my tone of voice for a joke. "What's the problem?"

"Now. We need to talk."

Moe's eyebrows shot up and he followed me into the office.

Once he closed the door, I grabbed the purchase orders off my desk and waved them in the air. "You want to tell me what's going on here. Where these Paradise Palms orders came from?"

The color drained from Moe's face. "They're old. I just happened to—"

"Don't bullshit me." It took all my self control not to reach across Moe's desk and slug him. "You'd undercut your own brother and drive us out of business for a lousy car?" I tossed the orders on his desk, ignoring the handful that slid to the floor. I slammed my hand on his desk. "You owe me five thousand bucks. Show up with the money by Friday or you're out. And I'll let Paradise Palms know what you've been up to."

Moe tried to break in, but I jabbed a finger at him. "If I have to, I'll go to the—"

Before I could finish, the phone rang. It was our direct line to the secretaries. I grabbed the receiver. "Can't you see we're busy ?" I listened to her then waited a few seconds as she transferred the call. My breathing grew heavy as I listened. I must have turned white because Moe stared at me with concern in his eyes.

I hung up and turned to my brother. "That was the police."

"And?"

"Landauer escaped from prison."

We stared at each other.

"I don't know what this means for us. It can't be good. But right now I don't give a damn. You have the dough here by Friday or you're out on your ass."

The next morning Moe walked into the office with five thousand bucks, cash. And I never saw the Mercedes again. But from that point on, I never trusted Moe. It's a lousy thing to say about your brother—but he was as crooked as they came.

30

A week after the Hanukkah dinner with Tootsie, I pull my car behind the block-long warehouse and showroom that used to house his business. He's been less than forthcoming about contacting Abe and Landauer and I've got to do something before the gangster shows up again. Finding the articles Tootsie mentioned at the bowling alley seems my best bet for learning what happened between him and Landauer. My father claims they're still in the warehouse. I've got no choice but to find them. Maybe there's something there I can use to force my father to face Abe or Landauer—or the police.

The neighborhood's even more blighted now than it was five years ago when my father retired and sold his business to a cocaine dealer who now calls federal prison home. The grass swale along the road is a patch of weeds. Paper cups, newspapers, and condom wrappers clog the gutters.

It's ten in the morning and the encampment of cardboard and makeshift tents on the lot across the street from the warehouse appears deserted. Within minutes of my arrival, though, a woman with a leathery, cracked face emerges from a pile of cardboard boxes and limps in my direction. Her clothes are a shabby assemblage of skirts, shirts, and more sweaters than I can count but the red coat that engulfs everything lends a note of cheer to the overcast wintry morning. As she draws near my car, I get out to greet her. Her hair is longer and grayer than I recall, but I recognize her as Mashed Potatoes, the name my father assigned her for her lumpy cheeks. His office adopted the lady, in a manner of speaking, years ago—bringing her food, clothing, and books to make survival on the streets more bearable. I'm not surprised she doesn't recognize me. The drugs that landed her here in the first place left her in a fog.

"Bless you," she says when I hand her five singles and ask how she's doing. "The good Lord will watch over you."

I'm tempted to ask if she and, perhaps, the good Lord, will watch over my car. But it's probably wasted breath.

The building's enclosed by a rusted chain-link fence that's four feet taller than I am. Once Mashed Potatoes hobbles back to her cardboard cottage, I walk around the fence looking for a way through. Apparently, I'm not the first person who's wanted in. A few feet from my car, a sprung metal lock lies on the ground where someone jimmied the gate open. When I push the fence, it slides reluctantly, emitting an arthritic groan. I slip through and walk to the building.

Bags of garbage rot against the back wall and I jump when a rat scurries across the parking lot. I approach the back door gingerly fearing what else may crawl from the disintegrating mass of wooden pallets to its left.

When I called Esther this morning and told her what I'd planned today, she said I was crazy. But this is something I have to do. Waiting for Tootsie to act is pointless; he doesn't answer when I ask if he's contacted Abe or Landauer. And after the lies he's handed me so far, I suspect the newspaper clippings hold all sorts of surprises.

The door appears to be securely closed but, when I turn the knob, it gives. Damn. Someone's been in there. Most likely, homeless people have broken in and I'm intruding—which they may not take too kindly. I draw a breath and inch the door open. It glides easily. I look over my shoulder and fight an urge to run to my car. I've come this far. There's no way I'd muster the guts to return.

The acrid odor of dead rodents accosts me when I step inside but no one responds to my loud "hello." I wait for my eyes to adjust to the dark. It's at least ten degrees colder inside the warehouse and I shiver as much from the temperature as from nerves. After a few minutes, I make out the shape of large brown puddles on the floor. I look up and notice that rain has seeped through the roof, leaving blotches of mold on the acoustic tiles on the ceiling. At the sound of scratching I hold my breath, expecting a herd of rats to race across the floor. When nothing moves, I tiptoe farther inside. The place is a disgusting mess.

The warehouse feels strange, familiar and foreign at the same time, as though I've come home to find my house ransacked by strangers. I spent hundreds of hours here during high school, helping my father take inventory. Half of the pots and pans, serving pieces and knives in my kitchen came from these shelves. The dark pools of shadow and raw cement-smell of the abandoned building fill me with sadness and dread.

The wooden pallets my father placed in the central section of the warehouse to keep equipment dry are still there, but sit empty. To my left and right, rows of metal shelving extend ten feet high, almost reaching the ceiling, and thirty feet to the wall.

I don't know where to begin. Thin rays of sunshine pierce ragged holes in the ceiling, providing enough light to see where I'm stepping, but the warehouse is a large empty space with shadowy corners that could hide full-sized men. I pull a flashlight out of my purse and run its beam across the shelves to my right. The bottom two are empty, but the top ones hold huge stockpots that glare down at me like squat malevolent ogres. My father'd need a ladder to put anything that high so I rule against searching the upper shelves.

The middle shelves hold metal baking sheets, industrial cooking pans, and giant stainless colanders. I run the beam between them, reaching with my hand to feel if there's paper stuffed where I can't see it. After a half hour, my nose itches from the dust and my hair is soaked in sweat. I'm dying to go home to a long hot shower.

I'm pushing a set of pans aside to look beneath it when I hear a door click. I freeze and keep my breathing shallow for a few seconds, then pop my head around the corner. The warehouse door is closed and no one moves. I consider making a run for it. But it may be a rodent and I hate the idea of giving up my chance to find the clippings. It took a lot of nerve to enter the warehouse and I'm resolved to go home with them.

"Anybody there," I call, forcing myself to sound brave.

No answer.

Then I remember. There's another door in the warehouse—to the bathroom. Brandishing the flashlight over my head, I tiptoe down the aisle, turn right and walk past a long shelf that holds clear plastic storage bins and food carts. I breathe heavily and my knees feel weak. When I reach the bathroom, I throw the door open.

Standing there, aiming a gun at my chest, is my father.

"Jesus Christ," we yell in unison and jump back. He trips and lands firmly on the toilet, dropping his gun on the floor. I remain on my feet and stare at him with my mouth open. He's managed to hang on to a manila folder, but a pile of newspaper clippings are scattered across the ground. As filthy as the cement floor is, I squat and pick them up while my father heaves himself off the toilet. I can hear him panting over the pounding of my heart.

"What are you doing here?" he says once he's caught his breath. "Don't you know this neighborhood's dangerous?"

"I could be asking you the same question."

He looks toward his gun, which I've left on the floor, and turns pale. My God, I could've shot you." He picks it up and slips it in his pants pocket. "I came to get my file. I didn't want it falling into the wrong hands."

"Who'd come to this dump looking for it?" I say, and then laugh. I'm the wrong hands to which he refers.

Tootsie shakes his head. "You are something else, Doll. Let's get the hell out of here before the ceiling falls in."

It's a relief to step outside into the fresh air. After we lock up, he gets in my car and we drive around the block to the S&S diner, where he left his car. Mashed Potatoes is manning her corner at Second and Sixteenth, schmoozing the drivers for a couple of bucks. She blesses my father when he hands her a ten and he blesses her back.

"So what's with all these articles?" I ask once we're settled at the U-shaped counter and Irma, a waitress who knows my father from the old days, has parked cups of coffee on our placemats. My father leafs through the manila file. Some of the articles have disintegrated to little more than piles of dust and quite a few are too faded to read. As I'm leaning in to look at a photo, my father slaps his hand over the clipping.

"What're you doing?" I say. "I spent a half hour in that filthy warehouse looking for those articles. I deserve to read them."

"No one invited you."

"That's not the point."

"Then what is?"

I take a moment to gather my thoughts. The clippings *are* his property after all. "When those articles were left in my bedroom and my house was ransacked—" I hesitate a moment—"they became *my* business."

Tootsie shrugs. "Fair enough." Then he rips the article he's holding into small pieces.

I'm so angry that I leap out of my seat and reach for the file. Tootsie anticipates my move and flips the manila folder closed before pulling it toward him.

"You son of a . . ." I stop at the look I get from Irma. Tootsie and I glare at each other.

"That's great," I say. "Keep your stupid folder. And your secrets. I'll talk to Abe and your hoodlum friends myself."

I stomp out of the restaurant, leaving my father alone with his precious file.

Then I drive home, where I take my time showering away the cobwebs, rat feces, and nasty mood I acquired in my father's warehouse.

31

It's six o'clock on Friday night and my head's pounding. I haven't eaten since seven this morning and I'm in no mood for Tootsie's games. He joined Congregation B'nai David a week ago and invited me to attend services with him. I figure he's changed his mind and is letting me read the clippings. When I press him about it on the ride over, he says they're none of my business. I'm tempted to drop him at the temple and take off. But I wouldn't feel right about letting him walk into the synagogue for the first time alone. He hasn't been in a temple since my mother's funeral.

The chairs at B'nai David are deep and seductively comfortable, with wide arm rests and plush, velvet-upholstered seats in which it's almost impossible to stay awake. But the cantor has an operatic voice and, judging from the stillness of the audience, the congregants are as enraptured as I am by his throaty baritone. His voice soars toward the rafters of the synagogue's tall beamed ceiling then descends in a series of arpeggios as he weaves his silken tones through the ancient melodies. I feel transported in time and imagine the chant emanating from the lips of a white-robed priest on a golden hill in Jerusalem.

When Tootsie elbows me in the ribs and leans over to whisper in my ear, I ignore him. I withdraw my elbow from our mutual armrest and turn so my back is toward him. Instead of taking the hint, his voice grows louder, rising to a hoarse whisper that draws a loud shush from the gentleman behind us. I blush. My father, if he notices, doesn't care.

"Itzhak Cohen," he says, pointing his chin at the front of the room and drawing an angry glare from the woman in front of us. Tootsie winks at her and she twists back around. "I haven't seen that *putz* in years."

I follow my father's gaze toward the bimah, the raised area at the front of the synagogue. An elderly man waits at the bottom of the richly carpeted purple stairs that lead to the ark, the ornamental enclosure where the Torah is kept. When the cantor's solo comes to a close, the old man mounts the steps. He's bent so far over he faces the floor and struggles to surmount each stair. His elbow is supported by a middle-aged man I assume is his son. The senior Cohen is well into his nineties and the overhead lights throw reflections across the pale freckled pate on which a tiny white yarmulke tenuously rests. It inches down the back of his head and slips toward his neck as he mounts the stairs. I'm surprised he reaches the bimah with the yarmulke still in place.

My father seems to be equally engaged by the yarmulke's progress because he doesn't speak until Cohen shuffles across the upraised stage.

"Fifty years ago, the old bastard probably led prayers at Sing Sing." My father speaks louder than he needs to. I don't know if it's deliberate or his hearing aid is set too low. Either way, he's attracted an audience.

"Dad, this is not the place," I whisper loud enough so people in adjacent seats know I'm not a party to his rudeness.

His eyebrows rise in mock surprise. "Who are *you*? The rebbetzin?" He picks up the prayer book and pretends to find his place. "I'll tell you about it on the way to the Marmelsteins."

I do my best to read responsively with the old man. But it does no good. I'm trying to picture this Itzhak Cohen in a jail cell at Sing Sing. And as my stomach lets out a growl that can be heard five seats down, I think longingly of the Shabbat dinner we're heading to once services are done.

Between Tootsie's stop in the men's room and his insistence on schmoozing with old friends in the lobby outside the sanctuary, it takes a good half hour to make our way to the car once services are over. The parking lot is empty, but a security guard mans the entrance and watches us get in the Mercedes.

The Marmelsteins don't attend Sabbath services but invited us to come over for dinner when we're through with ours. They still live in Coral Gables, down the street from the house in which I grew up. Neither Tootsie nor I have seen them since my mother's funeral years earlier and I'm looking forward to reminiscing about the old neighborhood and my mom. Mrs. Marmelstein, who played on my mother's tennis team, saw my food column two weeks earlier and invited me to join her family for Friday night dinner. It was obvious from her brief silence that she was caught off guard when I mentioned I was going to temple with Tootsie that night. She said to bring him along, which was generous given that she knows about his cheating. Naturally, I have not shared her hesitancy with my father.

"So who's this Itzhak Cohen?" I ask my father once we're on the expressway heading south. "It's pretty hard to picture the old guy in prison."

"He's not much to look at now but he was a big son of a bitch in the old days. I saw him two, maybe three times. Built like a barrel back then, thick through the chest and short. But all muscle." Tootsie wipes his forehead with a handkerchief, then aims the air-conditioning vent toward his face. "I met him in New York."

"Last year?"

He gives me a confused stare, then laughs. "Yeah sure. On the way to your cousin Harriet's wedding, I stopped to see Itzhak. Don't be an idiot. In the forties. Just after your sister was born."

"When you were working on the docks in New York?"

"You got a good memory, Doll. I had the occasional day off. And for once my boss, Sammy, had the decency to show me around."

My father fiddles with the vent again. I can't actually hear the cogs turning but from the way he flips his head from side to side, it's obvious he's mining his brain. Every time we get together now, he's got a new story for me. It's as though his revelations about Fat Louie opened the floodgates. I suspect he's trying to explain himself, to justify his behavior by walking me through his past.

"I don't want you to repeat this," he says as we mount the ramp onto I-95, "because I doubt his wife or son know the story."

I smile. There's not much chance of that.

"It was about halfway through my stint on the docks. I guess Sammy wanted to reward me for working so hard, because he called on a Friday to let me know he'd pick me up at my apartment Saturday night. He said we were going to see the *real* New York.

"That sounded good to me so I put on a fresh shirt, my best suit, and a red tie your mother bought for me before I left. I was waiting downstairs in front of my building when Sammy pulled up in a shiny black Packard driven by a man in a chauffeur outfit. Very classy. I didn't know my boss was such a big shot. I slid into the back seat next to Sammy, who wore a tux and looked sharp for an old guy." Tootsie laughs. "He was probably forty-five to my twenty-five.

"We headed north on the West Side Highway toward the Bronx but I was too busy checking out the car to notice where we were going. When I looked up from the wood paneling and leather seats, the driver was already cruising through a neighborhood I'd never been in. We drove for a while, maybe an hour, through a hilly area with estates set back from the road. I figured Sammy was taking me out to some ritzy restaurant in the suburbs so I was shocked when the driver headed up a long driveway to this dump. The paint was peeling and the lawn was infested with weeds. It was big but looked like nobody had taken care of it in years. At this point, I didn't feel so great. I could think of plenty of reasons Sammy'd drag me to a pit in the boondocks and none of them were good."

"Did you try to get away?"

"I considered it but there was nowhere to go. Plus when the driver maneuvered to the back of the house and parked in an open field packed with Caddys and Rolls Royces, I figured I'd be okay. Sammy wouldn't kill me around all these rich people. And he seemed jazzed, not angry. I was stunned when he knocked on the door of what looked like a two-car garage and a guy in white tails opened it.

"I couldn't believe it. Sammy'd taken me to a carpet joint. I'd heard about these swanky casinos that operated outside the law, but I'd never been to one. Men and women in tuxedos and evening gowns. Gorgeous broads. I'd never been there but it looked how I imagined the Palace of Versailles would look. Crystal chandeliers. Oil paintings. Could have been Old Masters for all I knew. Of course, I played it cool, didn't let on to Sammy that I was bowled over—even after he led me to this fancy buffet table loaded with caviar and champagne.

"Did you pay to go inside?" I say, imagining a scene from *The Great Gatsby*. We're ten minutes from the Marmelstein's and I'm eager to hear the end of the story.

"I didn't. But Sammy arranged everything. He may have.

"I'd never been much of a gambler but I did okay at blackjack so I played a couple of hands before losing twenty bucks and calling it quits. I looked around for Sammy, who'd started at the table with me but disappeared. I figured he was playing craps or poker so I roamed around the casino. It was larger than I'd figured, with a leather bar that ran the length of the room and a dozen tables that faced a stage where a fat broad sang. But Sammy was nowhere to be found. I didn't know a soul in the place and I was pretty uncomfortable around the swells with their tuxes and gorgeous dames. Which, I'm fairly certain, were not their wives."

"He left without you?"

"That's what I thought at first. Then I noticed a door to the left of the bar. It was set into a tufted burgundy leather wall. You couldn't see it unless you were looking hard, which I was. I figured it was the john and Sammy was in there so I went in. Well I found him all right, at a green baize table where he was talking to a couple of mugs. It didn't look like they were playing poker. This bull of a man—Itzhak Cohen—scowled when I entered the room. You could tell he was the boss because all the goons glanced at him. The room was small and windowless, with just enough space for the poker table and a couple of chairs. It stunk of cigar smoke. I mumbled "sorry" and turned to leave, but Sammy stopped me.

" 'It's okay, Tootsie,' he said, 'I got some friends you should meet.' "

"There wasn't much I could do at this point, so I stood by the table as Sammy made his introductions. I caught a couple of names, but Itzhak's was the only one that stuck. The men nodded at me but seemed relieved when Sammy said he'd join me in an hour. I went to the bar and lingered over a scotch and soda until he came out.

"On the drive home, Sammy looked at me, eyebrows scrunched and serious. 'I can count on you to keep your mouth shut, right?'

"I don't know what he's talking about but, of course, I agree."

The traffic becomes more congested as Tootsie and I leave I-95 for Dixie Highway and drive past a neighborhood with ten-foot walls. Fences crushed beneath trees when Hurricane Andrew struck eight years ago have been rebuilt and already are concealed by South

Florida's rapacious vegetation. It's remarkable how quickly Miami adjusts to change. People rarely spoke Spanish when I grew up here, but the thousands of Cubans who made it across the Straits of Florida changed that. Now more than half of Miami's citizens claim Spanish as their first language. And Brickell Avenue—once an elegant boulevard lined with gracious estates—has been taken over by behemoth banking institutions that house the wealth of Latin American oligarchs. Whatever grows here—foliage, culture, crime, money—expands rapidly and supplants what came before.

My father coughs, drawing my attention. "You listening?"

"Yes."

"As I was saying, in the tumult of working the docks and getting through a miserable winter without your mother, I didn't think much about the night at the casino. Sammy brought me to a few joints after that, but I never ran into any of those goons and kept my nose out of his business.

"When my job was over a few weeks later, I returned to Miami to your mother and sister. What a relief that was." He smiles. "Esther learned to sit up while I was gone and I spent every free moment with her. On my third day home, though, I was reading *The Miami News* and nearly gagged on my coffee. Right there on the front page was a mug shot of a clown I'd seen at the casino with Itzhak Cohen. The article said a fellow named Boom Boom Goldberg was charged in the murder of a Miami gangster, Harvey Pollock. I hadn't paid much attention to Boom Boom that night in the casino, but even I could tell the schmuck was a mouth-breather. I figured the other goons set this fat head up for the murder of Pollock, knowing he wouldn't rat them out."

"Did you tell the police?"

My father gives me his *what are you, stupid* sneer. "Hell, no. It wasn't my problem. I met the yuk once, in New York, what did I care? But when your mother read about Pollock's murder, she had her own ideas. She informed me we were going to the man's funeral. I almost fell off my chair. Turns out your mother knows his wife. Ethel Pollock belonged to her Hadassah chapter. They became friendly when Mrs. Pollock hosted a Hadassah luncheon and your mother, such a sweetheart, was the only one who showed up."

"Why didn't the other women attend?"

"Mrs. Pollock told your mother the old yentas snubbed her because of her husband's business associates. She didn't say the Jewish mob, mind you, but your mother figured it out. Ethel swore her husband was no longer involved in the game, but it didn't matter. The Hadassah ladies didn't want to knows from her."

"You think Mom knew before she went?"

"She was a generous person. I wouldn't be surprised.

"What could I do?" Tootsie continues. "I hadn't told your mother about that night in the casino, and I sure as hell wasn't saying anything about recognizing Boom Boom. So that Sunday we went to Congregation B'nai David for the funeral. I sent your mother inside to grab a seat while I had a cigarette. I was standing in front of the shul, minding my own business, when I felt a tap on my shoulder. I turned and almost jumped out of my shoes. It was Itzhak Cohen. He was in slacks and a polo shirt and it was obvious he wasn't heading into the temple.

" 'Can you offer my condolences?' he asked. I hadn't heard him talk before and was stunned by the falsetto that came out of this thick-chested ape. I was too surprised to do anything but nod. See, I didn't know that he was responsible for the hit on the deceased, but I had my suspicions.

" 'I can't go in,' he said. 'I'm a Cohen,' he told me then waited. When I didn't say anything, he tapped himself on the chest. 'A *kohanim*. Can't go near the dead. It's Jewish law. We can't defile ourselves.'

"I've heard about that." I say as I take a left off Dixie onto Bird Road. The street is lined with trees and, I guess, birds, but I don't hear them. "They're the Jewish priests, right?"

"Right. I'd heard of the *kohanim* too, but none of this bull about not going near a dead body. All the same, I was not going to argue Talmudic fine points with a big cheese from the syndicate. I told him I'd do it, and he got into the Cadillac idling in front of the temple and took off."

"Did you tell her?"

"I had to. I'd given my word. But I didn't want to upset Mrs. Pollock. I decided to postpone the message until after the funeral when we made a shiva call.

"We went to her house after the service. Your mother and I were the only ones who stayed for more than five minutes. People wandered in, had a quick cup of coffee, and left without more than a sorry to the widow. Even so, it was a half hour before I got my break. When your mother went to the powder room, I delivered Cohen's message including the part about his being a *kohanim*.

"I felt sick about it but I was worried about Cohen finding out if I didn't. Ethel Pollock stared at me a long time, her eyes wide and lower lip trembling. Then her eyes narrowed. That's when I realized what an idiot I was. I wasn't *sure* Cohen killed Pollock. But if he hadn't, he probably got another goon to do it. It disgusted me, his acting like some holier-than-thou yid, a big shot *kohanim* who's so devout he can't come near a dead body. Not even one whose hit he ordered. And he got me, the moron, to do his bidding.

"I was so ashamed I couldn't meet the woman's eyes. I apologized, found your mother and left."

"Was Cohen arrested for the murder?" I ask.

"Are you kidding?" Tootsie says as we pull into the Marmelstein driveway. "Boom Boom took the rap. When he got out, the mob set him up with a drift fishing business in Hallandale. Itzhak was convicted of tax evasion years later. Did a couple of months."

I turn off the engine. "So how'd he make enough money to get an *aliyah*?" I ask. Only the biggest contributors or most active members of a synagogue are given *aliyahs*—the honorary Torah readings and ark openings.

"He went legit. They all did, eventually. He opened a chain of men's clothing stores in Fort Lauderdale."

"And you? What'd you do then?"

"I told you. Your Uncle Moe and I opened the store. Went legit." He glances my way, then shifts his eyes. "After what happened to Pollock, I knew it was time to get out."

We leave the car and climb the steps to the Marmelstein's front porch. As I push the doorbell, Tootsie grabs my arm.

"Not a word of this to the Marmelsteins," he whispers. "I wouldn't want anyone to think your mother associated with gangsters."

Mrs. Marmelstein opens the door and we step inside before I can read his expression. Tootsie gives her a big hug before she leads us into the dining room where her husband, son, and daughter-in-law sit at a white linen-draped table. Sabbath candles blaze in silver holders and a braided challah rests, uncut, on a crystal platter.

32

Tootsie

The stormy look that sweeps Shoshanna Marmelstein's face as I reach to hug her would turn a lesser man to stone. I struggle to suppress a smile. Honest to God, I can't help myself. It's nice of the old broad to invite me for dinner but it's obvious I'm there through the grace of Becks. If my daughter sees how charming I am to Bernice's old friend, maybe she'll be more forgiving.

I chat about the stock market with Syd Marmelstein while Shoshanna goes to the kitchen to get dinner. In the meantime, Becks catches up with the Marmelstein's boy, Scott, and his wife, Ruth. The three went to high school together and run down a list of old friends, catching up on who's married and who's divorced. Becks seems animated, smiling warmly at everyone, and it's clear she feels at home with Shoshanna and Syd. When Shoshanna serves the Shabbat chicken and potatoes, the room grows silent before everyone starts talking again.

I try to join the conversation but have a hard time focusing. I don't remember most of the neighbors they talk about and my mind keeps returning to the image of Itzhak Cohen. It's hard to believe that old man was the gangster I met in New York. Yet another ghost from the past.

The hit on Pollock was my wake-up call. I'd never met him but knew he operated on the fringes of the syndicate. I don't know what he did to deserve the hit, but his murder scared the living daylights out of me. And not just because I saw my future in his death. Things were getting a little too close to home. Bernice said she met Mrs. Pollock through their Hadassah chapter, but there might have been more to it. Pollock could've set things up, suggested his wife get to know Bernice better. It would have been the perfect way to get me involved in whatever underhanded operation he was running.

The funny thing is I have no idea if Bernice knew what kind of business I was in or what Pollock did. Maybe she didn't want to know. She wasn't stupid— she must have suspected something.

Once I learned of Bernice's relationship with the widow, I worried people would think Pollock and I had been business associates. I asked Bernice to stay away from Ethel. She agreed. But who knows with dames? After my problems with Landauer and the illegal arms shipments in New York, I realized it was time to go straight.

Tonight, at dinner, I try to block those memories. Becks looks so happy and relaxed. I haven't seen her smile in months. I've been so wrapped up in my fear of losing her that I haven't given much thought to her separation. If only she wasn't so stubborn, if she could accept how little an affair means to a man. I've tried to convince her. But nothing I say helps.

It isn't easy being a father. My spirits drop as I reflect on how lonely and frightened she must be. I hate myself for all the pain I've caused her with Abe and Landauer's visits. Not that she didn't have a hand in it, sticking her nose where it doesn't belong.

"Dad?"

I startle at her voice and realize I've been staring at Becks.

"Are you okay?"

It takes a few seconds to answer. An unfamiliar ache constricts my chest and I realize I need to get away from the Marmelsteins and these memories. I put a hand over my heart and try to catch my breath.

"Becks, darling, I don't feel well." I stand but become light-headed and grab my chair. "I'm sure it's nothing, but I think it'd be better if we left now." I glance at my plate. I haven't eaten a bite.

Becks rises and makes our apologies. We've been there only forty-five minutes but the Marmelsteins are gracious. They assure us they're not offended and walk us to our car. It's chilly and I quickly slide into the passenger seat, my heart beating rapidly. I don't know what's going on, only that I have to get out of there fast. As Becks drives down the street on which we lived for thirty years, I let my eyes wander over the dimly-lit front porches and handsome landscaping. The houses sit far apart, separated by tall ficus hedges and ancient oaks that loom over the driveways. The neighborhood looks alien and forbidding—as though the shadows hide ghosts that'll catch up with us if we don't get out of there fast. I'm tense and nauseated and begin to calm down only after we've left the neighborhood and reached the brightly-lit strip malls along Dixie Highway.

33

My bedroom's pitch-black when the phone rings. In my stupor, I knock my glasses off the end table before grabbing the receiver.

"Becks? Are you awake?"

It's Daniel. The panic in his voice jolts me to a sitting position?

"What's the matter? Are the boys all right?"

"They're fine."

"Then what . . ."

"It's my father. He had a massive heart attack."

Fear grips my gut. My mother died the day after *her* heart attack.

Daniel and I may be separated but I still love his father, Milt. We hit it off the moment Daniel brought me to his parent's New York apartment for Thanksgiving our junior year at Amherst. Milt and I chat every few months, mostly about books, and I realize with a stab of guilt that I haven't talked to him since Daniel and I split up.

"I had no idea—"

"I tried to let you know but you never . . ." He lets the sentence hang. "My dad's been ill for a few months. Aunt Vivian phoned late last night from St. Luke's and I'm flying up this afternoon. Do you want to come? "

"Yes, of course." When I reach to the floor to retrieve my glasses, I glance at the alarm clock. Five in the morning. Almost seven hours since I dropped Tootsie off. "Does your father know about us?"

"I haven't said anything. I told him you were busy with a project when I visited last month. I thought we could work things out and didn't want to worry him."

He clears his throat. "There's no reason to tell him now. It'll upset him. I booked a flight that's leaving for LaGuardia at two this afternoon. I wanted to give you a chance to," he hesitates, "say goodbye."

We agree he'll book me onto the same flight and reserve hotel rooms. I spend the morning packing and arranging for a neighbor to feed Mulligan.

My elbow feels foreign as it brushes against Daniel's on our shared arm rest. The only seats he could find on the crowded plane were window and mid-row and I'm uncomfortable being crushed between him and the overweight man to my left.

I'm lost in a bewildering Alice in Wonderland world. Daniel and I haven't been together in months and here we sit, as if nothing had happened, on our way to visit his critically ill father. He offered to pick me up on his way to the airport but I turned him down, explaining it would be easier to take my own car. We might not fly home together. The truth is I knew any time we spent alone would be awkward, so why prolong it. When I met him at the boarding gate and he leaned down to peck my cheek, I hesitated before accepting his kiss.

What makes this trip particularly strange is the sense of déjà vu I've experienced the entire flight. Daniel, the boys, and I have flown to New York dozens of times to visit his parents and attend bar mitzvahs, anniversaries, and weddings. Our last trip, a year ago, was for his mother's funeral. We held hands the entire flight. One of the things I cherished about Daniel's and my relationship was our ability to see each other through tough times, to say the words that would bring comfort. Daniel is grieving and I want to console him. But every word out of my mouth sounds like a cliché. "It'll work out." "I'm sure he'll be fine." Words I'd offer a stranger.

Once the plane takes off, we chat about the boys' plans. We'll see how Milt's doing before scheduling their flights. Daniel and I catch up a little, though we're both careful to skirt any mention of our future. If we're going to be together for a few days, we need to get along. Halfway into the flight, the man in the aisle seat dozes off, and I tell Daniel about Florence Karpowsky's accusation. Daniel's not as horrified as I'd anticipated when I tell him Tootsie admitted that he worked for the syndicate and was forced to kill a man.

The ease I begin to feel with Daniel fades as the plane descends through dense gray clouds over LaGuardia. The reality of why we're in New York strikes me. Milt, my friend and the father of my estranged husband, is dying. I'm here to say goodbye. We grab our luggage from the overhead bin and race to the taxi stand. Though it's only five, the sky is dark and the streets are black and slushy with melted snow. Neither of us speaks during the ride to St. Luke's.

We find Milt on the cardiac floor, lying with his head elevated in an aluminum-barred hospital bed. His skin has a pasty gray tinge and he breathes with the help of a nasal cannula. His eyes are closed. Daniel's Aunt Vivian, Milt's sister, rises from a chair next to the bed and places a finger to her lips. We follow her into the deserted hallway. She's an attractive woman in her late seventies who dresses exquisitely and never leaves home without makeup. I'm shocked by how old and tired she looks without.

"He drifts in and out of sleep, but is lucid when he's awake. He asked for the two of you when he came off the heavy sedation this morning." She smiles at me and I avert my eyes. "Come in and wait. He'll awaken soon. He dozed off hours ago."

I sit in the small recliner at the foot of Milt's bed while Daniel takes the wooden chair next to his aunt. She tells us of receiving a call from a neighbor who was with Milt when the heart attack happened and of arriving at the hospital as the paramedics brought him in.

I don't join their whispered conversation. Instead, I study my father-in-law's face, now so passive, and remember the heated discussions we had about books and politics. Milt's a retired high school English teacher and loves to send me rare books he finds at estate sales and thrift stores. He grew up on New York's Lower East Side, not far from where my father lived, and dropped out of school at sixteen when his father died. Though he worked at a series of factory jobs to support his mother, he managed to finish high school and attend City College. He loves to tell stories about growing up on the Lower East Side and, later, organizing strikes to get New York teachers the benefits they deserved. Milt also likes to tease me about my father's youthful years as a tough.

It seems ironic that Tootsie and Milt came from similar backgrounds yet became such different men. Milt chose the world of the mind, while Tootsie decided to . . . these days I'm not sure what to call it.

I'm so lost in thought that I don't notice Milt watching me. When I catch his eye, he smiles. "How about that?" he says, his voice barely reaching a whisper, "Tootsie Plotnik's daughter visiting *me*."

It's as if he's reading my mind.

I go to his bedside to give him a kiss. His skin feels cool. "Would I miss a chance to see my favorite English teacher?" I smile and motion with my chin toward Daniel. "I brought your son the doctor along."

Daniel, already standing, says, "Hi Dad" and takes his father's hand.

"You kids okay?" Milt says. "I haven't seen you in a long time."

Daniel catches my eye.

"We're fine," I answer. "It's been a busy year."

"Does your father know about my heart attack?" Milt says. His voice is weak and I glance at Aunt Vivian to see if I should continue. She nods.

"I didn't get a chance to call yet. I'll let him know."

Milt smiles. "Who would have thought my Daniel would end up as the son-in-law of one of the toughest *mumsers* in the neighborhood?" He stops talking for a few minutes and I watch his chest rise and fall. "We both did okay."

"How are you feeling?" I ask.

He smiles gently. Then, with a vaudeville inflection, "How should I be feeling?"

I'm about to answer when he interrupts.

"I tell you about the time I tried to join your father's gang?"

I shake my head. I wonder if Milt should be expending so much energy but reason Daniel will end the conversation if it becomes too fatiguing. I can't imagine why he wants to discuss Tootsie, but he's the patient and I defer to him.

"Your dad led a gang of kids I wanted to hang out with. The big boys. He let me once. I went with him and his pals to Hester Street where your father stole an apple from a pushcart." He stops a minute and catches his breath. "When the vendor chased him, the rest of us grabbed our own apples. It was a con every kid in the neighborhood pulled at one time or another. Your Uncle Moe taught it to him."

I smile. Stealing apples is the least of my father's transgressions.

"How about the time your uncle beat up Reb Mottke?" Milt's voice seems weaker. "Your father tell you about our religious school teacher?"

As he's talking, a young doctor in a white coat enters the room and announces that visiting hours are over. He needs to examine *his* patient. Aunt Vivian and I exchange glances and retire to the hallway, but Daniel insists on remaining.

In the hall, she takes my hand in both of hers. "Don't listen to his old stories," she tells me. "Your father was a good boy. Your Uncle Moe." She presses her lips together. "A real hoodlum, that one."

I ask what she means, but she waves her hand in a vague circle as though dusting a stray cobweb from midair. "We all have family skeletons."

When Daniel and the doctor emerge, Daniel joins us in the corner of the hallway where Aunt Vivian has commandeered an abandoned wheelchair. "Dad's sleeping. I think we'd better get a bite before he wakes again," he says.

I glance at my watch. It's almost nine and I'm exhausted. Aunt Vivian demurs. She's too tired to join us, but recommends an Italian restaurant two blocks away. She suggests we leave our luggage in Milt's room and retrieve it when we return to say good night. Daniel and I kiss her and go downstairs.

I step through St. Luke's sliding glass doors into the dark of night and gasp. Living in Florida, I've forgotten the visceral shock of stepping from a warm building into frigid air. Noting my discomfort, Daniel runs into the street and hails a cab. We're going two blocks but I have no desire to fight the wind. It lashes my cheeks and stings my eyes.

Five minutes later, the cab stops in front of a small brick-fronted restaurant on Amsterdam Avenue. I run inside to get a table while Daniel pays the driver. The air is aromatic with the scent of roasting garlic and fresh-baked rolls and I fall gratefully into the cozy booth the host finds me. When Daniel enters, I wave to catch his attention. He towers over the other men in the room and carries himself with a dignity that belies the fear I know he's feeling. Without thinking, I stand and kiss his cheek. He pretends not to be as shocked as I feel.

Neither of us bother with the menu. Spaghetti and meatballs are fine. A house salad. We're alone with our thoughts until the food arrives, when we both lean forward and say "thanks."

I laugh and motion for him to speak.

"Dad seemed so grateful you came. He never told me those stories. It's almost as if he was saving them up for you."

"I'm glad I got to see him. He's a special man. A love."

Daniel nods and returns to his pasta.

After a few minutes, he lifts his head from the plate. "While my father was talking, I thought about what you said on the plane. About your dad."

He absentmindedly twists spaghetti onto his fork.

"I don't know that what your dad did was so unusual. Don't get me wrong. Running numbers and ratting on a friend are pretty lousy. But think about how our fathers grew up. My dad told me his mother was so desperate at one point that she rented a corner of their living room to a prostitute. The lady hung a blanket and serviced her customers behind it. Can you imagine living like that?"

I shake my head recalling similar stories told by my father.

"It's no wonder people who grew up in that neighborhood looked up to gangsters," Daniel continues. "Those were the guys who made it. No one hired Jews back then. It was the Depression and everyone was miserable. Who wouldn't want what the gangsters had?"

"Are you saying that what my father did was okay?" My voice rises.

"Not at all. I'm just suggesting that, given his background, there was some justification for hooking up with the syndicate. When your dad saw the kind of money gangsters made, of course he was tempted."

The waiter removes our plates and takes our order for tiramisu. When it comes, I take a bite of the creamy espresso dessert, then watch as Daniel devours the rest. What he says makes sense. My father had no idea Louie would cheat him and his boss or that Landauer would force the brothers to kill their friend. And he couldn't go to the police if what he said about Miami law enforcement being on the take then is true. He *had to* follow Landauer's orders.

Daniel's always been good at stepping back and analyzing a situation. He doesn't see things in black and white, as I often do. He knows how to confront the gray areas where compromise and understanding lie. He's made some good points. But I'm not buying his argument. At least not completely. If Milt could break out of the neighborhood and make an honest living, so could Tootsie.

I'm starting to yawn and, when I check my watch, realize we've been talking for two hours. We take a taxi back to St. Luke's, but Milt's asleep so we pick up our luggage without saying good night. Back outside, the sleet's turned into a soft, steady snowfall and our cabdriver, remarkably, takes his time driving to our hotel. When Daniel takes my hand in the darkened backseat. I don't pull it away.

Once I've hung up my clothes and arranged my toiletries in the hotel bathroom, I stretch out on the bed and call Esther. It's been a strange day and I need to share it with someone. The week before, she told me her hair was thinning from the chemotherapy but she thought she was going to be okay without a wig. She's still teaching. We talk almost every night now and I'm dying to get her take on what happened today. I tell her about Daniel's early morning call and the visit with Milt. She sends him her love.

"So how'd it go with Daniel?" she asks. "Was it strange?"

"Yes and no. Everything was familiar and unfamiliar at the same time. Whenever I start to feel comfortable with him, this gremlin on my shoulder whispers 'watch out.'"

"You can't let go, can you?"

"I've never been good at forgiving."

She laughs. "Me neither. Or mom. I wonder if resentment is genetic."

"It was nice of Daniel to bring me. He didn't have to, but he knows how much I love Milt."

I tell her about my impulsive kiss in the restaurant and holding hands with Daniel in the taxi.

Esther releases a long low whistle followed by "And?"

"And nothing. He went to his room and I went to mine."

"You're a fool."

"Maybe."

"So what happens next?"

"I'm not sure. Do you ever think about how Mom and Dad's relationship affected you and Bruce?"

"It's one reason I stay away from Tootsie. I'm afraid our marriage will become like theirs if I spend too much time around him. That I'll treat Bruce the way mom treated Dad."

"You're not saying Mom drove Dad to cheat?"

"Of course not. It's just that after a while, she became so bitter she couldn't see beyond her pain. Everything she did was ruled by resentment. She'd snap at him the moment he opened his mouth. And he'd do the same. They expected the worst from one another and that's what they got."

What she says is frightening. It hits too close to what's happening to me.

"It's scary how often I notice myself thinking about Mom since Daniel cheated," I say. "I'm so afraid our marriage will be like theirs—that I'll take Daniel back and he'll cheat again. Then I'll become bitter and snap at him all the time. I don't want that."

"It's hard to believe Daniel would do that."

"It's hard to believe he cheated with Dawn."

"Sometimes you have to go on faith."

We're silent. I've heard all the clichés about how no one knows what goes in other people's relationships. I assume everyone is as happy as they seem. It upsets me that I didn't realize my marriage was falling apart. Daniel was unhappy, but he kept it from me. He became a stranger and cut me off. That feels like almost as great a betrayal as his affair.

"I can't help suspecting I overreacted to Daniel's affair because Dad treated Mom so abominably," I say. "She made me feel that it was up to me to create her happiness, like I had to live the life she couldn't."

"What's that got to do with Daniel?"

"Maybe I *am* punishing him because I can't do anything about Dad. I can't erase the pain he caused Mom but I can prevent Daniel from doing the same to me. Daniel accused me of that a few weeks ago and I told him he was crazy. Now I don't know. We're different from Mom. We're not stuck with men like Dad. We can leave our husbands. And if we stay, it's because we want to."

"So you're taking Daniel back?"

"I'm not sure."

"You just got through telling me . . . "

She sounds annoyed and I realize how confused I sound. "I'm talking from my head, not my heart," I say. "I'm not sure I've forgiven Daniel. It just means I think I can. What would you do?"

"That's an impossible question."

Esther says nothing for a few seconds. A police siren thirty stories below emits a piercing wail that reverberates off the towers of Midtown. Holding the phone to my ear, I walk to the window and look for the cruiser. It's long gone. The snow's given way to sleet and rain and the street below shimmers with the dappled reflection of red, green and white lights. A couple bundled in heavy coats crosses the street at a crosswalk.

"Okay, Beckygirl," Esther says, using my mother's pet name. It makes me feel safe and reminds me I've got at least one person in my corner. She may not have the answers I need but she's there to help me find them. "You know what's best. Give Milt my love. And good luck with Daniel."

I hang up and, after changing into my flannel nightgown, slide between the cool, silken sheets. As I pick up my novel, I realize I've never stayed in a New York hotel without Daniel. I wonder if he's thinking about me.

34

My father takes a long time getting to our table tonight. It's *my* birthday and we're celebrating at *his* favorite restaurant, the Circus Diner. I'd hoped Gabe would join us but, when I invited him yesterday, he said he had an exam Monday and promised to celebrate another night. I don't believe him. He can't forgive me for making Daniel move out.

"Can't you just let it go, Mom?" he said this morning, a refrain I've heard at least a dozen times since Daniel left. "It's over and Dad wants to be back with you"

"I know, Sweetie, but I'm not ready."

"When do you expect to be ready? What's it been, three or four months? It's cruel to make him live in that stupid apartment. And think about what it's costing."

So now *I'm* the cruel one. I take a deep breath. I don't want to play the drama queen but he needs to know how deeply it pains me that he's taking Daniel's side.

"I love your Dad but he hurt me and I need time to forgive him." I don't add *if I ever do.* "Try to see things my way. I trusted your father and his actions stung."

It seems that every conversation we have ends with him shutting down and finding an excuse to get off the phone. Birthday or not, this is no different. A friend, he says, is waiting downstairs to leave for the library. He has to go.

On a more positive note, Joshua called this morning and sang happy birthday, after which we chatted for fifteen minutes. He has a new girlfriend, a freshman from Atlanta, and sounds happy. I'm lucky to have him in my life. He has the sensitivity, or maybe it's maturity, to understand what I'm going through. If he thinks I'm being stubborn, he has the insight not to say so. Both boys talk to their father every week. I'm relieved they have a good relationship.

Five minutes after Josh hung up, Daniel phoned. He wanted to take me out for my birthday. I declined, explaining I was meeting Tootsie. Daniel's called twice since returning home from New York last week. Milt's making a remarkably fast recovery and should be going home in a day or two. Daniel seems as hesitant as I am about discussing the connection—I don't know what to call it—we made while visiting Milt. It's like a bubble that'll burst if we prod it too closely. Better to let it float and see where it lands.

I'm still not sure I can trust him the way I used to and I enjoy my independence. No waiting for a phone call to start dinner. In fact, no making dinner. I spend almost every night testing recipes for my cookbook and, last week, got a letter from an editor who wants the first fifty pages.

At any rate, my father and I have worked our way down the diner's narrow aisle, squeezing between the chrome-topped bar and the row of symmetrically-spaced, linen-draped tables. It's just after five on a Sunday and the two white-aproned waiters behind the bar are caught up in a game of soccer on the overhead screen. Neither glances up when my father and I enter so we seat ourselves.

My father looks every bit his eighty-six years. He spruced up a bit in new khakis and a crisply-pressed, button-down shirt. But his eyes are redder and rheumier than when I ran into him during our warehouse "break-in" and he shuffles slowly down the aisle. I'm dying to ask about running across his picture in the newspaper this morning but decide to hold off.

I rose early this morning, leaving plenty of time to get through the headlines, circulars, and advice columns before testing recipes. I don't usually read the society section, but today it caught my eye. In fact, I almost dropped my coffee. Smiling out from the front page was an eight-by-ten inch photograph of Tootsie. He sat at a table at what was obviously a formal affair with a middle-aged man wearing a goatee and a tuxedo, a slim blonde in a red silk gown, and a rather mousy teenage girl. My father's arm draped the shoulder of a small boy, who looked at him adoringly.

The caption on the inside front cover offered little, just that Ira Nudelman, the man in the photo, was being honored at an Israel Bonds dinner. The story that ran inside mentioned he was a financial advisor who'd made a long list of contributions to the Jewish community.

I searched my memory for the name. Nudelman? It meant nothing. It was too early to phone Tootsie, so I rang Esther.

"You ever hear of this Nudelman?" I asked after telling her about our father's star billing on the society page. "Because I haven't."

"I can't recall anyone. What's in the article?"

"Not much. Nudelman's an investment advisor, a big shot in the Jewish community. The article says he used to be president of The Jewish Federation. He must be doing okay. You've got to give big bucks to get invited to the Israeli Bonds dinner."

"Tootsie sure as hell didn't do that."

I laugh. My father made a nice income, but he never spent it supporting Jewish causes. Or, as far as I can remember, any cause before the Karpowsky Foundation.

"We're going out for my birthday tonight," I said. "I'll find out what's going on."

"Do that."

I waited for her to send her regards, maybe a hello to her father. But she clicked off with just a goodbye.

We order dinner—snapper for me, roast duckling for him—and I wait for the server to bring our iced tea before pulling the article out of my purse.

"What's this all about?" I slide the circular across to him, orienting the page so he can read it. The newsprint leaves a smear on the white linen tablecloth.

I expect Tootsie to be embarrassed or apologize for not alerting me to his society section coverage. Instead, he seems pleased with himself.

"Oh you saw it," he says, not missing a beat. "My new family." He leans back in his heavy walnut chair and flashes the grin he wears in the photo. Then, he places two fingers on the article and draws it closer. "The front page, huh? Bet you didn't know your old man was such a society big shot."

"Who are these people?"

He looks at me in mock horror, "I never told you about the Nudelmans? The nice people who adopted me." He laughs and turns the photo so I can see it clearly. "Those are my new grandchildren." He taps the image of the girl. "Mindy." Then the boy. "Bobby."

I know he's playing a game and he knows I know. But we keep it going.

"Adorable," I say.

"And smart," he adds. "They're both on the honor roll."

"You should be proud."

"I'm kvelling." He uses the Yiddish term for pride.

"Okay," I concede. "How'd you meet the Nudelmans and what were you doing at the Israel Bonds dinner?"

He smiles and picks up his napkin, setting the flatware aside. I wait while he tucks the cloth into his pants and smooths the fabric over his thighs. I suspect he's giving himself time to invent a story.

"You remember my trip to Turkey last year?"

Has it been that long? He saw a television special about Turkey over a year ago and immediately booked a trip. Esther and I worried he'd become ill while overseas. He went anyway, joining an American tour. He sent me half a dozen postcards but never mentioned anything about the other travelers.

"What about it?" I ask. "You meet them there?"

"I ended up eating with them most nights. The little girl's a doll and the boy stuck to my side the whole time. It turns out they're from Miami. We've stayed in touch ever since."

"You never told *me* about them."

"I've got to tell you everything that goes on in my life?"

He must see the hurt in my face because he continues. "I love you, Doll, but an old man's allowed to have a few secrets." He takes a sip of iced tea, then sets his glass on the table. "You want to meet the Nudelmans? Fine. We're getting together next Sunday night at their synagogue. It's a planning session for our trip to Israel."

I don't bother to hide my surprise. "You're going to Israel?"

"Did I forget to mention that?" He gets a big kick out of my shock. "Their boy, Bobby, is having his bar mitzvah on Masada in two weeks and he wants me there. How can I say no?"

The phone's ringing when I unlock my front door. In the rush to answer, I stumble over Mulligan in the hall. It's Esther. I tell her what I learned.

"That's just weird," she says. "What do these people want from him? It's not like he's the most charming guy in the world."

In fact, I tell her, he can be. How else would he have become so successful in a business that depended on sales?

"You said this guy was an investor. Maybe he's after Tootsie's money?"

The thought has crossed my mind but I've pushed it into the background. "I don't think so. It *is* possible this family likes Dad."

Esther snorts. "You don't believe that anymore than I do. Dad's got plenty and I'll bet this Nudelman knows it. Maybe we should hire a detective. Find out if he's legitimate. You read about these financial shysters who scam old people."

"Dad's smarter than that. And they're going to Israel with a tour. Nothing will happen."

"Don't be naïve. An older man has a heart attack while overseas, no one's going to ask questions. For all we know, Nudelman's convinced Tootsie to rewrite his will."

"You're getting carried away."

"Maybe not."

Neither of us speak.

"So what do you want me to do?" I ask.

"Meet Nudelman. And let me know what you think."

The following week is busy. My editor's asked me to write weekly restaurant reviews and the trip to see Milt has forced me to play catch-up. So far, I've written essays to go along with twenty of my mother's recipes so the cookbook's going well. Friday, after I email an article in to the paper, I run a search on Ira Nudelman. He looks fine to me. He's on the boards of a handful of Jewish organizations. I figure my dad knows what he's doing, traveling to Israel with the Nudelman family. Esther and I are being paranoid.

That Sunday, Tootsie and I grab a quick bite at Zimmerman's Deli, then drive south to Coral Gables. I assume we're meeting at a synagogue, but my father directs me to an office building.

"It's a new congregation," he says as we ride the elevator to the tenth floor, "and they're still working on a building fund. Nudelman owns this place and lets the congregation use it for free."

We step off the elevator and travel down a freshly-carpeted hallway to a room the size of an Olympic swimming pool. The chemical smell of paint and drywall permeates the air and strips of brown paper lie along the corners of the room. A coffee urn sits on a folding table at the front, next to a stack of paper cups, a jar of creamer, and a handful of sugar packets. A man in his early thirties wearing a black yarmulke over close-cropped black hair—I assume he's the rabbi—stands next to the table talking to a dozen adults and children. The chairs are set out in semicircular rows. My father waves to a man I recognize as Nudelman and we seat ourselves a few rows behind him and his children.

I struggle to stay awake as the rabbi explains that the group will base itself in Jerusalem and Tel Aviv but visit religious sites throughout the country. When the meeting's over, Nudelman strides across the room to Tootsie and gives him a bear hug. Releasing my father, he turns to me. "You must be Becks. You're lucky to have such a sweet guy for a father."

I glance at Tootsie. No one ever calls him sweet. The best I can offer is "Thanks."

"Don't worry about your dad. We'll take good care of him. Though I suspect, with his energy, he'll take care of us."

I don't have a response. It's a cliché and doesn't deserve an answer, so I smile blandly.

My father introduces me to Nudelman's kids, an attractive girl named Mindy and Bobby, the bar mitzvah boy. He's small for thirteen with thin legs and arms that look like stick figures emerging from his shorts and tee shirt. I find myself comparing this fair, delicate child to my sons, who were clumsy, noisy creatures at that age. Nudelman leads us to the elevator and he and Tootsie talk about hotel accommodations on the ride down. The whole time,

Bobby hangs on to my father's hand. I'm surprised when he gives Tootsie a kiss before leaving for his father's car. My father's not demonstrative and he rarely gave his grandsons more than a quick hug. I'm jealous but still touched by his affection for the child.

On the ride to my father's apartment, he talks about the trip. He's excited about visiting Israel for the first time. I drop Tootsie off at his apartment and head home, uneasy. I didn't get a chance to talk to Nudelman although he seemed pleasant enough. If my Google search is to be believed, he's a successful and generous man who supports Jewish causes all over town. Maybe I'm jealous that my father has a better relationship with a strange family than with his own and concerned about his traveling so far. But I can't shake my skepticism over Nudelman's willingness to include Tootsie—and Tootsie's eagerness to attend—such an intimate and far-flung family event. Traveling to Israel for the bar mitzvah of a child he's just met seems odd, even for my father.

That night, it takes me awhile to doze off. When I do, I dream of my father riding a camel—alone and far from civilization—along red desert sand dunes.

35

The Saturday night after Tootsie leaves for Israel, Daniel calls. It's almost ten when the phone rings, interrupting work on an essay I'm writing about my mother's potato kugel. I'm miffed at his interruption and assumption I'll be home alone on a Saturday night. But his voice holds the soft timbre that means he's lonely. I haven't heard that since early in our marriage, when we were apart for weeks at a time while he did clinical rotations in Tennessee. And his good news trumps my resentment. Milt, he tells me, is leaving the hospital Monday. He'll spend a week or two at his sister's apartment while Aunt Vivian nurses him back to health. It looks like my father-in-law will be around a few more years.

The last time Daniel phoned, he insisted we take the boys out to dinner together when they're home for spring break. I told him I wasn't ready for that. I do miss Daniel. But sometimes, when I hear his voice, my resentment and bitterness flare. The most innocuous question—about whether I paid a bill or hired a new lawn man—sets me on edge. It's as if he doesn't trust me to take care of matters I've handled for years. I wonder if I'll get past this. Tonight, he asks if I've paid our mortgage this month.

About five minutes into our conversation, Daniel coughs and grows silent.

"Are you there?" I ask.

"Hold on a sec?"

I hear water running. Daniel's first impulse is to reach for a drink—water or coffee—when he's angry or nervous. I wonder what I said to upset him.

The sound of running water stops and I wait as he takes a sip and clears his throat. "Any chance of meeting for breakfast tomorrow?" The words come quickly. "We could go to Lester's? Share an order of blintzes."

I hesitate. Lester's has the best blintzes in South Florida.

"I promise not to pester you. Tootsie called before he left for Israel so I figured you'd be free."

Mulligan jumps onto the desk and rubs against the receiver, no doubt recognizing Daniel's voice. My dad won't be back for a week and I don't relish the prospect of a Sunday alone. Most of my friends spend the day with family or have standing tennis games. It would be nice to have something to do, something to which I can look forward. The thought startles me. I *do* look forward to seeing Daniel. But I don't want to be trapped in a restaurant where I'll be embarrassed to leave if he angers me.

"How about a walk in Delray Beach?" I say. "We could meet in the tiki hut across from Atlantic Avenue?" That's where we used to stop to rest on our Sunday morning walks along the beach. "Ten thirty," I add before I can change my mind.

"I'll pick you up?"

"No. I'll meet you there."

I get to the beach fifteen minutes early and park along A1A, managing to snag a spot near the water a quarter of a mile south of the tiki hut. The wind blowing in from the ocean sends sprays of sand across the grassy dunes, slicing my face with sharp-edged grains. I didn't check the weather before leaving my house and the sky hangs low and forbidding over the slate ocean. Large rollers strike the beach, which is lined with rows of dark sargassum that last night's storm threw on shore. Even so, the usual crazies are in the ocean—surfboarders in their black wet suit shorties and kite surfers in colorful bathing trunks. When I stop to watch a kite surfer flip his board in the air and execute a tight turn, I'm almost struck by an inline skater.

Daniel's waiting on a bench inside the tiki hut when I arrive. His black nylon running shirt shows his graying temples and high cheekbones to advantage and I'm struck by how distinguished he looks. He rises and there's an awkward "should we kiss" moment before I seat myself and he drops onto the wooden planks beside me. We're the only ones inside the hut. The cooler weather and gray day have apparently discouraged other walkers.

"I'm glad you could make it," he says.

I smile and shrug. The two of us stare out to sea at a surfer struggling to catch a wave. He's young, about Gabriel's age, and lies flat on his stomach as he paddles fifty yards over breaking surf. Then he orients the board toward shore and watches the waves over his shoulder. A few of the waves he catches die beneath him but he turns the board, paddles out, and tries yet again. I admire his persistence.

"You want to grab a bite? Go for a walk?" Daniel asks once the surfer skims to shore on the crest of a breaking whitecap.

"Let's walk."

We head north along the sidewalk. Our pace adjusts, as it always has, with him slowing down to compensate for my shorter stride. In less than a minute, we're back in sync. We make good time, which means I'm breathing hard from the effort of keeping up.

As we walk, we chat about nothing in particular. Tootsie's relationship with the Nudelmans. Josh's decision to remain in Atlanta for the summer term. He tells me Gabe decided to double major in engineering and computer science and may remain in Miami over the summer. I realize I haven't talked to the boys in a week and experience a moment of guilt. My last conversation with Gabe ended in an argument. As usual, he contended it was time for me to let go of my anger and take his father back. I snapped that it was none of his business. I tried to explain that it was up to his father and me to work things out but he sounded hurt. We haven't spoken since. I hope Daniel's and my separation isn't behind the kids' decision to spend their summer away.

"About the boys . . ." He interrupts my thoughts.

"What about them?"

"They've called me a few times in the last week."

I feel a stab of jealousy. They don't call me that often.

"They asked me to talk to you. They . . . " We jump back as a bicyclist in sleek black jerseys zips within inches of us. "They want me to convince you we should be a family again. That we should reconcile." He hesitates. "We'd all like things to go back to the way they were."

My cheeks grow warm but I'm too dumbfounded to speak. *I'm* being blamed for our separation. Yes, I threw Daniel out. But I had a good reason. Why am I the bad guy in this? He's the one who chose to cheat and break up our family. I break into a jog but Daniel trails close. When I stop and turn around, he almost runs into me.

"I can't believe you're having this conversation with the boys. This is between us. I don't need the three of you ganging up on me. Or you manipulating the kids. You saw what happened to my family."

Daniel rolls his eyes.

"Don't start," I warn. "You know perfectly well how my mother forced Esther and me to interfere. Don't do that to our kids."

I turn my back to him and retrace my steps toward the tiki hut.

"Becks."

I keep walking.

"Becks."

His voice is closer. Daniel grabs my arm and spins me around. "Don't do this. I love you and hate myself for what I did to you. I can barely sleep at night because of my guilt. The boys know that and want us to be a family. I'll do anything you want. But you've punished me enough. You can't believe I'd cheat on you again."

I pull my arm away. "Why not? I didn't think you'd cheat in the first place. Why'd you do it?"

The question has plagued me for months, draping me in a cloud of anger and despair each time I think about it. I've been afraid to hear the answer. That sex was no longer good? That I've let myself go? That I've become boring. I've been beating myself up searching for reasons. But frustration and Daniel's determination to reunite have given me the nerve to ask.

Daniel winces, then studies his hands. "I don't know. I've been struggling with it myself. After my mother died, I felt lost. We were pretty close. You remember?"

I nod. Daniel and Sylvia spoke two or three times a week, more often after she was diagnosed with pancreatic cancer. They didn't talk long, but it was enough to feel connected. I hope my sons will be as devoted when I'm older.

"Then Dawn showed up and I was flattered by her attention. I couldn't believe a girl like that was interested in me. She was young. She made *me* feel desirable and young. I think she helped me block the depression I felt after my mother died. Around her, everything was easy and mindless. I guess I needed that."

Easy and mindless? Was I difficult and depressing to be around?

He continues. "But after a few weeks, it wasn't fun. I knew I was deluding myself, pretending to be someone I wasn't. And I missed us. I'd come home at night and feel sick with remorse but couldn't say anything. I felt isolated from everyone, even you. I hated that and wanted so much to get closer to you. We *were* starting to get closer when Eva called. By then Dawn and I were long over. All I wanted then and now is to be with you."

I search his face, seeking evidence of truth. Yellow flecks dot his irises and his crow's-feet crinkle with concern. We're silent for a moment and, with a jolt, I realize he means what he says. His skin is pale and he chews his lower lip. I want to forgive him. But something holds me back.

A light flickers behind his pupils. "It's your father, isn't it?"

I glance toward the beach to escape his gaze. Row upon row of sailboat masts dot the shore, emerging from behind the dunes like popsicle sticks in tufts of grass.

"I'm not Tootsie. Do you understand that?" He speaks slowly and his voice embraces me like a warm breeze. "I'd never treat you the way he treated your mother." He stands closer to me and I take in the familiar scent of car leather and shaving cream. "I love you and always will. When you're ready to come back, I'll be here."

I nod and step back, torn between the urge to hug him and the compulsion to run. A lump fills my throat, choking off any possibility of speech. I wave a hand ambiguously and shake my head. He squeezes my arm.

I turn away and walk to my car. When I've gone a hundred yards, I glance over my shoulder. He stands on the sidewalk, arms hanging at his sides, smiling. Driving home along the ocean, I feel a lightness I haven't known in months.

36

My father's back from Israel for two days before he calls. We argued before he left, but he dismissed my concerns about getting sick while so far from home. I didn't mention Esther's suspicion that Nudelman was running a con. The last time she accused Tootsie of getting scammed—by a woman half his age—Tootsie didn't talk to her for three months. I don't need that. Apparently, my nagging's forgiven. Tootsie invites me for dinner Sunday night.

He's still jet-lagged when I show up, so we send out for Chinese food.

"How was Israel?" I ask after he calls in our order. "Any problem keeping up?"

"It was tiring but I enjoyed the trip." He tells me about exploring the Old City in Jerusalem and gives a brief roundup of the bar mitzvah at Masada.

"And the Nudelmans?" I say when he's through. "They have a good time?"

My father laughs, a short staccato bark, and walks into the kitchen.

"What is it?"

He looks at me, shakes his head, and laughs even harder. Each time he glances at me, he starts in again. In seconds, he's bracing himself, palms on the counter and arms straight, laughing so hard tears run down his cheeks.

I watch, amused and dumbfounded. "What's so funny about a trip to Israel?"

"I'm sorry," he says once he catches his breath. "The answer to your question—at least for Ira Nudelman—is nothing."

I raise an eyebrow and he motions me to the couch.

"I don't know where to begin." He eases himself into the armchair across from me. "I told you about meeting Ira on the trip to Turkey."

"Yeah, with his family."

"There's more to the story. I knew his father."

"You didn't tell me that."

"Of course not. With your big mouth, it would've been all over Miami. I didn't want Ira to know. It's so crazy. Ira's father was a big time hoodlum on the Lower East Side. Everyone called him Boots because he'd kick over your fruit or vegetable stand if you didn't pay protection. It wasn't a sophisticated scheme, just a pain in the butt. At least until my father, who had a small grocery store, refused to pay. The son of a bitch beat him up and put Grandpa Leo in the hospital for a couple of days."

I don't remember my grandfather, who died when I was five, but family photos show him as a big guy who could handle himself. Nudelman's father had to be pretty tough to beat him up.

"Moe and I were too young to do anything about it. Luckily, at least for my dad, Boots had bigger fish to fry. He joined a gang and left the neighborhood peddlers alone."

"But how did you figure Ira— "

"Let me finish, will you. You don't meet many Nudelmans in this world. So when I got back from Turkey, I called friends in New Jersey. Sure enough, he *was* Boot's son. And a con man like his father. Got caught scamming a couple of investors in New Jersey and managed a plea deal. Made a new start in Florida. I wasn't surprised. The bastard was sizing me up in Turkey, asking about my business, my family. I bet he looked into my finances when we got home. The wife and kids are sweethearts. But I can spot a con artist a mile away."

"So why'd you go to Israel with him?"

He holds up a finger in answer. "About a month after we got back from Turkey, I met Ira for lunch and mentioned I needed a lawyer to update my will. Figured I'd play the half-witted old geezer who needed advice. He bit and gave me a name, Juan Perez. Then, when Ira invited me to Israel, I reeled him in. My guess is he thought I'd update my will before the trip and he'd arrange for Perez to give him a piece of the fee. I didn't think he was planning to knock me off or anything like that, but I took measures. Told him I had an appointment with Perez to work on the will the week I got back."

He leans in my direction and plants his hands on his knees. "Did I mention that Ira advanced the money for my trip? Ten thousand bucks with first class seating on El Al. I told him I'd pay him back a few days after we returned. That I had a certificate of deposit coming due."

"Dad, are you telling me you went to Israel just to—"

"Hold on, Doll, I'm not done. And in case you think I'm some kind of cheapskate, I bought the boy a beautiful gift. A prayer shawl and yarmulke from the Holy Land."

He waits for me to comment, express my admiration for his generosity. I say nothing.

"We flew back Thursday night and got in about four Friday morning. At the baggage carousel, I pulled Ira aside. The bastard was all smiles, thinking I was going to thank him." My father curls his lip. "I told him the same thing I told you. What his father did to mine. What I know about him. And how I'm not paying him back.

"You should have seen his face." My father sighs and shakes his head. He looks genuinely sad. "I could tell he was scared. I'm not going to kid you, Becks, I was out for revenge. But the guy's got a wife and two great kids. I couldn't ruin it for them. Nudelman knows I'm watching. And he can't be sure I haven't told anyone about his past. That should be enough to keep him straight."

My father rises bracing both hands on the arms of his chair and eases himself up. He goes into the kitchen, gets two paper plates and two plastic forks, and sets the table.

I don't know what to make of his story. He planned this carefully and went to great lengths to exact revenge. But why? It's been forty-five years since Grandpa Leo died. What good does it do Tootsie conning the son of a man who, no doubt, has been dead for decades?

His story makes me uncomfortable. How many people would go to such lengths for revenge? It's vindictive and cruel. The con he pulled on Nudelman isn't as bad as what he did to Fat Louie. But it's criminal all the same—stealing from a victim who can't go to the police. Whether Nudelman deserved that or not isn't my—or Tootsie's—place to judge. I suspect the crazy thinking that helped him justify Louie's murder is the same kind of reasoning that spurred him to con Nudelman.

I'm about to suggest as much when the doorbell rings. It's the deliveryman with the Chinese food. My father brings the brown paper bag to the table.

"I should have taken you out for a nice steak," he says as we pull warm aluminum containers from the bag, releasing the honeyed scent of General Tso's chicken and fried rice. "After all the money I saved on the trip."

He looks up from the table and frowns. "What? You don't like the way I finance my travel."

I'm tempted to make a smart-aleck comment about the fruits of criminal labor but hold my tongue. I haven't seen him in two weeks and don't want to argue. He's eighty-six and operates under his own set of rules. And if I want to continue to spend time with him, I have to keep my mouth shut.

37

Tootsie

I'm clearing the table after Becks leaves when I realize she completely missed the point I was trying to make. The whole time I talked about Nudelman, she chewed her lower lip and threw me sidelong glances. A son would've understood. You don't take crap from anyone. And you don't let anyone get away with shit—even if it means waiting fifty years. What I did was justice, pure and simple. No better and no worse than what happened to Fat Louie. That's how the game is played.

I'm hunched over, loading cartons of leftover rice and chicken into the fridge, when an idea strikes me. I stand so fast I bang my head on the freezer door. Maybe *that's* how Landauer felt—that the bad blood between us gave *him* the right to intrude in Becks' life. That it was perfectly legitimate for him to confront my daughter.

But the situation with Nudleman is different. I settled my accounts with Landauer years ago. And offered to pay him extra to leave Becks alone. But Landauer hasn't responded. I tried to reach Abe before leaving for Israel but he didn't return my call. Bastards. They know I'm sweating it out and want to keep me hanging. I'm sick of waiting. I've got to bring this business to a close.

It's past ten, but there's no point in delaying. I hate begging Abe to contact Landauer but have no choice. I feel like a heel for making Becks wait so long but figured I'd hear from them eventually. I dig through the junk mail on my cocktail table for the scrap with Abe's number and dial.

"What is it now?" Abe says. "I'm in the middle of a football game."

"Did you hear from Landauer?"

"About what?"

"My offer. Will he take my money and leave Becks alone?"

"He's not interested."

"What did he say?"

"He doesn't want your, quote, fucking money."

"Then what does he want?"

"You miserable. And alone."

"Don't be stupid."

"Then don't ask."

I think about it for a minute. "Did he tell you *that*?"

"Why would I lie?"

"So what am I supposed to do?"

"You're the big shot businessman. Figure it out. Then tell me."

Abe hangs up the phone.

I pace the living room puzzling out what he meant. Me miserable? Like things can get worse. I'm losing sleep and ruining my health over Landauer's plans for Becks. Maybe that's Abe's point. Landauer wants me to stew. Keep me dangling, then do nothing. It'd be like that son of a bitch.

I'm not biting. The bastards have better things to do with their lives than torment me and Becks. Hell, Abe barely remembered my asking him to call Landauer. And Lord knows Landauer doesn't need the money. He stashed plenty away before being sent to prison and probably made a fortune in the Bahamas. He wants the satisfaction of knowing I'm sweating it out more than he wants my dough.

It's been four months since Landauer visited Becks. If he hasn't done anything yet, he's got to be bored with this whole cat and mouse game. He's had his sick fun and it's over. If he wants to leave me up in the air, fine. I'm not wasting any more of my time on his bullshit. When he's ready to call, he'll call. And if he doesn't, so what. Becks will be fine.

38

It's early March and I've established myself as the newspaper's "Jewish epicure," which means my stories make it to the food section's front page when there's a religious holiday. I've been so busy trying to meet my editor's deadline and working on my cookbook that I haven't seen much of my father. Passover will be here in less than a month and my article is due Friday. I've decided to write a piece on dishes traditionally made by Sephardim, especially Iraqi Jews—baked eggplant, date haroset, spinach soufflé. The kitchen is redolent with the aroma of roasting leg of lamb I started earlier.

Last night, Daniel called to tell me he had dinner with Tootsie. When he asked about Fat Louie's murder, my father said it was no big deal and that I'd blown things out of proportion. All of that happened long ago. Daniel's shocked by Tootsie's attitude. So am I. I can't believe the old man has the nerve to minimize what I've been through. I haven't told Daniel about Landauer's unexpected visit or his threat. And neither, apparently, has my father.

I still haven't heard from Landauer and Tootsie refuses to tell me whether he's contacted the gangster. I suspect he has but doesn't want me to know. Maybe he paid the old gangster off and is loath to tell me. Afraid I'll be upset that he spent his so-called fortune buying "protection." At this point, I'm so frustrated by Tootsie's obfuscations that I don't know what to do. I've yelled and screamed at him and all I've gotten is reassurance he'll take care of it. Like, I ask, he took care of Fat Louie? He gives me a dirty look, but says nothing. It's hard to imagine the old man killing Landauer. But Tootsie had no problem carrying out his vindictive plan of revenge against Nudelman.

As I slice the eggplant and sprinkle it with salt, I find myself growing angrier and more disgusted with my father *and* Landauer. I replay the gangster's visit and become incensed at the memory of the old bloodhound planting himself at *my* kitchen table and threatening *me*. When I toss a knife too forcefully in the sink and break a glass, I realize I've got to act. It's been nearly five months since Landauer threatened me and I'm still edgy when I enter my home. It does no good to tell myself he's lost interest, as my father claims. He could show up at any time.

This is no way to live. As I slide the breaded eggplant into the oven, I resolve to settle things and get on with my life. There's no choice. I'm going to meet Landauer and tell him what I've learned about my father. I decide to do it that afternoon.

There's one snag. The road to Landauer passes through Abe, the last person I want to contact. I'm sure he won't talk to me over the phone or, if I give him warning, answer the door. I need to surprise him. I call my friend Aviva, who assures me her mother will tell the Harbour Villas guard to admit me that afternoon. Then I take a quick shower and steel myself for the meeting.

I idle fifteen minutes in line behind five cars waiting to get through Harbour Villas' gated entrance. The same elderly commando who let me in before mans the guardhouse. Today he wears a sparse red toupee that's slipped forward and perched above his eyes. He looks like a demented swimmer in a burgundy bathing cap. It's hard to keep a straight face when he asks who I'm going to visit and if I'm making a social call. As if it's any of his business. I feel like an alien life form going through customs in a Woody Allen film.

This time, I find Abe's building right away and, after parking, rehearse what I'll say. The parking lot and sidewalk are deserted even though a light breeze blows from the east. It's a perfect afternoon for a walk. But Mother Nature and a gentle wind aren't much competition for the canasta tournament or water aerobics class Harbour Villas recreational mavens have, no doubt, scheduled that afternoon.

I drag my feet climbing the stairs and shift my shoulders to release the knot in my back. I don't know if he'll talk to me. And if he does, if he'll give me Landauer's phone number. But I am certain of another angry outburst when the door opens.

When I reach his door, I knock, wait a minute, then knock harder. A muscle in my back twitches. It takes Abe a few minutes to open up. His eyes narrow and his face reddens.

"What do you want?" He spits out the words.

"I'm sorry to bother you, but I need your help. I'm not sure what you know about this." I realize I'm blathering but can't stop. "After I met with you, I got a . . ."

The door to the neighboring apartment flies open and a woman in a red house robe splashed with black-and-yellow ladybugs sticks out her head. She looks me over, curiosity stamped across her leathery features. "Everything okay, Abe? I heard banging and voices."

"Not to worry, Millie," he says, then takes my elbow and draws me inside. He pulls the door closed behind him. "What's this about?"

I don't know how much time he's willing to give me, so I talk fast. I tell him about finding my house ransacked and a warning slashed across my mirror. About Landauer showing up in my kitchen and threatening me. I tell him I've complied with Landauer's demand that I learn the truth from my father.

"So what's this got to do with me?" he says when I'm through.

"I think you know where I can reach him."

Abe looks at me, shakes his head. "You and your father. What am I? Fucking directory assistance?"

"Will you give me his phone number so I can tell him what I've learned."

Abe considers a moment, then motions with his cane toward the sofa. "Here's the deal. Tell me what you want Mr. Landauer to know. I'll pass your message along."

I follow him into the living room, where he settles into the recliner. Sitting opposite him on the sofa, ready to sprint, I tell him about my father's confession. He listens to the story with a bland expression, nodding now and then. I tell him what I know about Tootsie and Uncle Moe luring Fat Louie to their mother's home and disposing of the body near the Miami River. I also mention my father's admission that Landauer took the rap. My voice breaks and I stop every few minutes to swallow my fear. I could be reciting Japanese haiku for all the emotion Abe shows.

When I'm through, he raises his eyebrows and looks at me expectantly. We seem to be at an impasse. "And that's it?" he says.

"What do you mean?"

"That's all he told you?" He sounds incredulous.

"That's all there is."

At that he seizes the lever of his recliner and propels himself upright. He grabs his cane and hunkers over the stick, hands clasped on its wooden grip. "The old bastard." He runs a hand through his hair. "Even lied to his kid. *I'll* tell you the truth."

I perch on the edge of the sofa. Adrenaline courses through my veins and my hands tingle. I'm stunned. Not so much by the news that my father lied. He's done that often enough. But it's hard to take in the fact that there's more. And, from Abe's sneer, possibly worse.

"You got some of it right." Abe says. He sounds sad and resigned and shakes his head as though in disbelief. "Including the part about Mr. Landauer taking the rap for Louie's death. But you're an idiot if you think Mr. Landauer let your father and uncle off that easy. I worked for him then but, unlike your uncle and father, I knew the meaning of loyalty. Before he went away, he asked me to make *arrangements*."

He looks at me, eyes widened, to confirm I'm following him. I nod.

"Here's how it worked. I made phone calls, let Mr. Landauer's friends know your father and uncle had a restaurant supply store and should send business their way. A lot of the casino operators who opened restaurants in Hallandale and Miami Beach owed Landauer for . . . services rendered. Mr. Landauer told Tootsie and Moe to deposit seventy percent of their earnings in his wife's bank account. He figured it'd be enough to take care of his family while he was away. Your father and uncle had to live on the other thirty percent, if they could. That wasn't Landauer's problem."

I recall the news clippings left at my house. S&G, the name penciled on one of the clips, must have been a casino operator Abe contacted to do business with my father.

"Things were okay for a while," Abe continues. "Moe and Tootsie were grateful for the restaurant contracts not to mention being alive. Landauer chewed over the idea of having them knocked off, but figured he'd arrange that later if need be. Meanwhile they were cash cows. They deposited money in Estelle's bank account and she and the kids, a boy and girl, did okay. Then one day, the ungrateful broad decides a nice girl from New Jersey shouldn't be married to a bum who's doing time in Raiford. She divorces Mr. Landauer and takes the kids back to Jersey. Won't let them visit their father, write him, nothing.

Turns out Estelle has an old flame in Newark. In less than a year, they're married.

"Then, as if that's not bad enough, your father and uncle decided that the broad's remarriage took *them* off the hook. Which it did not. They stopped depositing money for Estelle. When Mr. Landauer got out of prison and found an empty bank account, he went nuts. Told me to put a hit on Moe and Tootsie."

I flinch as I realize how close my father came to being killed. The room feels chilly, as though someone opened a window and let in an icy breeze. I wrap my arms around my shoulders and shiver. He may be a pain in the neck, but I can't imagine growing up without my father. If Tootsie'd been murdered, I would've ended up like my cousin Zvi, fatherless and flipping burgers in high school. Still—and I feel guilty at the thought—my mother might have remarried a man who treated her well.

"What happened?" My voice is shaky. "Did he . . . order the hit?"

"Obviously not. Landauer'd been in prison for fifteen years and didn't know the score. I told him we didn't have as many friends on the police force as we used to. And most of the guys we hired for these jobs were doing time or had gone legit. Maybe he should consider a financial settlement. I argued with him, explained how things stood, and he finally bought it. I told Moe and Tootsie to meet us at the Miami River, same place they took Louie's body, with a half million bucks. They had three days. Your father and uncle agreed. What choice did they have?"

He looks at me and I shrug. My stomach aches at the prospect of where this is going.

"It was raining the night of our meeting and the only shelter was a stinking shed bums used as an outhouse. Landauer and I waited a half hour in the rain before Moe showed up with a briefcase. He apologized over and over, said he and his brother had a hard time raising the dough. Tootsie'd assured him it was all there. Landauer didn't give a damn. He made Moe take the cash out of the briefcase and count it in the rain."

Abe takes a deep breath and rubs his chest. "Moe came up short. A hundred thousand. I could smell his fear as he counted a second time. He swore he was as shocked as we were. Then he promised he'd get the rest of the money the next day. But Landauer was having none of it. He'd worked himself into a rage waiting in the rain. And your father and uncle stiffed him. Next thing I knew, Landauer was holding Moe by the collar and using his face as a punching bag."

I cringe, but Abe continues.

"Your uncle fought back but it only made things worse. Landauer was out of control. Seemed like all the anger he'd stored up in prison exploded. He went crazy, punching and kicking your uncle. Moe was a big guy, but no match for Landauer. After five minutes, Moe collapsed on the dock. I tried to help him up but he didn't move. We didn't know if he was unconscious or dead. But we got out of there fast."

Abe settles back in his recliner and stares at me, his upper lip curled. I struggle to keep my expression neutral, but swallow repeatedly to restrain my sobs.

"Was he . . .?"

"Yes."

My uncle may have been loudmouthed and crude, but I loved him. The image of him being savagely beaten and dying alone behind an abandoned building is more than I can bear. I lose control.

"After that, I gave up the rackets for good," Abe says, ignoring my sobs. "Moe and Tootsie had been my friends. So had Louie. I'd had enough of the stupid killing."

"But the police, didn't they . . . ?"

"Forget about the police. We didn't have a lot of friends in law enforcement then, but we had enough. Including a medical examiner with a gambling debt that disappeared after your uncle's death. And if you're thinking of going to the cops, forget it. The doctor died fifteen years ago."

I'm panting as though I've run a marathon. As I catch my breath, I stare at Abe's hands, still grasping his cane. His fingers are as crooked as the roots of a banyan tree and the knuckles look painfully swollen. The skin on the back of his hands is crepe paper thin and splotched with purple age spots.

I try to remember what I was told about Uncle Moe's death. He died of a heart attack. Maybe so. But only after being brutally beaten. Then the implications sink in and my stomach heaves. My father let Moe deliver the money to these animals, knowing how they'd react when he came up short. Tootsie knew his brother would be beaten, maybe killed. Intentionally or not, Tootsie sent Moe to his death. My heart races and the knot between my shoulders spasms. My God. No wonder he didn't leave his study for two weeks after his brother died. He couldn't face anyone after what he'd done.

And how can I face him now?

When I look up, Abe's contempt is tinged with satisfaction. I feel like lashing out at him. *I* don't deserve his scorn. My father's appalling behavior has nothing to do with *me*. What Tootsie did was the act of a monster, not the father I thought I knew. There's no point in challenging Abe's story. It's too consistent with what I've learned about my father. A cold blue flame dances behind Abe's pupils. He revels in my horror.

I grab my purse and run from the apartment, rattling the glass jalousies as I slam the door. My stomach heaves and my chest grows tight as I descend the concrete stairs. Before I reach the parking lot, I duck behind a hedge and throw up, hunched over, hands on my knees. Once. Twice. A third time. My body feels drained and my blouse is plastered to my back with sweat.

My father sent his brother to his death.

I can't escape that reality. I crawl inside the car and cry for fifteen minutes before recovering enough to start the engine.

I want to run home and hide, to collapse on the couch with a blanket over my head. But halfway there I change my mind and, instead of taking a left toward my neighborhood, continue east on Glades. My heart races as I mount the I-95 ramp to Miami. Enough already. I'm fed up with my father's lies. I've made too many excuses for his behavior. Why have I forgiven him? Because I'm desperate for his love and companionship. How pathetic does that make me? Esther's right. The man *is* evil. I need to cut him out of my life.

I blast down I-95 in a whirlwind of rage. Damp hair plasters my skull and my eyes grow gritty from crying. When I arrive at the Schmuel Bernstein, the front porch is empty and I wave myself past the guard at the entrance. I get off the elevator at my father's floor and find the long, narrow hallway deserted. The sound of my fist pounding on his door reverberates in the corridor. When Tootsie pulls it open, I collapse into him.

"What's the big deal?" he says, grabbing my arm and pulling me in. "What's so awful you couldn't wait?

"You," I say. "I know the truth."

His eyebrows rise and he steps back. "Calm down. You look like shit. I'll get you a glass of water and we'll talk."

I sit at the kitchen table and watch him fill a blue plastic tumbler. His hand trembles and my anger flags as pity takes over. But I catch myself. That's been my problem all along. He's old. And vulnerable. And he knows how to manipulate me. I've been too willing to listen and forgive—and buy into his lies.

When he brings the glass, I take a sip and motion him to sit. He does so, slowly.

"I went to Abe's today." I keep my voice even. "He told me about Moe. Everything. Including how he died."

Tootsie's eyes narrow. We stare at each other for a few seconds. He leans forward as if to talk.

I hold up a hand. "I don't want to hear it. Let me finish. Then you'll have your say."

He sags back in his seat and picks up a napkin.

I repeat what Abe said about Tootsie and Moe using their mob contacts to start a business, then failing to pay Landauer. As I speak, my father tears bits of napkin and rolls them into tiny balls. He looks through the sliding glass doors and at the floor, but never at me. When I tell him about Landauer beating Uncle Moe to death, his eyes redden. I don't think he'd heard the details before. I feel a morose satisfaction in witnessing my father's anguish.

When I'm through, I feel drained and empty. My father holds his head in his hands. He looks shrunken and old.

After a few minutes, he shakes his head. "Becks. Darling. There are a lot of things you don't know. Things you can never understand."

"So tell me," I say. "Go ahead. Come up with an excuse for killing your brother. I'm dying to hear it."

He takes a deep breath. "Your Uncle Moe." He hesitates before starting again. "What I did was wrong, horribly wrong, but I couldn't raise the cash and had no idea Landauer'd kill Moe. He was my own brother, for crying out loud. I'd never do anything to harm him."

He looks at me out of the corner of his eye. I sit with my arms crossed on my chest.

"Sure I came up a little short but I ran all over town and called everyone I knew. I couldn't come up with that kind of dough in the three lousy days Landauer gave us. He had to know that. I figured he'd take the money and leave. Or wait for the extra cash. It sounds crazy now, but I thought I could come up with more—sell my car or my watch—before Landauer knew what was what."

"That was one hell of a gamble," I say, "and Moe lost." I rise to leave, but he grabs my arm. He's crying. I've never seen him like this, eyes red and hands trembling. I'm shocked and drop back in my chair.

"Listen to me. I did everything I could for Moe's family after he died. I told your Aunt Gert we'd taken life insurance on Moe and supported her until she remarried. I paid for Zvi's college and law school. What more could I do? Your uncle wouldn't have taken care of my family. He was a gonif. He was doing business on the side, selling our equipment and pocketing the profits. I caught him filching cash from the safe when he thought I wasn't looking. The bastard was robbing me blind."

Our gazes lock. Then he looks away, realizing what he's admitted. Maybe he didn't do it consciously. But he sent Moe to Landauer, intending to settle the business's debts and avenge his brother's thievery. And whether or not it was intentional, my uncle paid with his life.

I rise. When I reach the door, I glance over my shoulder. Tootsie remains at the table, his head in his hands and his shoulders heaving. I burn the image in my brain, suspecting this will be the last I see him, and leave. He doesn't stop me.

39

The next morning, as I drive to Ft. Lauderdale International Airport to pick up Esther, I consider how to tell her about Uncle Moe's death. She may already be aware—she seems to know more about our family's dark side than I do. She finished chemotherapy and has an appointment with Daniel at nine to decide on the next course of action. I've decided to stop for breakfast on the way to his office and fill her in.

I'm killing time in front of the Delta terminal when a fat cop with a nasty sneer moseys over to my car. He wears knee-length boots and a holstered gun and walks with the bowlegged stance of an overweight broncobuster. I'm in no mood for his attitude.

"Move on," he says, snapping his head to the left.

I glance around. Mine is one of two cars pulled to the curb. The terminal's deserted at this ungodly hour. The sun isn't up yet and no one in her right mind—except my sister Esther—flies into Ft. Lauderdale at six on a Wednesday morning.

"I'm waiting for my sister. She should be in the baggage area." I say. He purses his lip and crosses his arms. "She's been ill and I'd rather she not stand too long waiting for me."

He doesn't give a damn. "Look lady," he says, "there's no stopping here so get going."

I'm in a lousy mood to begin with, having stayed up most of the night. I'm ready to leap from my car and tell the officer what I think of power hungry cops hassling drivers at empty airports. Then it hits me. I'm doing exactly what my father would've done. Gone straight for the jugular. It's a frightening notion and stops me as I reach for the door handle. Fortunately, the cop's too busy harassing the other driver to notice my anger. I put the car in drive, then leave Esther a message I'm circling the airport.

It was torture getting out of bed this morning. My anger had subsided marginally by the time I got home from Tootsie's but I was too charged up to go to sleep. Once I got into bed, I spent the night struggling to suppress disturbing images of my uncle's last hours. Uncle Moe was a big man who laughed from his gut and whose unrestrained use of four-letter words made my mother blush. But he was also a kind, gentle person who told me I was the prettiest girl in Coral Gables. Lying in bed, I tormented myself with the image of him bloodied and pleading with Landauer. It was like being trapped in an endless loop of 1940-era film noir. At three in the morning, I took a sleeping pill. Now I'm groggy and confused.

"Becks." I look up. I wasn't conscious of pulling up to the terminal. Esther's standing at the open passenger door with her brows drawn together. "What happened to you?" She throws her suitcase in the backseat, then crawls in beside me. "Ever hear of a brush?"

I laugh and slide my fingers through my hair. It's matted. I forgot to brush it. "Hard night," I say, then pull on to the road. "I'll tell you over breakfast."

Ray's Diner is ten minutes from the airport so we stop there. I pull up to the metal-framed structure and park between Ford F-150s that dwarf my Mercedes. It's six thirty and the place is deserted except for a handful of bulky men on their way to construction sites. Three women in heavy makeup enter after we're seated. I figure they're dancers coming off work at the strip club next door. We order buttermilk pancakes from an Amazon of a blond in a pink uniform.

While we're waiting, Esther takes a sip of the coffee the waitress drops at our table. "So what happened?" she says. "You get mugged?"

I grunt. "Might as well have been. You remember I told you about dad's old mob boss showing up at my house?"

"He came back?"

"God, no."

"Then what? Please tell me you worked things out with him?"

I grab a napkin from the metal dispenser that anchors the salt and pepper shakers and blow my nose. It could be allergies. Or relief Esther's here. But my nose is stuffier than usual this morning.

"Not yet. Dad told me he'd take care of Landauer, but when I asked if he'd talked to the man, he wouldn't give me a straight answer."

"Sounds familiar."

"I've been a wreck for the last few months. Each time I walk in the house, I expect to find him waiting. I couldn't take it anymore so I went to see Abe yesterday and asked him to put me in touch with Landauer. I figured I'd tell Landauer what Dad said about killing Fat Louie and get the creep off my back."

"You *are* brave."

"No kidding. I never got that far though. Abe wanted to hear what I was going to say first."

"Did Abe know about Fat Louie's murder?"

"Every detail. The big shock yesterday was that there's a lot more than Dad told us. It didn't end with Louie's death."

"What didn't?"

"The killing."

"Are you telling me Dad . . . ?" We glance up as the waitress drops platters of pancakes and stomps away. I wait until she's out of earshot, then lean in and speak quietly across the table. I tell Esther what Abe said about helping our father and Uncle Moe start their business. About their decision to stop depositing money in Landauer's account. And about Tootsie's failure to give Uncle Moe the money the mobster demanded. Her eyes grow wide when I describe Landauer's brutal murder of Uncle Moe.

When I'm done, she stares out the window, then returns her gaze to me. Her face is pale and her expression resigned. "I should have known."

"Known what?"

She sections her pancakes into neat rows, stabbing lines into the plate, then sets her fork and knife down. "Remember how Dad acted at Uncle Moe's funeral. He couldn't stop sobbing and embarrassed everyone, including Aunt Gert. Zvi pushed him out of the chapel during the service. I don't know what he said, but Dad stayed in the lobby until the rabbi was through."

"I don't remember that."

"The old man was sick with remorse. He couldn't tell anyone. Mom would've left him or turned him in to the police if she knew. He had to live with it."

"What about Landauer? Dad had to be afraid the guy would come for him next."

"Maybe. But I'd be willing to bet Tootsie had the extra money all along. Probably gave it to Landauer the next day."

I stare at her, horrified. "You think he would've done that?"

Esther stabs a forkful of pancake. "You bet!"

Daniel's waiting area is empty when we arrive at eight thirty and his nurse, Mary, escorts us to the examining room. The space looks like every other examining room in the world. Beige Formica cabinets and a sink fill one wall and a matching examining table rests against the other. I sit in Daniel's low-slung rolling stool and Esther takes the room's only chair. We chat about her treatment. The surgeon is confident he removed all of the affected tissue and her oncologist feels that the chemotherapy was successful. Esther's hair is growing back and she looks striking, if a little gaunt, with her new short hairstyle. She tells me she wants to talk to Daniel about starting long-term hormone therapy.

Five minutes after we arrive, Daniel enters the room. He leans in to give Esther a kiss and I allow him to peck my cheek. We haven't spoken since our walk on the beach and I'm ill at ease in his presence. In any event, we have more important issues to discuss. He wraps the blood pressure cuff around Esther's arm and takes a reading. That's normally Mary's job and I wonder if he feels as awkward as I do.

Esther, no doubt sensing our discomfort, breaks the silence. "Did you tell Daniel about your meeting with Abe yesterday?"

I stare at her, raising my eyebrows to express disapproval. I told Daniel about the vandalism to our house and, during a late-night conversation, Landauer's visit, but I haven't had a chance to discuss Uncle Moe's murder. This is hardly the time to do so, Plus I don't want more pressure from Daniel about moving home. When Daniel turns his back to us, I give a quick shake of my head, hoping she'll understand. Esther ignores me and, after Daniel assures her he'll consider her options and discuss them later, she tells him everything. When she messes up the story, I break in.

"My God, it's beyond imagining," Daniel says when I'm through. "I can't believe Tootsie did that. He must have been insane. It's a wonder you two turned out normal."

"I'm not sure we did," Esther says.

Daniel laughs. Then, as usual, he gets to the crux of the matter.

"What happens now? Perhaps it's time you told the police about Moe's and Louie's murders? At least mention Landauer's threat. Not reporting what you've learned could put you at risk."

"I thought about that last night, along with about a hundred different options. I can't report Landauer for killing Uncle Moe. There's no proof." I explain about Abe's crooked medical examiner.

"Then you need to make sure Landauer knows what Abe told you—and that you're aware there's no proof he killed your uncle. That has to be what he meant with the ask your father note," Daniel says. "Do you have Landauer's number?"

"Damn. I was so upset yesterday I forgot to get it. I'll call Abe, then Landauer, as soon as I get home. That should be the end of it, but who knows." I slide my hands under my thighs so Daniel and Esther can't see them trembling.

"These guys sound like sickos," Daniel says. "Maybe you should move out of the house, leave town for a while."

"I'm not going anywhere." I appreciate Daniel's concern but I'm fed up with letting these mobsters rule my life.

He's silent a moment. "Thank goodness Esther's here. At least you're not alone."

The two exchange glances—no doubt, agreeing Daniel should move back in.

I pretend not to notice their interchange, but consider the possibility. It no longer sounds like such a terrible idea.

40

Esther and I have been home less than ten minutes and are carrying her bags into Josh's room when the doorbell rings. We're on our way downstairs when our visitor starts stabbing the bell. It creates a high-pitched racket. Then the pounding starts.

My sister and I freeze at the bottom of the stairs and exchange frightened glances. We've got to be thinking the same thing. Landauer. I approach the door, stepping lightly to hide the sound of my footfall.

When I peer through the peephole, the sight, though not entirely comforting, is a relief. Standing on my front porch in a heavy wool suit and with a dense black beard is my cousin Zvi. He looks like a throwback to a seventeenth century Polish ghetto.

When I open the door, the scent of mothballs wafts into the hall.

"I'll dance on your father's grave." His voice is gravelly with anger.

"Hello, Zvi. Why don't you come in and tell me what you're talking about?"

He doesn't budge. "You know damn well what I'm talking about. Your father called this morning and spilled his guts about my dad's death. He said you'd been digging around. It sounded like he wanted to beat you to the punch."

Esther, who's standing behind me, pushes the door farther open. "Come inside or leave. We're not putting on a show for the neighbors."

Zvi hesitates, then steps into the hall and follows us into the kitchen. I gather up the newspaper I've left on the table and motion for everyone to pull out a chair. I offer coffee, but Zvi refuses.

"So what's going on?" I hand Esther a cup and pour myself one. Zvi doesn't say a word as I serve the coffee. Instead, he glowers at me from beneath thick black brows.

"I got off the phone," he says, "and headed straight over. The old bastard was sobbing. Told me how he'd double-crossed my father. And how that *may have* led to his death. I told him I already knew and that he was lucky I hadn't gone to the police."

"You knew?"

"My father was thirty-five when he died. He never had heart trouble. I was young, but I wasn't stupid. I wanted to believe my mother when she said it was a heart attack. But I went with her to identify my dad's body. His arms were bruised. And I knew there was trouble between him and your dad."

"What kind of trouble?" This from Esther.

"My father said your dad didn't trust him, that Tootsie treated him like a criminal and tried to steal the business from him."

"I never heard that," I lie.

"Why would you? My father claimed he was the one with the connections that brought in business. And that your father wanted to cut him out."

"If they were having so much trouble, why didn't they split up the business?"

"Your father wouldn't have it. Didn't want to share the profits. I guess that's why he sent my father to meet those mobsters."

Zvi was a teenager when his father died and may have known more than I did about our fathers' business affairs. But I find it hard to believe Uncle Moe told Zvi about his connections with the Jewish syndicate. I consider sharing what I learned about my father and Uncle Moe, but decide to leave well enough alone. Why sully memories of his father? And who knows if my father *was* telling the truth? It's just as likely he brought Uncle Moe into the syndicate.

"After the funeral, your father didn't visit for more than a month." He glowers at us across the table. "And I knew the story about having life insurance on my father was a crock because the checks he sent to my mother came from your dad's personal account. There's no way he'd have done that unless he was guilty."

"Are you going to tell the police?"

"I should. But what's the point? The old bastard only has a few years left."

Despite my determination to cut my father out of my life, I'm relieved.

"I don't know what to say," I tell Zvi, then turn to Esther to see if she has anything to add. She doesn't. "I'm sorry. It's been horrible for us, but I guess it's worse for you."

"No kidding." He rises. "I just wanted to warn you. When the old bastard kicks the bucket, I'll be there in my tap shoes."

Between the cowboy cop, the appointment with Daniel, and Zvi's visit, my day is off to a terrible start. I get Esther upstairs, where she takes a nap, and go to my study. As I'm organizing the papers that threaten to engulf my desk, I consider what Zvi said. I picture my father in his apartment, alone and miserable. Pity wells up in my chest but I swallow and suppress it. *My father killed his own brother.* It's become a mantra. A wave of exhaustion washes over me. Then fear hits. I still have to call the scum who set this whole thing in motion.

I punch in Abe's number. He answers right away. "Mr. Kravitz? It's Becks Ruchinsky."

"What now?"

"You said you'd give me Mr. Landauer's number. I forgot to get it yesterday."

Abe grunts. "I'm not surprised. You tell your father what you learned?"

"Yes." I barely whisper the word.

"What happened?"

"He admitted it." My voice is stronger.

"All right, then, here's what you do. I told Mr. Landauer about our meeting. He wants to talk to you, but it's got to be on his terms. He'll meet you at the Mad Grouper Grill Thursday night at seven. It's on the Miami River."

I hesitate. The invitation sounds forbidding. The Miami River's a polluted watercourse used mainly by cargo ships. Who would open a restaurant on its banks? The idea of meeting Landauer frightens me.

"Can I bring my husband?" The words come out on impulse.

Abe hesitates. "Sure."

I hang up the phone and release my breath.

When Esther wakes up and comes downstairs, I tell her my plan. She's furious. "You can't meet that man. He'll kill you. And Daniel too. Why are you doing this?"

"To put it behind me—get his reassurance he'll leave me alone."

"Can't you call the police?"

"And tell them what? That I'm meeting the octogenarian gangster who knocked off my uncle fifty years ago? Even if they buy it, it'll raise all sorts of questions, maybe lead to Dad's arrest."

"Aren't you worried about getting hurt? Or getting Daniel hurt?"

"Landauer could've killed me when he broke into my house. Why do it now?"

We argue for a few minutes before she realizes I've got to do this. When she stomps into the kitchen, I do an internet search on the Mad Grouper Grill. There's no website but I find an article from the *Sun-Sentinel* that describes it as a small fish restaurant that's become a popular late night hangout for young professionals. How bad could it be?

Then I call Daniel. I'm prepared for the worst. That he'll try to dissuade me or turn me down.

"You're meeting the man?" he says after I tell him my plan. He sounds incredulous. I repeat what I told Esther about putting this behind me. When I ask if he'll come, he's silent for thirty seconds. I understand his reluctance. It is *my* father who set this in motion. Why should Daniel jeopardize himself? Not that I think we're in danger. But he may not see it that way. Landauer is a gangster and a killer, but without his acknowledgment I've fulfilled my part of the bargain— learned the truth about my father—I won't feel safe.

When Daniel gets back on the phone, his voice is deep and determined. "All right. Let's do it. I emailed Mary to cancel my late-afternoon appointments. I'll pick you up at five thirty tomorrow. Maybe we can settle this once and for all."

I'm so relieved that I'm near tears. "Daniel," is all I can choke out, "I . . . thanks."

41

Tootsie

I can barely muster the energy to pull myself out of the armchair and walk into the kitchen. It's dark outside and there's no telling how long I've been asleep. I catch my reflection in the sliding glass doors and freeze at the dark rings around my eyes. My jaw's swollen. I look like I've gone five rounds in the ring.

When I woke up a half hour ago, it took a few minutes to figure out why I felt so foggy. My stomach sank as I remembered. I'd taken a succession of sleeping pills over the past two days, downing another each time I awakened. It seemed the only way to cope with the mind-numbing despair that overwhelmed me after Becks left.

In a small way, I am relieved. No more hiding the truth from Becks or Esther. The worst has happened. They know. Neither will speak to me again. I tried to prevent them from learning about my past. And I succeeded—for fifty years. But the game's over. Which leaves me with what? Bowling on Tuesday nights. Poker with Winchell and his pals. It's something. But they're not family. There's nothing like family.

I rummage beneath the sink for the bottle of Scotch. Shuddering with impatience and frustration, I remember finishing it after Becks left. I'm hungry but the fetid odor of sour milk assaults me when I open the fridge. Two shriveled apples at the back of the produce bin will have to suffice for dinner.

When I finish eating, I return to the living room and pick up the remote control. I toss it on the cocktail table. Watching television doesn't help. Nothing does. I have to face the raw ugly truth. All those decades of hiding my past have come to nothing. I had a few good years. But now I'm alone. I struggle through my fog to figure out how I reached this point. I was a good father and I still don't understand why Becks felt she had to prod into my past. Now I'm paying for mistakes made long before she was born. I don't deserve that.

And that bastard Abe. Telling Becks stories she didn't need to hear. I'm not proud of my past. I've been too weak, too ready to take orders from schmucks like Moe and Schatzi and Landauer. Maybe if I'd refused to kill Louie? Tried harder to get Moe the money Landauer demanded? And the broads. Who the hell knows? After Moe's death, I fell into a depression and sought comfort in the arms of strange women. Even that didn't help.

I walk to the sliding glass doors, open them, and stumble out to the concrete patio. Across the open lawn, three old men slump in wheelchairs on the red brick porch of the nursing home. Two stare blankly ahead, their hands folded on their lap robes. A third sleeps with his head tilted and his mouth agape. A ribbon of saliva drips from his lips to his shoulder. Nursing assistants in white uniforms sit on the lawn chairs behind them, chatting.

My intestines knot up like a snake, constricting my bowel and forcing acid into my throat. I turn away from the old men. Sobbing, I go back inside my apartment.

42

I'm so grateful when Daniel pulls in front of the house at five thirty Thursday night that I almost cry. I couldn't sleep the night before, envisioning Landauer shooting Daniel and me and dumping our bodies into the Miami River. In the dark of the night, I let my imagination run wild and picture Josh and Gabriel getting a call from the police informing them their parents' bodies were found floating in the bay. As I lay in bed, I tried to remember if I told them where I keep my will and good jewelry. When the sun rises, the fears that assailed me in the night subside. Even so, exhaustion and tension have left me foggy and confused.

"You have no idea what this means to me," I say as I slip into the passenger seat of Daniel's Volkswagen. "I was too frightened to go alone."

"I'd be hurt if you hadn't asked me."

I'm touched by his response, but feel guilty. "This . . . it's dangerous. And Tootsie's not your father. If anything were to happen to you, I'd kill myself."

He laughs. "I'm flattered." Then, more seriously, "It'll be fine. We'll wrap things up tonight and get on with our lives."

I look at him, then back at the road. He seems so calm. My stomach aches and my palms are clammy. We're silent for most of the drive and I find myself mulling over his choice of the words—our lives. Daniel's right. We need to get on with our life together. My father may have been a serial cheater, but Daniel's not. I know he loves me and regrets what he did. And who else but Daniel would endanger his life for me. Though he may joke and act unconcerned, he's too smart not to realize what we're up against. A warm rush of affection washes over me. I reach over and touch his shoulder. He glances over and returns my smile.

The traffic to Miami is heavy and when we pull off I-95 onto Biscayne Boulevard it's six forty-five. Only fifteen minutes to locate the Mad Grouper. We speed up along Biscayne Boulevard as it merges into Brickell Avenue, then make a right into a neighborhood of narrow streets and industrial buildings. Block after block of abandoned warehouses lead to a stretch of wooden shacks that back up to the Miami River. It's starting to get dark and the cargo ships docked behind the ramshackle structures look like haunted galleons against the night sky. When I spot a bungalow that's in nominally better shape than the others, I tell Daniel to pull over. A single exposed bulb throws harsh white light across the front porch. I get out of the car to read a handwritten sign taped to the front door. "Mad Grouper Grill." I wave at Daniel to join me.

No one responds when I knock, so I try the knob—figuring most restaurants are open at this hour. But the door is locked. I'm ready to give up and retrace my steps to the car when I spot a handwritten sign propped against a rickety wooden chair at the far end of the front porch. It reads "Around Side to Mad Grouper."

"This is starting to feel like *Alice in Wonderland*," I whisper to Daniel.

We cross the sparse lawn to the side of the house, where a narrow gravel path leads past four beat-up metal garbage cans to the rear of the shack. I hold my breath, expecting to find Landauer and Pinky waiting. Instead, we step out to a waterfront restaurant that on any other night would be charming. Six rough-hewn picnic tables rest atop an unfinished wooden deck that extends from the shack to the river. Fishnets and colorful glass floats hang on the rear wall. The minute we seat ourselves, a stooped, elderly black man emerges from the back of the house. He nods then disappears inside.

"You think they're open tonight?" I ask Daniel. He stares across the muddy brown water of the Miami River.

"I doubt it."

I follow his gaze and strain to see in the deepening twilight. Three men in kayaks paddle to the rocky shore a hundred feet across the river. They lodge themselves onto the landing, slip out of their kayaks, then pull the narrow boats ashore. A bungalow, no doubt built before the neighborhood became a warehouse district, sits thirty feet back from the water. The kayakers look like college kids, scraggly and unkempt with long hair, but I find comfort in knowing people are near. The only sound is the rasp of the boats being dragged across the graveled backyard up to the house.

I glance at my watch—it's seven thirty—then check my cell phone. No messages. I wonder if Landauer's deliberately making us wait—playing a power game. Daniel and I don't speak. Fifteen minutes later, I'm sitting with my back to the house, watching the river, when I sense movement. I look to my right and almost jump.

Old as he is, Landauer has managed to creep up to our table in silence. His jowls hang lower than I remember and his face has the mournful, hangdog mien I noticed when I encountered him in my kitchen. I nudge Daniel, who looks up quickly, then stands.

"Daniel Ruchinsky," he says, offering a hand. His voice sounds formal, as though introducing himself to a business associate. "Becks asked me to come."

"That's fine," Landauer says, his voice expressionless. He eases himself on to the bench, sitting with his side against the table, half facing Daniel and me. He yells toward the house for three glasses of red wine, which the black waiter brings in less than two minutes. I glance around for Pinky. If he's here, he must be inside.

"So you know about your father now." Landauer speaks slowly and lugubriously, meeting my eyes.

"Abe told me."

He shakes his head. "It must be hard to admit to your own kid that you're a rat and a murderer. I was no angel. But your father. My God. His own brother!"

I'm tempted to point out *he's* the one who beat Uncle Moe. But this isn't the time or place to argue semantics.

"It's taken a long time but the truth is out."

I realize I should let him have his say and take off. But curiosity gets the better of me. I want to know why he's gone to all this trouble just so I'll know about my father's past. If he were the monster Tootsie painted him to be, it seems he'd have done something more brutal—though ransacking my home and showing up in my kitchen uninvited felt violent enough. He's too old to do much damage, but he's got Pinky to do the dirty work. Maybe the cruelty and barbarism my father spoke of have aged out of Landauer, and his years on the lam have taken their toll.

"Why" I ask, "is it so important to you that I know about my father's past?"

He looks at me and the edges of his lips rise, drawing up the loose folds of skin beneath his chin. He's even more terrifying with the smile.

"That's the most intelligent thing you've asked since we met."

I shrug and set my wineglass on the table. Neither Daniel nor I have taken a sip.

"I don't know what Abe told you about me. Your father knows what happened. When I went away, I lost everything. My wife left me. She took our kids and let another man raise them as his own. When I got out, I couldn't contact them. The police could track me down through family. Can you imagine what that was like?"

I nod. Maybe I should feel sympathy, but it's hard to picture him a husband or a father, let alone a man who'd let his wife betray him with impunity. He's too forbidding, too cold and distant.

"Years later, I found out where my son and daughter lived and drove by. But I never knocked on their door. I didn't want to complicate their lives. I hoped that at some point, the little ingrates would track me down. They never did."

His jowls sway as he shakes his head.

"Your father was lucky, though. He had it all. A legitimate business. A wife who stuck by him. Daughters who knew their dad. It wasn't right, not after he betrayed me. I tried to leave the bastard alone, let bygones be bygones. But I kept an eye on him. On you girls, too, I knew when each of you got married, had kids."

Daniel and I exchange glances. If Landauer notices, he doesn't let on.

"When Abe told me you were snooping around, I took it as my opening. I'm not getting any younger. I waited a long time for your family to catch on to what your father did. I heard through one of my sources that your sister abandoned him a couple of years ago. That left you."

Landauer's eyes gleam in the dim light that escapes through the shack's screen door. The sclera is mapped with veins and the lids are red.

"I thought about killing you or your sister," he says. "Taking from Tootsie what he took from me. And I came close to murdering him years ago. But the bastard wasn't worth it. I'd done enough time."

Hearing him speak so casually about murdering my family jolts me. What kind of brute is so indifferent to taking another human being's life? My spasm of fear becomes repulsion and I ball my hands into fists. Who does this bully think he is, acting as though our lives have no value beyond the time *he'd* have to spend in jail. I beat a fist against my thigh. But I keep my mouth shut.

Landauer rises and, turning his back on Daniel and me, trundles into the building. He lets the screen door slam behind him. No goodbye. His fifty-year vendetta is over. I stare at Daniel. *This* is what five decades of criminal living add up to? A paid bodyguard for companionship and meager vengeance behind a shack in a Miami slum.

I glance around the wooden patio. It smells of newly-cut timber and sawdust. Then it strikes me. This has to be where my father and Moe dumped Fat Louie's body. Where Landauer brutally beat my uncle to death. I glance at the shack and wonder if the old gangster thinks he won—if living a bitter, lonely life and ensuring my father is miserable count as winning.

Looking at the river, I make out the shapes of the plastic bags, beer cans, and bloated fish that float by on the incoming tide. There's a certain irony to turning this shack, the scene of who knows how many murders, into a late-night hangout for young men and women. I doubt any realize their Miami—their city of flashy neon nightclubs, marble skyscrapers, and landscaped boulevards—was built with the filthy lucre of violent gangsters. I'll never come here again. And with a pang, I realize I may not see my father either. I steel myself to accept the truth. He made terrible choices and the blood that flowed from them is embedded in the wood rotting beneath this deck. I'll miss the old man. But he isn't the father I thought I knew.

When I return my gaze to the picnic table, Daniel's leaning against it, his hands in his pockets. "You ready to go?" he asks. I nod and take a step in his direction. He takes my hand and we walk through the dark to our car.

If you enjoyed
The Yiddish Gangster's Daughter,
your review in Amazon, Goodreads, and other social
media would most certainly
be appreciated.

Acknowledgements

Few novels are the work of one person and I'd like to recognize those who helped bring *The Yiddish Gangster's Daughter* to fruition. I'd like to acknowledge the guidance provided by my critique group, Prudy Taylor Board, Buck Buchanan, Joe Frarraci, Mary Yuhas and Maria DeSoto as well as Debbie Shlian and Eileen O'Brien, whose editorial remarks and encouragement proved invaluable. I'd also like to express my gratitude for the support, guidance and patience of my professors in Florida International University's Creative Writing Program: my thesis advisers Dan Wakefield, Les Standiford, and Bruce Harvey along with John Dufresne and Lynn Barrett. David Morrell generously offered advice on structuring the novel and upping the stakes.

Many of the scenes in this novel revisit historical events documented by authors and researchers who did the real hard digging on the Jewish syndicate. I'd like to recognize Robert A. Rockaway's *But He Was Good to his Mother: The Lives and Crimes of Jewish Gangster,* Albert Fried's *The Rise and Fall of the Jewish Gangster in America and* Leonard Slater's *The Pledge.* Thanks to Dr. Deborah Shlian, Dr. Albert Begas and Sharon Plotkin for technical advice and to readers Stephen J. Forman, Susan Lebrun and Shelley Little.